Mindhealer

* * *

Lilith Saintcrow

Mindhealer
Published by ImaJinn Books

13 Digit ISBN: 978-1-933417-36-3
10 Digit ISBN: 1-933417-36-6

10 9 8 7 6 5 4 3 2 1

PUBLISHER'S NOTE:
This book is a work of fiction. Names, characters, places and incidents are products of the author's imagination or are used fictitiously. Any resemblance to actual events or locales or persons, living or dead, is entirely coincidental.

Books are available at quantity discounts when used to promote products or services. For information please write to: Marketing Division, ImaJinn Books, P.O. Box 545, Canon City, CO 81212, or call toll free 1-877-625-3592.

Cover design by Patricia Lazarus

ImaJinn Books
P.O. Box 545, Canon City, CO 81212
Toll Free: 1-877-625-3592
http://www.imajinnbooks.com

One

Caro closed the suitcase and clicked the locks down. "I'll call as soon as I get to the safehouse," she repeated, soothingly.

"I can't believe you're doing this." Trev folded his arms over his narrow chest. His fingers tapped at his black shirtsleeves—it was a ragged *Tragic Diamonds* shirt, artistically ripped. His freckles ran together on his nose, as if they had been baked on. Jeans clung to his narrow hips, he wore scuffed blue Doc Martens and a leather bracelet on his right wrist. One of Caro's gold hoop earrings curved in his left ear—a small one, peeping through dark hair. Caro hadn't worn small earrings for years, and wondered how long it would be before Trev started raiding her longer ones.

"They need me." *And you've got a life here, Trev. Never thought I'd see that.* "I'll be driving, it will only take me about eight hours, and I'll be *fine*. I'll be inside a safehouse before dark. I'll call."

She hefted the suitcase experimentally. Her heels clicked against the hardwood as she carried it to the door, set it down with the two other suitcases, the duffel bag of bathroom necessities and emergency items, and the large canvas bag that held her professional tools. "I'll examine these cases they're so worried about and spend a few weeks specialist-training the Mindhealers and Seers there. I'll be back by Yule." *I can also shop for a present for you there and you won't ransack my room trying to find it, for once.*

Trev actually came out and said what most of them had to be thinking. "I wish you'd just take a Watcher with you."

Caro glanced up, sweeping a long strand of golden-brown hair away. No matter how tightly she braided it, her hair had a mind of its own. *It would be even worse if I cut it. Curling around and getting in my face all the time, I'd end up eating a mouthful of it every time there's a breath of wind.*

The safehouse was just beginning to wake up, the heavy walls—each nail, each piece of wood, each bit of drywall and each block of stone covered with Watcher wards and spells of protection—almost seeming to breathe. Under the heavy warding the air sometimes turned thick and unmoving, and Caro couldn't wait to be out on the road, windows down a little and the heater turned up against the chill, singing along with the radio as she drove. Traveling between one place and the next was her favorite part of the job of being a Mindhealer. If you could call it a job, that was.

Well, I get paid, and I work myself hard. That's a job, isn't it?

"Why?" She managed a light tone. "You think I need a babysitter? I'm thirty blessed years old, Trev. I think I can handle the drive to Altamira and finding the safehouse there. I have excellent directions, and I promise not to get carried away and make a run for the Mexican border. All right?" She made it back to the bed, pulling the hem of her blue silk sweater down, picked up her cream pashmina scarf and draped it around her shoulders. "Though I must say I'm tempted, with the weather the way it is."

Outside, gray icy drizzle drifted down desultorily; the city below looked just as lifeless and blanched. The trees were losing their leaves, October wind ruffling the thin naked branches. Samhain was right around the corner, the beginning of the witch's year.

The season of the dead. The thought of her teacher Eleanor rose, Caro pushed it down. Dead only two years, and it still was a hurtful jab every time she thought about Eleanor. She was the closest to a mother Caroline ever had. She supposed the grief was natural, even if it still felt like getting punched in the stomach each time a stray memory rose.

Trev didn't rise to the conversational bait. "It's not safe, Caro. I'd feel better if you'd just this once—"

You don't step outside without a bruiser looming over you. My little brother the chicken. But that was unfair, and she chided herself as soon as she thought it. Since the incident with the *kalak*, Trev shuddered whenever he smelled smoke and stayed well within the safehouse walls, accepting without demur the presence of a Watcher every time he ventured out. Given that he'd always been the wild child, it was faintly unnerving—but also a relief. At least Caro didn't have to worry about him all the time now.

Though she did. It was, she supposed, reflex after twenty-six years of worrying about your baby brother night and day.

"—give in and let the Council put a Watcher on you. Just this once," she finished, chapter and verse. She'd hoped to get out of here without having this talk *again*. "No, Trev. I'll be inside a safehouse before dark. That's the bargain. The Council keeps the Watchers away from me, and in return I take every reasonable precaution. Nothing's changed."

Nothing is ever going to change. I will not cause another man's death.

She glanced around. She was going to miss this suite; she'd made Santiago City home base for the last three years, venturing to other cities to train novice Mindhealers and take a look at cases that required a specialist but always coming home. She liked this set of rooms, loved how the kitchenette, hung with ferns, glowed with yellow walls and oak cabinets. How the sun slanted through the big window in summer, redolent of spice and lavender from the garden below as she sat on the window seat. How her desk and her bookshelves had come to assume the character of permanent residents rather than uneasy guests. It was a far cry from where she'd spent the first ten years of her existence, and the further away Caro got, the happier she was.

Not bad for a foster kid who heard voices, she thought as she did every time, with a small leap of grateful anxiety in the middle of her chest. Say what you would about Circle Lightfall's anachronistic rules and regulations, they took their duty seriously. They had saved her life.

And, more importantly, saved Trev's.

"Eleanor would have a fit," Trev muttered darkly.

"Then we'll just be glad she can't see me now that I'm such a disappointment." Caro's tone turned sharp. The pretty blue linen curtains Mari had given her ruffled slightly as her voice touched them. Rain whispered against the window.

"That's not what I meant and you know it." Trevor frowned. His aura turned lemon-yellow, a trailing scarf of indignation unfurling like a bright banner. Caro herself had applied a layer of shielding to him, careful almost-maternal wards to help bolster her brother's weak talent. He was an air witch, the most common type; male Lightbringers didn't often have considerable gifts. But even if he'd been normal, Circle Lightfall would have taken him in when they took Caro. They didn't believe in splitting up siblings. Not like the foster system.

The sharp pinch of guilt began right under Caro's collarbone. It felt like indigestion, only a few inches too high. She'd hoped to go at least a few hours without feeling it.

Well, I managed forty-five minutes. That's a good sign, wouldn't you say? "Of course that's not what you meant," she agreed briskly. "Though that's what it sounds like, Trev. Let's not ruin a movie-worthy good-bye with bad feelings. I'm sorry I'm going to miss your Samhain show."

"So's Elise. She loves watching you squirm on a barstool while she sings."

"It's not her singing I object to; it's the drunkards around me." The point-counterpoint was so familiar Caro could have done it in her sleep. "Help me carry this, will you?"

"Keenan's outside. He'll help too." Trev's eyes sparkled with mischief. "I thought you might overpack. As usual."

"I *never* overpack." She rose to the bait gratefully. "I just like to be prepared."

"For what, an invasion?" Trev sniffed. He made a show of hauling up two of the suitcases, making a face. "Good gods above, Caro, what'd you put in here? Rocks?"

"Weakling." She checked her purse one more time. Everything in its place.

"Teacher's pet." Trev was grinning broadly.

"Irresponsible."

"Anal-retentive."

"Jerk."

"Witch."

"You too." Caro actually grinned back, unable to help herself. "Want to keep going, pot calling the kettle black?"

Trev muttered something she was sure was a good-natured obscenity, dropping one of the suitcases so he could jerk the door open. The smile fell from Caro's face.

Outside in the hall, with the light glowing in his dark hair, stood Keenan. The broad-shouldered man, his face expressionless, leaned against the far wall, his hands in the pockets of his long black leather coat, blue eyes scanning the room once. He had, with perfect Watcher tact, stayed outside. It was just as well, the sword hilt sticking up over his right shoulder and the knives strapped to his chest—as well as the silver guns at his hips—were reminders Caro did *not* need.

The familiar crimson-black whirl of a Watcher's aura slid over him briefly, Caro had to look *under* it for a moment to see him. Keenan wasn't happy, any more than any other Watcher Caro met; the dragging pain from the Dark symbiote melded to his body teased briefly at her own consciousness before her shields thickened reflexively. She saw his eyes flare with blue for a moment; he would be sensitive to any change in Caro's bright aura.

And Caro, of course, would be sensitive to that pain. It was part of being a Mindhealer.

"Morning, Keenan," she said politely.

He ducked his head, mumbled something suspiciously like *morning, ma'am.* He was one of her favorite Watchers, if she could be said to have any, because he generally knew when to keep his mouth shut and never, ever suggested he go with her anywhere. Not that any of the other Watchers would suggest it either, but sometimes they looked as though they might.

Stop it, Caro. Watchers aren't your problem. Not anymore.

"Come on, Keen, Caro's overpacked again and wants us to haul all her crap around. Up to it?"

Trev handed over the two suitcases. The Watcher handled them easily. That brought Trevor back to pick up the duffel and the third suitcase, but he left her work bag. *Nobody* touched Caro's tools unless she gave specific permission. It was a courtesy other Circle Lightfall witches unconsciously gave her, and one she was grateful for. It was so good to live with other psychics, people who *understood* what it was like to have the thoughts of the outside world screaming at you every waking—and sleeping—moment.

She followed him out the door, letting out a small sigh. *I love traveling, but leaving here is getting harder and harder each time. Why? Because my bookshelves are starting to look like they belong, or because I'm beginning to wish I could go out at night again? Or wishing I could just . . . who knows? Leave it all behind. I suppose every woman who's ever hit thirty has the urge to run away sometimes.*

She swept the door closed, and sketched a little rune over the doorknob—not that she thought anyone would mess with her belongings in a safehouse. It wouldn't occur to anyone here to trouble her things. It was just habit, a sort of good luck charm.

The little buzz of Power trembled away from her fingertip and grew firm as she set it against the doorknob. She set off down the hall after her brother and the Watcher, who were conversing in low conspiratorial tones. Her heels clicked against the floor—sharp little cracks of frustration when she lengthened her stride; precise little taps marking out time when she observed a decorous pace. Which she did now, letting Trevor and Keenan go ahead of her. Otherwise Keenan might try to hold the door for her, and Caro wasn't sure her temper would keep down for *that.* She wanted to be out of here. Gone. Already on the road with the radio playing.

Driving between places is the only time I really feel happy anymore.

The work was fine and she was lucky to get it, she told herself again as she entered the echoing stairwell, hearing Trev's light footsteps and sensing Keenan's silent step continuing down. The safehouse had elevators, of course, but the Watchers rarely used them. Too easy to get caught, Vincent had told her once.

Will you stop thinking about Vince? Annoyed with herself, she rested her hand on the railing. She'd chosen the suite in this hall because it gave onto the stairwell going directly down to the west parking level, and when she needed to get somewhere quickly the stairs were the best bet.

Trev's laugh rang out below, making her smile. Trevor was happy now. He had all the drumsticks he could break, a steady gig with the Tragic Diamonds, and a job working in a music store out on Magen Boulevard. It took so little to make him completely at peace.

And what would it take to make me at peace? She discarded the question as useless. Here in Circle Lightfall, her talents were put to good use. She was a Mindhealer, capable of healing the traumatized and shattered, and it was her great good luck that she'd come to the attention of the Circle and received the training to corral her talent instead of ending up in a mental asylum screaming about things nobody else could hear.

Or eaten by the Dark.

Caro shivered. The stairwell suddenly seemed to draw close and go dim.

But Trevor's laughter floated up to her, and Caro gave herself a little shake. She was a fully-trained witch and Mindhealer, and she had survived quite well on her own for years now. She had even gone toe-to-toe with the High Council and won the right to be the only witch without a Watcher, as long as she stayed in a safehouse and wasn't outside after dusk. Unless, of course, she went out after dark with a bonded pair, witch and Watcher. That concession had been won grudgingly from her, but she didn't mind.

Lately, though, the Council had been making little noises. Little noises like they wanted to put Caro under guard again.

She made it down to the parking level and opened the door into the garage. Echoes boomed off concrete. Her heels made lovely little sounds as she strode, determined, between the aisle of parked cars.

Trev sounded horrified. "What the hell? *Caro!*"

She rounded the corner and saw him staring at the little blue Miata, only its open trunk marring the low perfect profile. A smile teased at the corners of Caro's lips, she banished it. "What? You can't find the keys? I signed it out this morning and it has a full tank."

"You're not driving *this!*"

"Of course I am." She saw Keenan fading back into the shadows, retreating to a defensible position, away from the hurtful glow of her aura. Close enough that should something happen, he would spring out of the shadows and banish it the traditional way: with steel. There was precious little chance of anything being here inside a safehouse, but a Watcher never relaxed. "What's wrong with it? It's perfectly serviceable, it has an engine, and the suitcases go in the trunk."

"Caro, if you get into an accident—"

She folded her arms. "You think I'm a bad driver? What, because I'm female, or because I'm your sister?"

Trev spluttered. She liked to make him splutter. It was when Trev got quiet and sneaky you had to watch out for him.

In short order, the luggage was stowed in the trunk and Caro had placed her purse and work bag in the passenger's seat. Trev scolded her all the while, and she gave him a kiss on the cheek. He flung his arms around her, hugging her tight the way he used to do when they were children. She hugged him back, ignoring the wrinkles it would put in her skirt and sweater. Her earring pressed between his cheek and hers, she shut her eyes and breathed in, deeply and quietly. It was always hard to leave him, a habit left over from an uncertain childhood of clinging to each other for support.

"Be careful," he whispered in her ear. "Please, Caro. Be safe."

"I'll be fine. I always have been. It's an eight-hour drive, and I'll be well inside before nightfall. I'll call. Don't be such a little worrywart, baby boy."

"Witch." He mock-glared then, untangling his arms from around her. Caro smoothed her skirt.

"You too. Remember to water my ferns." She touched his shoulder, stroked gently. "I'll be fine, I promise. I'll call."

"Okay. Get going." He wiped angrily at his eyes. "You'd *better* call."

"I will," she soothed. "Go on, you know how you hate this part."

"Dammit." But he paced away, Keenan following like a

dark shadow with one indecipherable look over his shoulder. But he didn't say anything, thus confirming himself in Caro's opinion as her favorite Watcher.

She got in the car, digging the keys out of her purse. It started with a smooth restful purr, and she touched the stick shift, curling her hand around it. Put the car in reverse, pulled out and set about sedately navigating out of the parking level. The Watcher on duty at the entrance didn't make a move, simply watched her go past from his niche, and she pulled out into the gray of early morning and turned on the wipers. The freeway was close, and she could open up the Miata once she was free of the snarl of traffic. If he knew, Trev would have a heart attack.

Caro turned on the radio, and her heart began to lighten.

* * * *

She stopped in Grenade Bay for lunch in a café that looked over a small marina where sea lions sometimes congregated. There was heavy weather moving in from the Pacific, a winter storm that would wash agates free on the beaches and make the waves pile up like moving gray laundry. She was oddly thankful she didn't have a Watcher hanging around. If she did, he might want her to go back, since a day with heavy cloud cover wasn't really safe. Not as unsafe as night, but still . . . not as safe as a sunny day. Even assuming a sunny day was safe.

She told herself not to think about unpleasant things and watched the glimmer of gray water, seagulls skimming in a white line offshore. *Wish I had time for some beachcombing. That would be nice.*

Vincent would have been sitting across from her, would have eaten if pressed, and would have let his dark eyes travel across the café and the street beyond—only two lanes, with a short scallop of beach below the opposite pavement, and a wall to keep people from falling onto the sand. He would have waited for her to finish her coffee, then shepherded her out to the car with only a faint, ironclad smile. His worry would have been tightly controlled but still like static spilling out from his aura, and she would have been glad to feel it. He had been unfailingly patient, of course—all Watchers were; but Vincent's quality of patience hadn't irritated her. It had been rather pleasant, since he mostly *asked* instead of *told* her what to do. His hair had been getting long, and sometimes, just before she fell asleep, she would think how she needed to take him for a trim, since it was a witch's duty to do things like that for a

Watcher.

Then her stomach would churn, like it was churning now, and she would remember the shattered bowl and the sound of her own screams.

And the smell of the Bane as it killed her Watcher.

Caro paid and left a good tip, with a faint relieved feeling that she never had to worry about money, and found the Miata parked on the street. Rain lashed down, spotting her sweater, and she hadn't bothered with a coat. She rarely did unless it was snowing or icy, which almost never happened in Saint City.

Home.

I was right. I do feel better when I'm traveling. Why is that? Maybe because I'm not being reminded every moment of what I am. Here on the road, I'm just another car. If it wasn't for travel I'd probably go nuts.

She shivered and turned the heat up. The thought of insanity, after seeing so much of it, was chilling and comforting in equal measure. She could be fairly sure she wasn't insane. Maybe wound a little too tight, but not *insane*.

And that was another thing, it was the travel she enjoyed, not arriving at the destination and certainly not arriving home. It was the state in-between that appealed to her.

She drove south, listening to oldies on the radio, tapping her fingers on the wheel, and singing along as the rain poured down. She was ahead of schedule and doing fine. When she reached Altamira and the safehouse there she would spend the night listening to rain falling on the roof, maybe getting up for a midnight cup of hot chocolate since she would probably have trouble sleeping, as she did in every new room.

Hold that thought, she told herself, humming along to the music as the highway dipped and curved along the humps of the coastline, priceless scenery unrolling out the passenger's side, scenery she was too busy driving to appreciate but soaked in nonetheless. *A whole new city to be an insomniac witch in. Who says life isn't fun?*

Two

The storm had arrived, lightning and thunder sweeping inland and penned by the coastal range into dumping its fury here. Merrick crouched in the lee of a HVAC vent, watching the last scraps of daylight succumb to the double assault of storm and night. His face burned in three stripes, the scars seamed and stitched with fire. Dark-made scars reacting to the Dark. It was coming out early to play in the concrete canyons.

He crouched easily, a big man in a long black leather coat, the sword riding his back and the guns—dull black instead of the shiny silver most Watchers used—low on his hips. An onlooker would have only seen an indistinct dark shape, thanks to the glamour, better camouflage than he'd ever had before. There was a trick to staying unseen he'd known since his first mission: *believing* yourself invisible. That the Watchers had a magickal method only made it easier.

The city sat under a pall of cloud, rain washing down. The wind was rising. This was his part of the city; he'd patrolled for three months now. It didn't take long for a Watcher to get to know a quadrant, know all the little alleyways and the deep wells of blackness, all the places Dark liked to hide. Just like tracking back in the jungle, really, learning the habits of a different wilderness and hunting through its labyrinths. It was why they called him the Tracker. He was famous for hunting down and dispatching the most dangerous and difficult Dark.

For all the good it bloody well does me. Don't think about that, Merrick old man.

Being on patrol was restful in its own way, and he was taking double shifts. Weariness wasn't a problem, not with the *tanak* burning inside him. The Watchers were, as always, stretched thin, barely enough of them to keep the city under control. Things were a little different up north in what the Watchers were calling Hope City, but that wasn't for him. Patrol, more patrol, endless patrol, and maybe sometime soon he would meet a piece of Dark and get careless, and that would be the end of him. Might even be a relief.

After the sun slipped below the horizon and full night covered the streets, he moved out onto the roof, ignoring the sudden heavy stinging of rain, and reached the edge, scanning

Fourth Avenue below. He was restless tonight, something was happening. Expectancy brushed at him, maybe his very slight precognitive ability warning him of a fight ahead. But this wasn't the cold lethal tension of a situation about to get critical. It was just . . . electricity. A type of call, as if he were tracking. But he hadn't been called upon to track anything—or anyone—for a few months now. The last prey had been a *belrakan*, difficult, dangerous, and causing havoc all through Altamira. He'd taken a team and found its lair. Lost two good men in that stinking cave, lucky not to have lost more.

Still, it had been a little quieter since they'd rooted out the last of the Bane. More time to think, and that was the worst part about being a Watcher. The adrenaline and crises he could deal with. It was having so much bloody time to *brood* that got to him.

His hair tangled over his eyes as he glared at the city, daring it to throw another enemy at him. He was off kilter, hadn't felt this strange since . . . When? The feeling had been growing for a good fortnight. He'd almost gone to the infirmary to get checked out, but another Watcher had bonded, and they needed someone to pull a double shift on patrol until the replacement could get here. Still, he wondered about the odd sensation.

Then again, nothing about being a Watcher was *normal*. Nothing about what he was had ever been normal. He seemed to have missed the normal train, so to speak.

The north end of the city wasn't technically his zone, but he moved toward it anyway. The few normals out on the street tonight wouldn't be able to see the sword hilt over his right shoulder. They would only see a man in a black trenchcoat, a man their instincts would warn them not to mess with. Of course, a Dark predator would see him for what he was: a lethal crimson-black swirl, tightly controlled, *trouble* written all over the night with neon, in capitals and underlined. Given how he felt tonight, he might almost welcome a fight.

The voice of his trainer echoed as he cut through a close, dim alley reeking of garbage, allowing himself a single nose-wrinkle. *Don't go out looking for a battle. That's the best way to give us one less Watcher. Stay cool, stay controlled, don't back away from a fight, but don't start one either. Always remember your first duty is to the Lightbringer in your care. And the less Watchers, the more danger for*

Lightbringers.

Here Stone had smiled, a brief bitter expression that wasn't amused at all. He'd looked at his two students, noting Calhoun's attention and Merrick's seeming inattention, and the smile had turned back into a habitual straight mask. *Of course, every now and again you have to keep the iron sharp,* he'd remarked, and gone on.

Merrick was almost to Ulvill Street when the sense of danger returned, thickening and swirling through wet air, making the scars on his face tingle and run with hot pain. Thunder crackled, he smelled salt wind from the coast. Altamira was thirty miles inland, up the curve of a great river. The sea seemed to reach up that long sheaf of water and drain the city of all color. Still, it wasn't a bad place. Not really. Less crowded than Seoul and more relaxed than New York, with the mountains and the beach close for nature buffs. No architecture, but then, nowhere in America had decent architecture.

He faded into another alley. A few moments of effort on the rusted-out fire escape brought him to another rooftop, this one unprotected. The full fury of the wind boiled across the roof as he peered down into the street below, the freeway offramp melding with the rest of Chess Street and creating a traffic nightmare during rush hour. Now, though, there was only a washed-clean street glimmering in the darkness. Nine o'clock, just barely into his second shift of patrol, and not usually a time for any heavy Dark activity. Not yet.

A sword of headlights jutted through the rain. It was a sports car, dark and sleek, going slowly as if the driver was uncertain. As Merrick watched, it pulled over, and the dome light inside went on. Someone lost, maybe?

His eyebrows pulled together. *Wait a minute. Just one goddamn minute.*

But there wasn't time for waiting, because he saw the flicker between shadows two blocks up. Long, low, and lean with a reptilian snout and claw-tipped legs, the thing lifted its head and sniffed like a dog. Only it wasn't a dog, not precisely. The dome light flicked off, but the car stayed in place, idling. There was a deeper glow behind the screen of warding on the car, and Merrick had to tear his eyes away to track the shape two blocks down.

It was *koroi*, a cross between dog, lizard, and Dark, with needle-sharp teeth that could make a wound septic and a habit of roaming in packs. Merrick swore to himself, reaching for a knife hilt. Paused. The thing slunk forward, its hide gleaming wetly, far more physical than it should have been. Like some other Dark predators, the *koroi* was mostly insubstantial until just before it struck, not wasting the energy to keep a physical form together until it could be sure of a return on the investment. His eyes scanned the street in one smooth arc, and Merrick swore to himself. There were more of them, of course, moving in on the car in a pattern he recognized. They had probably been chasing for a while, herding the occupant through a tangle of side streets. *Koroi* just didn't do that unless they were sure their prey was helpless. They stalked like jackals, moving in on other predators' kills, and only taking the weak or unwary.

Like a lone Lightbringer in a little toy of a sports car, with a cloth top a set of claws could easily rip through.

The screams rose again in Merrick's memory, He shoved them down with an effort of will. He'd seen what happened to a Lightbringer when a pack of lizard-dogs descended.

That was why he was on patrol. It was a sight he never wanted to see again.

His hand blurred for his sword hilt and he hurled himself forward, out into empty air. He was going to hit hard and braced himself for it, spending Power as the laws of physics bent just a little to let him land without breaking a bone. Not like it mattered, but a broken bone might slow him for a few critical seconds. And that Merrick wouldn't allow.

The glow coming from inside the sports car dimmed slightly, as if the Lightbringer inside was concentrating. What the hell was a Lightbringer doing out alone? Maybe she was a flyer, moving from place to place, a few steps ahead of the Dark. Maybe she was just visiting.

He hit and whirled, sword ringing free and cleaving through Dark not-flesh. Four *koroi*, sneaking up from this side of Chess Street. He could take these out and get to her before the others did—maybe.

Then the sound of crunching metal jerked him around in a tight half-circle, bright blade tearing through another lizard-dog's body. It gave out a shattering psychic squeal, and he heard smoking tires, an engine revving.

Get out of here, he thought, wishing she could hear him. *I'll hold them, you just get the hell out of here!*

Another crunch of metal. He dispatched the last *koroi*

and whirled to see the car skewed across the road under three of the lizard things. One of them leapt with scary, nimble grace to rend at the cloth top, but something sparked and smoked, driving it back. She'd tried to get away from them and been stopped, the lizard-dogs spending Power recklessly to bring her down.

That's Watcher work on the car. What's going on? He flung himself at the car, blurring through space with all the preternatural speed the *tanak* could give him, tasting adrenaline as the symbiote jacked his hormonal balance to make him sharper. His left hand, full of the knife, drove forward as he landed, black rune-chased metal smoking as it tore through the insubstantial bonds holding the lizard-thing to the world. It let out another deafening psychic screech, ringing through Merrick's head. He ignored it and dropped a few layers of camouflage, letting what he was shine through the landscape of Power.

The two remaining *koroi* retreated, hissing, step by step. Merrick hopped down from the car's bonnet, sword held level, knife hilt tucked in his hand, the blade lying against his forearm. Ready for anything.

The rest of the lizard dogs—*Christ, there's bloody ten of them, must be a nest around here somewhere. Got to get together a sweeps detail*—regarded him with their orange eyes. Then, deciding he was too much for them, they faded back. His breath came harsh and tearing as his attention swept the street, making sure. They were retreating. He was more than they'd bargained for.

At least, for now.

Merrick dug in his pocket for the cell phone, fished it out. His attention followed the retreating *koroi* as the lamps of their eyes extinguished two by two. There would be other Dark predators on the way, attracted by the mess and noise of battle, as well as by the stench of death.

The phone came to life in his ear. "Report." It was a Watcher, thank God. He placed the voice. Drake, the one with the tattoo of a scorpion. Quiet man, good Watcher, even if he did have a death wish.

I'm not far away from that myself. Merrick's heart thumped against his ribs, coming down from the redline of combat. The thought was there and gone in a moment, so familiar he barely noticed it.

"Merrick, Zone 45. I'm at Chess and Hollworth with a possible flyer in a sports car and a bunch of bloody *koroi*." His voice sliced the air, steamed sharply between raindrops. Thunder ruffled the clouds overhead. "I need cleanup and possibly a tow truck. Not to mention a little backup, if we've got any."

"How many Lightbringers?"

"Just one, maybe two. Can't fit more into that car. I'm going to secure it and stand guard."

"Help's on the way." Just like that. And the connection was terminated.

Merrick turned back to the car. There was definitely a Lightbringer in there, the clear glow pulsing and stuttering. It was subtly wrong, and he paused, trying to think of *why*. Nothing that glowed that brightly could be Dark. But instead of a jewel-toned shine, this was a sheer golden aura, full of golden pinwheels. He let out a soft breath.

Mindhealer. Of course. He'd met a few, back in the day when he was on guard duty, before he'd requested to be put on patrol. Difficult, vulnerable to Darksickness, and exquisitely sensitive to Watchers.

In other words, a real joy.

His scars twinged. Now that the battle was over—or at least, taking a breather—he could feel that he'd almost pulled something in his leg, leaping over the car like that. His shoulder hurt, he'd pulled a tendon meeting the *koroi* head-on. The *tanak* twisted at the pain, bathing the slight wounds with Power from the spent deaths of the lizard-dogs. It *hurt*, but the pain was so natural by now that he ignored it.

The driver's door rocketed open. He caught sight of light hair, glowing under the streetlamp, and braced himself to deal with a hysterical witch who had no idea why a man with a sword had just fought off nightmare creatures. She'd probably cry, too. He hated to see Lightbringers cry. They were such gentle souls, it was hard to watch them suffer.

He'd reached the front end of the car, headlamps still uselessly burning and the bonnet dented and crumpled, when she made it all the way out, moving shakily. He wanted to tell her to stay down in case she had any injuries, but she held grimly on to the door and a pair of dark eyes met his.

The shock stopped him midstride. Outside the Watcher warding that still sparked and fizzed against the structure of the car, bleeding energy into the wet air, she glowed all the more brightly. The force of that light should have brought Merrick to his knees, if not literally then damn close, especially when he was still smarting from the battle. Her aura, pure Light, should have made the scars on his face and the deep channels of his bones fill with acid. Should have hurt him, in short, the way every other Lightbringer did. The brighter the glow, the more pain—after all, the *tanak* was a creature of Darkness, for all it was symbiotic to a Watcher. The *tanak* got a safe harbor, food, and physical *being*. A Watcher got superhuman strength, endurance, and a level of Power to work the combat magicks that gave him a chance against other Dark predators.

It should have been agony.

It wasn't, and that brought him up short, blinking at a woman who was almost incandescent with anger. Her hair was rapidly being lashed down and darkened with the rising wind and water. She wore a flimsy blue sweater and a pencil skirt, drew herself up to her full height and glared at him with dark eyes that threatened to strip their way past his skull and right into the center of his brain. "Who the *hell* are you?" she demanded, and her voice was another surprise, clear and firm. Beautiful, with the same bell-like quality other Lightbringers had, but also with a snap of command. "Have you been following me?"

"No ma'am." Training rose under his skin. When a Lightbringer spoke, you damn well listened. *Duty. Honor. Obedience.* "I'm out on patrol. Those things—"

"*Koroi.*" She shivered. "Gods above and below, how I hate *koroi.* I suppose you've already called in?"

Relief flooded him. She was a Circle Lightfall witch. He wouldn't have to contend with giving The Speech, hopefully calming her down while he tried to explain he wasn't the enemy, even though he was armed and looked like a piece of Dark to otherSight himself.

Then where's her Watcher? Hurt? In the car? AWOL? "Of course, ma'am. I—"

"Great. Just *great.* I suppose they deliberately *planned* this city to be impossible to navigate even with *directions!*" Her dark eyes were almost spitting sparks. Her aura sparkled, fizzed, and sent a jolt of sugary heat through Merrick's entire body.

No. Can't be. Impossible. He stood frozen to the drenched

street, staring at her. It was *im*-bloody-*possible*. The only thing
that could ever, possibly, conceivably feel like that was . . .

"I asked you a question, Watcher. Who the hell are you,
and why were you following me?"

That snapped him out of it. She looked just about ready to
fillet him with words alone. He would have far rather faced
another batch of *koroi*. "Merrick, ma'am. Attached to the Blue
Street Safehouse, Altamira. On patrol. I wasn't following you,
I saw the *koroi* just as you happened along."

She eyed him with barely contained suspicion. "Perfect.
Wonderful. *Outstanding!*" She suddenly stopped, clapped her
hand over her mouth, and closed her eyes. Merrick observed
this, curious, scanning the street. He had to get her under cover.
The lure of a Lightbringer, as well as recent combat, would
bring all *sorts* of Dark out to play.

"Oh, *gods* . . ." She made a low, hurt noise and swayed,
holding onto the door. He suddenly understood why her aura
was sparking so badly. Shock, and exposure to the Dark. She
was probably skirting the edge of Darksickness.

Where's my backup? Where's her Watcher? Bloody hell.

"Ma'am?" He made his voice softer, attempting to lessen
the harsh tone. "Maybe you'd best sit down."

She swayed again, her knuckles white on the car door, and
he made it to her just as her knees buckled. Caught her and
lowered her down so she sat in the driver's seat, automatically
moving to block the worst of the rain as best he could. Between
him and the bulk of metal, she was a little safer. Her aura
touched his, slid along the edges of the red-black stain, and
Merrick shivered. The feeling taunted the Dark in him, made it
retreat growling.

He held his hand a scant inch above her shoulder—she
was going to be soaked in a minute, the rain had intensified—
and sent a flush of heat through her, the small Power charge
slamming visibly through her aura. Her head dropped forward,
and Merrick almost went to his knees, catching her shoulder
and bracing her.

"I think I'm going to throw up." Now she sounded very
young. Who *was* this witch?

"If you must." He tried to sound comforting. There was
nobody else in the car. "Where's your Watcher, ma'am? Is he
hurt?"

She managed to give him an extraordinary, almost vengeful

look before she dropped her head again, random curls of her hair falling down. Her braid was getting much the worse for wear, and Merrick was suddenly shaken with the uncharacteristic desire to smooth her hair back and say something comforting.

"I don't have a Watcher," she said to the pavement. The car was so low-slung he had no difficulty kneeling as he held her up. Damp soaked into the knee of his jeans. "I told the High Council to take them off me. I won't—I won't . . . oh, *gods*."

No Watcher? But that was impossible. How could she be a Circle Lightfall witch, out alone after sundown, with no Watcher? Who had allowed that?

A flare of proprietary anger shocked him. He shook his head, his hair falling in his eyes and dripping down to his cheekbones. Her aura didn't hurt him. There was only one reason why that could be. Only one, single, solitary reason why, even this close to her, the force of her light didn't make his bones scream in agonized pain.

She was his witch.

Can't be. I didn't ever think I'd get a witch. It can't be. Merrick glanced up. He scanned the street again, suddenly unaccountably nervous. "Does the car still run?"

"I th-think so, it j-j-just . . . I s-st-stalled it by standing on the brake when the k-k-kor—" Little shudders raced through her. Merrick glanced at the interior. A purse, spilled out, and a canvas bag on the passenger side floor. No room for anything else.

"Keys," he said briskly, and checked the ignition. They were still there. The bonnet of the car was dented, and the cloth top would probably never be the same, but it appeared less damaged than he'd thought. "All right, ma'am. I'll bring you in. You don't have to worry. You're safe now."

Just as he said it, warning bells went off. He scanned the street again, and cursed to himself. The instinct of a hunted animal rose under his skin. Something else out there. If he was lucky it was only *something,* singular instead of plural.

"Safe?" She gave out a laugh that now sounded older than he would have thought. "Nothing's safe, Watcher. N-nothing."

She seemed too young to know that much about the world. "You're safe now," he said shortly, and pushed her upright to sit—but gently. "Can you climb over into the passenger seat?"

"I-I'll dr-dr—"

Not right now, you'll kill us both. It wasn't strictly true, he could survive far more damage than she could. But his primary objective was to get her *out* of here, and one shocked and almost-Darksick witch wasn't likely to be able to drive the way he could. "Can you get into the passenger seat?"

She raised her head and glared at him, then glanced down the street. Her pupils dilated, and her aura gave another extraordinary flash. Merrick bit down, his jaw freezing as she stared at the gathering patch of darkness scuttling between streetlamps, coming past the freeway offramp on Chess Street. It was a Slider, and a big one, most definitely attracted by the fight and her broadcasting. Her distress rang in the wet air like a gong, and his scars lit up with pain. But this time the pain had a softer edge—it was honeyed and spiked, and it made him suddenly acutely aware that her sweater was thin, damp, and clinging to her.

"Into the other seat." He pushed her gently and she complied, scrambling. He saw she was wearing expensive-looking black heels, and was surprised to see her ankle under the nylons, slim and delicate and fascinating.

Goddammit, keep your mind on your work. Merrick slid into the driver's seat and took a moment to push the seat back, she was much smaller than him and the car was tiny. But it started when he twisted the key, so he jerked the door shut, shifted, and gave it some petrol.

The car leapt forward as if it had never intended to stay still. He shifted once, twice, fished the cell phone out and hit redial with his thumb as the Slider broke into a lope behind them. With any luck, it would stop and feed on the psychic sludge of the *koroi* he hadn't had time to cleanse from the air.

"Report." It was Drake again.

"Merrick. Eastbound on Chess Street. Cancel the tow. I'm bringing the witch in. She's in shock and I'm bloody well halfway there myself."

"Pursuit?" Drake sounded calm. Of course, he was a Watcher.

"One Slider I can see. Nothing else. I'm going to take Eighteenth up to Blue and come in that way; less traffic and more chances to dodge."

"Be careful. There's a team coming out to bring you in."

Merrick dropped the phone, shifted again, and stole a glance at the witch. She was pale, and in the dim light he could see the high arch of her cheekbone, the fans of her eyelashes as she closed her eyes, the sweet sculpted mouth pulled down as she fought nausea. A thin thread of something dark he hoped wasn't blood traced down her chin.

"Just hang on, ma'am." He tried to sound reassuring while glancing in the rearview mirror. The Slider had hunkered down over the remains of the *koroi*. "You're safe."

"Caro." She gulped in air, reached over blindly, and held onto the door while he manipulated the car around a turn. The tires were a trifle splashy, but other than that everything seemed fine. He hoped it stayed that way, hoped nothing in the engine had been damaged. Power tended to make engines behave a little funny. "My name's Caro."

"Hallo, Caro." He checked the street again and cursed to himself. There was something else following them, something that didn't seem interested in the remains of the *koroi*. "Don't worry. You're going to be all right."

"Oh, I know that." Did she actually sound irritated? "It's *you* I'm worried about."

The statement was so absurd he almost missed another turn up Sixteenth. He drifted the car into it, the scabbarded sword digging into his back. He was a Watcher, meant and trained for one thing: protection. He carried enough hardware to take on anything Dark and fight himself and a Lightbringer free; he had been taught to disregard pain very early, before he had even known Watchers existed. Why would she be worried about him?

He had no time to ask, because the Dark trailing them dove out of the night sky, and Caro screamed, a high thin sound that broke at the end. It was a *s'lin*, fully grown, and the air inside the car turned thick and choking as the torn Watcher wards tried ineffectually to beat the thing away. The cloth top ripped, Merrick slammed both the clutch and brakes at the same time, tearing the car into a tight circle and cutting across three lanes of traffic before slamming down on the petrol again. The street was almost deserted, headlights down at the other end, but nobody near enough to see. He reached over, his hand closing around her nape and forcing her head down just in case the claws tearing through the top of the car came close to her.

A jolt of agonized, narcotic pleasure tore up his arm.

Merrick set his jaw and pumped all the Power he could spare into the torn and bleeding wards. The combination of the car's sudden change of momentum and the flare of energy threw the *s'lin* free. Rubber screamed, he juggled trajectory and friction and came up with an answer he didn't much like, twisted the wheel again. He would have to take a sharp turn on Doren to get over to Eighteenth, and there was plenty of time for the *s'lin* to catch them again.

Where's my backup? And where's her goddamn Watcher? No Lightbringer this bright should be without a Watcher. Well, don't worry about it, not going to be a problem. If I can just get her to the safehouse it will be enough.

He considered praying, discarded it. Didn't have time. Besides, the gods could be pleaded with, might even lend a hand, but it was up to this Watcher to make *sure* no harm came to her.

Cold wet air poured in through the rents in the top of the car. He let go of her, his fingers reluctant to slide free. The feel of her skin was such a relief from the constant grinding pain of the *tanak* that he was severely distracted, a distraction he couldn't afford with a *s'lin* chasing them and the car's engine suddenly making a sound he didn't very much like at all.

"Don't you worry about me, witch." He made the turn onto Doren. Traffic was heavier here, and he hoped he could avoid police notice. That would be the very last thing he needed. "Just stay calm, and breathe deep."

And you can pray, if you like, he added silently. *The gods will listen to you more than me.*

Then the *s'lin* drifted overhead for another pass, and Merrick forgot all about praying.

Three

She had only wanted to examine the directions again. She *would* have been on time, but had somehow gotten tangled up in a maze of streets and ended up getting progressively later and later, more and more lost in this strange city, and hungrier as well. Caro never thought well when she was hungry anyway. The lack of physical food detracted from her ability to keep the walls between herself and the emotions of other people swirling around her strong enough. And the lower the sun sank in the sky, the more frantic she'd become.

Then she'd been slowly aware of something lurking in the streets, something that was taking an active interest in her. The weather moving in from the sea had made dusk arrive early, and she wasn't sure when she'd come to the attention of the *koroi* She'd just looked up from the map and seen the low, slinking shape between two streetlamps, recognition making her heart hammer and her palms go wet. Her instinctive reflex to get away, stamping on the gas and twisting the wheel, had probably saved her life.

Caro squeezed her eyes shut, hearing the Watcher beside her curse under his breath as rubber screamed and the car twisted around a corner. *I should have my seat belt on. He should have his on too.* It was a useless thought. Warmth filled her nose; she was bleeding. A nosebleed, probably spurred by the Dark.

"Backup," he muttered. "Any time now, mates."

The cell phone, wedged between Caro's hip and the console between the two seats, buzzed insistently. Caro reached blindly for it—the Watcher had his hands full, and if someone was calling it was probably important. The car slewed again, and she felt the scraping, awful passage of the thing chasing them overhead, like a serrated knife slipping under the skin of an apple, tearing. Her hand closed around the phone's sleek exterior, and she stole a glance at the man who had appeared out of nowhere.

He was much bigger than her. Most Watchers were, since the *tanak* gave them denser bone and muscle structure, and constant combat kept them in shape. But this Watcher had a shock of dark hair, longer than most other Watchers wore theirs, falling over his face. He glared through it with a pair of bright-green eyes glowing with furious intensity. Most Watchers developed a piercing gaze after a while, the *tanak* bleaching out their irises. The rest of his face was shadowed, and the concentric rings of awareness he sent out—a kind of Watcher radar—were familiar to her from a childhood spent in Circle Lightfall. He sounded a bit odd when he talked, a clipped foreign accent she hadn't had time to place yet.

She got the cell phone free, pressed the talk button. "What?" she snapped. Images spun by outside the window: a laundromat, a teriyaki restaurant, a liquor store. Streetlamps flashed past. He seemed to know where he was going, thank the gods. Something wet and warm trickled down her cheeks—tears. More wet warm trickles on her upper lip—it was the way she always reacted to the proximity of anything Dark, with a stupid nosebleed. *Thank goodness I didn't wear the linen suit. Blood never comes out of linen.*

There was a brief pause. "Ma'am?" Another Watcher's voice. "Tell him to take Ferne instead of Blue. There's police presence on Blue he needs to avoid."

"Hold on." Caro lowered the phone. "He says to take Ferne instead of Blue, because of police." Her voice shook, tremulous. She cursed herself for being weak. He sounded so goddamn *competent*. It was strange to be so close to a Watcher again, hear that absolute confidence.

"Got it." He held out his hand for the phone, Caro relinquished it, careful not to touch his skin with hers. He must be in pain from her nearness, but he didn't show it.

He downshifted, lifted the phone to his ear. "Talk fast." A pause. "Not yet. I've got a *s'lin* on my tail and the engine's giving out." Another short pause. "You got it. Thanks." Clipped, brief, he dropped the phone again, and all but stood on the clutch and the brake. Caro let out a traitorous shriek, grabbing for the door handle to right herself.

"Sorry." He really did sound genuinely sorry.

There was a sour taste in Caro's mouth; she finally placed his accent and almost sighed in relief. He sounded British. Or Australian.

Well, at least I've figured that out. Was he following me? He said he wasn't. He was on patrol, I was out after dark, dammit, they're going to have a Watcher on me now. Gods, what did I do to deserve this? I just got lost, that's all.

Her mind shivered, the chill creeping up her fingers and toes. It was a chill she was all-too-familiar with, a sign that the Dark was close, and closing in.

Then she felt it, an almost physical release of pressure. More Watchers, driving off the *s'lin*. The man in the driver's seat let out a short, harsh breath, the car's speed slackening just a bit but not nearly enough for her to let go of the door. The Miata sounded like an overworked sewing machine now—the way he drove, she wasn't surprised. Plus, the *koroi* had hit with both physical and psychic force. Car engines didn't do too well with psychic tampering, especially engines with computer chips. The car swerved, squealing, and he fought to keep it on the road. It sounded like one of the tires had blown.

"Where did you learn to drive?" she managed around the sour nausea rising behind her breastbone.

"Army. We're only a few blocks away, you can feel the safehouse from here. Almost there."

"Great," Caro mumbled, collapsing forward. She put her head on her knees, trying to remember to breathe, and promptly passed out.

* * * *

A brief starry period of unconsciousness, then Caro was vaguely aware of the car braking to a stop. The air was close and still, with the breathless feeling of Watcher wards. She heard the car door open, and women's voices, quiet and gentle— Lightbringer voices. She tried to open her eyes, couldn't, felt soft hands on her. Power flooded in, the softness of healers. Healers?

She was safe, then. The confusion, as she was drawn out of the car and clucked over, was equally soft.

"Is she all right?"

"Who is it? Goddess, she's *bleeding.*"

"What's that? Oh, her purse. Be careful with that."

"Hold on. Here comes Fran."

Running feet, more soft auras crowding around her, running with jewel-toned light. "Here, hold this, she'll want it. And this . . . oh, my. Oh my. She's bleeding, she must be Darksick."

"I'm here!" *This* voice, at least, was familiar. She'd heard it both on the phone and in person, and it was a welcome relief. "I'm here. What's—Oh, gods above and below! Caro!"

"It's her?"

Fran sounded relieved. "The Mindhealer, in the flesh.

Someone call up and let Drusilla know."

Caro tried to make her eyes open again. Failed. Power curled around her, worked into her aura, trying to dispel the spreading stain of Darksickness. The trickle of blood from her nose had eased, someone wiped it away with a soft cloth.

"You found her?" Fran's tone sharpened.

"I did, ma'am." The Watcher's tone was respectful, each word pulled out of him as if by force. The accent made him sound very educated, very precise. "Begging your pardon, but I have to report."

"Oh?" A rustle went through the women. Watchers didn't usually say that.

No, Caro thought. They were wiping her face again. Someone hummed a snatch of a chant. *Please, no. No more. Don't give them any reports, just go away!*

Caro sagged and managed to drag in a deep, endless breath. "Ow," she said, to stop him from speaking. "I *don't* want to do that again."

"Caro?" It was Fran, stroking her forehead, gently wiping blood away from her cheek.

She found, to her relief, that she could open her eyes.

The fluorescents and dark roof of a parking garage met her gaze. Claustrophobia tore briefly at her throat, released. Why did she feel so weak? Five women, all with the bright emerald auras of earth witches, were clustered around her. And leaning over her was Francine, a familiar sharp face topped with a braided coronet of blonde hair streaked with gray. Amber drops hung in Fran's ears; she looked, as usual, greatly amused. She wore a long purple sweater and a yellow scarf. *Dreadful taste, as usual, Fran. Goddess, I am so glad to see you.*

"Well, thank Brigid. You're alive. I was afraid of the worst." Fran had her hands on her hips, trying to look disapproving and not managing it through the relief.

"So was I." Caro's eyes hurt. Her fingers were cold. "I'm cold."

"Darksick, it looks like. You and your nosebleeds." Fran leaned down, touched Caro's forehead. "Are you all right?"

"I got lost," she mumbled. "You gave me bad directions." *I sound like a three-year-old.*

"I think I did," Fran said gravely. "No wonder you're late. Good thing Merrick stumbled across you."

The Watcher? Don't mention him, Frannie. Please. "You

didn't sic him on me?"

"Of course not." Now Fran looked severe. "I'll overlook that, since you're so obviously sick. Let's get you up to a comfortable room. Merrick?"

"Yes, ma'am." But he wasn't done with thinking he had to report. "Ma'am?"

It was so unheard of for a Watcher to persist like this that all the women stilled. Caro heard footsteps, felt the air disturbance. The other Watchers, having driven off the *s'lin*, coming back in. This was so messy and *public*, she'd been out after dark and attacked. All the noises the regional and High Councils had been making lately about sticking her with another Watcher would get louder. She would be lucky to avoid it now.

It was so absurd she could have laughed.

Gods, I'm a mess. Her nylons were torn, she was almost sure she'd lost a shoe, and her head ached savagely. The chill had now reached her knees and elbows, concrete cold and hard under her one stockinged foot. The women she leaned against were soft, and one of them smelled wonderfully of jasmine through the thick reek of copper in Caro's nose.

"Yes?" Fran sounded guarded. One eyebrow rose as she looked over Caro's head, at the Watcher.

"I need to be taken off patrol duty," he said, from behind Caro's shoulder. "This is my witch."

Oh, fantastic. Caro sagged against the women holding her up. "Perfect," she muttered. "He's lost his mind. Just what I need. I'd really like to lie down now. And if someone can get my bags, that would be nice."

She would have said more, but the chill swept through her, shaking her like an animal would shake something caught in its teeth. Little shivers raced down her arms and legs.

"Enough," the jasmine-scented healer said. "She's Darksick. Help me."

I'm not Darksick, Caro wanted to object, but her teeth were chattering too hard and a wave of weakness poured over through her. Too much excitement, and too close to the Dark. The better-trained and more powerful a Mindhealer was, the more vulnerable to the psychic contagion of the Dark. Yet another price she paid for her gifts. *I wouldn't mind if the nosebleeds weren't so messy.*

"Here, hold her," the jasmine-scented healer said. "Follow me. You three, get her luggage."

"It's all right, Caro." Fran patted her hand. "We'll get this sorted out. I'm glad you're here. We need you, it's getting worse."

What's getting worse? she would have replied, but the darkness closed over her head again. Before it closed completely, though, she felt herself picked up and carried, as if she were a child. The cold worked all the way down to her bones, and she wondered if this time it might freeze her all the way through.

Four

Merrick stood just inside the door, hands in his pockets, watching. The healers worked on Caro, murmuring, the glow of their auras scraping at him. This was a pretty room, wide windows kissed with false dawn, blue carpeting, a Cezanne print over the fireplace, curtains drawn back and pale gray almost-dawn smoothing over the small kitchenette . . . and one pale Lightbringer on the bed, her blonde hair spilling over the pillows. Only it wasn't truly blonde, it was a rich chestnut thickly streaked with pure gold. The nosebleed had stopped, thank the gods. Merrick wasn't sure how she'd started bleeding and didn't want to think about it. The sight of her blood made his stomach churn.

The healers were doing their best, *had* been doing their best all night. Her aura was stained with Darksickness, and each time the stain retreated, it then returned.

And Merrick's hands would tighten inside his pockets, his scars pulsing with pain. He wanted to stalk over to the bed and force Power through her, flood her with enough to make the stain retreat. Or if all else failed, bring her out of shock and Darksickness the old way. If she died . . .

She's not going to die. We're in a bloody safehouse with four healers right here. She's not going to die.

He hadn't failed. She was safe.

When the stain faded for good, he breathed a little easier. And finally, when the healers left, each of them passing close enough to Merrick for his bones to grind with agony, she was sleeping peacefully, the danger averted. The Council liaison— an air witch with a coronet of gray-threaded hair—stood near the window, watching, obviously reluctant to go just yet. She crossed to the bed, took the Mindhealer's pulse, and stroked a stray curl back from her face.

"Poor child," she said, quietly. "Do you have any idea who you've brought in, Watcher?"

It was a direct question. No way he could get around answering. "No ma'am." *A Mindhealer. Someone said her name but I didn't catch it. I was too busy carrying suitcases and trying to see what they were doing to her. Caro. She said, Caro.* "I found her on Chess Street and—"

"I'm well aware of that. Drake told me. You're asking to

be pulled from patrol."

He drew himself up but still didn't take his hands out of his pockets, afraid she would see how tight his fists were clenched. "Yes ma'am."

"Because?" Her eyebrow arched. She had a strong face, beauty pared down to the bone. They were all pretty, the Lightbringers, but a few of them approached pure loveliness. None of them seemed to consider themselves extraordinary. More often than not, they felt more cursed than blessed by their gifts.

"Because she's my witch." There. That was as simple as he could make it. *It doesn't hurt when she's near me. And when I touch her I feel like my entire nervous system's been wired to a car battery in a good way.*

"You're certain?"

You think I'd lie about something like this? Of course not. I'm a Watcher. Honor, duty, obedience. I might not have had any honor before, but I'm not a liar now. "Her light doesn't hurt me, ma'am." It was the traditional understatement, implying a Watcher had found his witch.

Amazingly enough, the Council liaison began to laugh. It was more of a helpless chuckle than anything else. "This is Caroline Robbins, the Mindhealer."

His jaw threatened to drop. "*The* Caroline?" *The Mindhealer that travels around teaching everyone? The one they've called in to take a look at all those cases on the North Side?* "Eleanor D'Arcy's protégé?"

She managed to swallow her laughter, but her eyes were watering. Her mouth twitched. Merrick dropped his eyes uncertainly. Whatever she was amused over, it had nothing to do with him. Witches sometimes had the oddest sense of humor.

"The very same. Some time ago she made an agreement with the High Council. She would stay at safehouses in lieu of having a Watcher. Another Watcher—one she was quite attached to, the same one that brought her in—was killed by a *belrakan.* Caro's never forgotten that." The Council witch sighed. "So she's now your responsibility, and you're no longer under the jurisdiction of Circle Lightfall."

Her blue eyes met Merrick's, a searching, significant glance. He wished he could shake his hair down over his face to hide the burning scars.

"Yes ma'am." *For all the good it does me. I barely got*

her loose of that s'lin. *I should have done something else,
gotten her free before she was Darksick.*

The Council witch folded her arms. "You are no longer
under the jurisdiction of Circle Lightfall. We can't order you
back on patrol."

Why is she repeating that? "Yes ma'am."

She gave him another significant look, then sighed, glancing
back down at the sleeping witch on the bed. "She'll be all right.
If she starts to run a fever, or if the Darksickness comes back,
do what you can and call for a healer immediately." She headed
for the door, her glow tearing and scraping at him. "And if she
wakes up and starts talking, remember she doesn't mean it.
And remember you're twice her size. Though it won't feel like
it."

What does that mean? "Ma'am?"

She didn't explain, just waved her fingers at him as she
drifted out the door. He thought he heard her laughing out in
the hall, uncontrollable giggles that sounded much younger than
she looked.

Mystified, Merrick checked the door and the wards on the
walls and windows again. Here, in a safehouse, with him
standing guard, his witch was as safe as it was possible to be.
But still . . . He looked at her, carefully, stealing little glances
out from under his hair, his scars throbbing with the aftermath
of the other Lightbringers.

She lay on her side, curled around the canvas bag one of
the healers had brought from the car. Her hair tangled along
the pillow, golden streaks glowing in the rainy dawn light. The
tanak growled inside him, shifted, and settled back, satisfied.

Her hands were small, delicate; her wrists finely made
and fragile-looking. She'd seemed taller. It was a shock to see
how small she was. Short, unpolished nails, a thin classic gold
bracelet against her pale skin. Her black sweater and pencil
skirt were still damp, her nylons torn and ragged. Someone
had found her shoes and laid them neatly by the bed. The healers
hadn't pulled a blanket over her—the room was warm with
the bleed-off from Merrick's aura and heat through the vents.
Besides, they had to be able to touch her.

Merrick worked the down coverlet loose, settled it carefully
over her as soon as he'd freed it from beneath her feet. She
was thinner than she should be, and the dark circles under her
eyes spoke of exhaustion. She had a soft mouth, still tinged

with a ghost of lipstick, and her mascara was smudged. A faint shadow of dried blood clung to her cheek. Her eyes, if he remembered right, were dark.

Of course I remember. It seemed he'd done nothing but replay the moment over and over, feeling the shock—when her eyes met his and the whole world stopped—like a punch to the gut.

She'd gone to the High Council and gotten them to agree to let her run around without a Watcher. Why? Though Lightbringers were wary of Watchers, there were precious few who didn't want the protection Circle Lightfall could offer. There were invisible operations going on all the time, protecting Lightbringers from afar until a Circle witch could make contact and gently introduce them to the organization.

Was that what this witch would require of him? Invisibility? It was no less than he deserved. He'd never for a moment thought he would get the reward most Watchers lived for.

Surprise, Merrick old man.

The light was kind to her, sliding lovingly across the planes and curves of her face. The fragile arc of her throat taunted him, her winged collarbones, the delicate shape of her shoulder. The sweater clung to her torso, but he was trying like hell not to look at that.

Bloody hell. If he stood there much longer he was going to be tempted to touch her again. Just once, to feel that shock of agonized pleasure rocketing through his nervous system again. *I don't deserve this.*

It was why he'd asked for patrol, damn near begged for it. He couldn't stand to see another Lightbringer hurt. He'd seen too much pain and suffering inflicted on these gentle souls, helpless against a world that was all too brutal and infested with Dark, not to mention the Crusade and the Brotherhood, as well as other organizations who would love to harness the psychic abilities of the Lightbringers for themselves. Or the normals, who would fear and therefore hate the different, the talented, the strange. The Watchers were the best defense against the accidents of Fate and the lunacy of the Crusade, as well as the greed of the Brotherhood ... but it was too much. He never wanted to see another Lightbringer suffer. And besides, there was no goddamn redemption for *him*, he knew all too well. Not for him, not for what he'd done.

So why? Maybe it was a mistake. But no other Mindhealer

had been able to get within a few yards without him feeling the agonizing pain of the *tanak* struggling in allergic reaction to their light. It seemed bloody unlikely.

Touch her again. Just one more time, just to be sure. Come on, you can do it. Nobody will ever know. She's out cold.

He watched her aura spark with golden pinwheels, the distinctive mark of a Mindhealer. When she woke up, what would she think of him?

Doesn't matter, the deep voice of his conscience replied. *Only thing that matters now is not screwing up. She's your witch. It's up to you to keep her alive. End of story.*

Merrick retreated to his spot by the door and took a deep breath. His hands shook, and his scars felt like liquid fire had been pressed into the flesh of his face, the regular low-level grinding pain of a Dark symbiote wedded to his body. If he needed a reminder of what he was, that burning would do just fine. He was a flawed Watcher, hadn't even come by his knives honestly, and maybe this had all been just a fluke. But he'd committed to this course, and whether or not it was a fluke, he was now responsible for one fragile-looking Mindhealer.

Should be no problem. How hard can it be to handle one little witch?

* * * *

She didn't wake up until evening, when the darkness thickened against the window and slid into the corners of the room. It was the longest day of Merrick's life, listening to each deep soft breath, watching her aura for the stain of Darksickness. Each breath was a gift, but the longer she slept, the more worry taunted him.

Then again, she must have been exhausted. And the nosebleed had stopped.

A healer came to check on her every two hours, nodding at Merrick. None of them brought a Watcher. Apparently the Mindhealer's aversion to Watchers was well-known.

Great.

When she did stir, rolling over onto her back and making a soft noise that turned into a stretch and a yawn, he pulled himself further back into the shadows near the door. He hadn't cared what he looked like in years, but he didn't want her to see the scars. He scowled at the thought, shaking his hair down. He wasn't here to look pretty. He was cannon fodder. In any case, if this witch didn't like Watchers, his face wouldn't matter.

He made sure his hands were out of his pockets, hanging loose and easy. Wouldn't do to frighten her. Get things off on the wrong foot, that would.

"Gods," she said quietly, stretched again, and propped herself on her elbows, blinking in the rainy dusk filling the room. Her aura sparked, then brightened, little fingers of gold waving gently like sea anemones, testing the air. She was fully-trained, excellent shielding, and likely to be disoriented.

He shivered as her attention brushed the air inside the room, wrapping around him briefly. The brief contact sent a rill of unexpected pleasure up his spine.

Then her gaze swung over, rested on him. "What on earth are *you* still doing here?"

As a greeting, it wasn't as bad as he'd feared. He cleared his throat. "Merrick," he reminded her. "Brought you in last night, ma'am. The Council liaison released me from patrol duty."

She yawned again, hugely and delicately, like a cat. Blinked. "Hit by a train," she muttered.

What? "Beg your pardon?"

She made it up to sitting, grimacing, and glanced around the room again. Her hair tangled down, random curls falling in her face, she sighed and tucked a few behind her ear. "I feel like I've been hit by a train. I'll be all right, you don't need to stay. Go on."

It was an extraordinary moment. *Does she not understand?* "You want me to go invisible?" He tried not to feel his heart sink at the thought. It wasn't unheard of. Plenty of Watchers had done their duty invisibly. He'd done it himself, watching over witches who were unaware of his very existence. But she . . .

Obedience, Watcher. Stay still.

She slid from beneath the coverlet, wincing, and contemplated her ragged nylons. "What the hell are you talking about? I covered this with the Council. I don't need a Watcher, I don't *want* a Watcher. Though I'm very grateful to you for saving my life—*very* grateful. I'll put you in for a commendation."

I don't want a bloody commendation. "You're my witch."

He shouldn't have said it, especially not so flatly and with such force the curtains rustled and he heard the wall groan, sharply. But his patience only stretched so far, and this was a Circle Lightfall witch. She should understand, shouldn't she?

As soon as he thought it, he was ashamed of himself. It was his *job* to be patient, and she'd just been dragged through the city with a *s'lin* trying to open up her car like a soda can and messily devour her, not to mention the *koroi*. She was justifiably a little upset, and probably disoriented from shock and Darksickness. And he'd been warned she probably wouldn't react well to a Watcher.

You are no longer under the jurisdiction of Circle Lightfall. We can't order you back on patrol.

So the Council witch had been trying to warn him and let him know his duty was to stay with the Mindhealer, no matter how upset she was. He cursed himself for not seeing it sooner. *I used to be quicker on the uptake. Am I slipping?*

The Mindhealer stared at him, her eyes wide. She'd probably never been interrupted by a Watcher before. *Obedience, dammit. How many times do I have to tell myself, obedience? I swore.*

But he hadn't sworn to lend himself to idiocy, and her wandering around without any protection was idiocy of the highest order. She could have died last night if he hadn't run across her. Whether it was luck, precognition, or the gods taking a hand, who knew? But the thought of what *could* have happened chilled him right down to the bottom of his guts.

My witch. And I'll be damned if I let anything happen to her.

"What?" She didn't sound angry, thank the gods, only baffled.

Merrick took a deep breath. "You don't hurt me. Ma'am."

She was speechless for a full thirty seconds, staring at him. Her aura hardened, closing her off from the outside world. He could catch no whisper of what she was thinking, but her face was blank, pale, and she bit at her top lip, a movement that made her chin jut slightly, made her look younger. How old was she? She seemed to swing between old and young alarmingly quickly. He wondered if it was a Mindhealer trait.

Now that she was awake, he could see how her serious, puzzled expression made her only solemnly pretty instead of heartbreakingly beautiful. And her clear golden glow, pinwheels rising in concentric patterns, swirled more slowly as she stared, puzzling over this. Dark eyes, tangled hair, the curves of her cheekbones, the shape of her mouth as she worried at her top lip with her teeth—

Oh, gods help me. I'm in deep water.

It didn't help that her aura made the Dark grumble and subside inside his bones. The *tanak* sometimes gave a Watcher what relief it could from the constant wrenching pain of the body bearing a creature that was basically a helpful parasite. The mind-resting trance a Watcher could use in lieu of sleep was deep and dark enough to provide a little haven. But to be awake, and thinking, and not feeling the low-level grinding that became so much a part of daily life—that was damn near priceless. He would do just about *anything* to stay near this witch and feel that relief.

She made it to her feet, her skirt making a low sliding noise as she pushed herself free of the bed. "Are you telling me what I think you're telling me?"

Chalk one up for him, she didn't sound angry. What she *did* sound was sad, and that made his chest tighten.

"Ma'am?" He said it carefully. *How would I know what you think I'm telling you? I'm just a stupid Watcher.*

"Oh, don't play dumb with me. My name's *Caro*, not ma'am, and I'm not fooled by that sleepy little façade of yours." Her tone sharpened. Merrick winced. She swayed slightly, as if her balance was unsteady, then stalked across the blue carpet, her feet shuffling in their ruined nylons. And the Watcher, used to facing down horror in all its Dark faces, actually considered retreating from this one tangle-haired, slim-shouldered witch.

She ended up right in front of him, hands on hips, dark eyes searching his face. "Well?"

Well, what? He was beginning to feel decidedly out of his depth. Caution was probably the best route. "Ma'am?"

Her hand shot out, and Merrick almost flinched. But her fingers only closed around his wrist, her soft skin against his, and the jolt of sensation nailed him in place. Velvet fire rolled up his arm from the touch, taking a short break in his shoulder, before spilling down through his chest and making him extremely aware that he was standing right next to a woman who smelled like green tea and spice. It was a scent he had never come across before, and he drew it in, all the way down to the bottom of his lungs, his eyes half-closing. The pleasure spiked, driving through his nervous system like a collection of hammers, each one tipped with barbed honey. Every muscle in his body tensed against the onslaught.

She dropped his wrist and backed away, her hand coming up to her mouth. She stumbled, he stepped forward to catch her, and she flinched. That stopped him, acutely aware that he was taller, and quite probably menacing. They faced each other in the dim room, Merrick perfectly able to see thanks to Dark-enhanced sight. He suspected she couldn't see much of him. Only a large shape in a leather coat, eyes glittering under the messy dark hair. He winced at the thought of what he must look like, to her. "Don't be afraid." He pitched his voice low. He couldn't sound comforting, but he'd try.

For her sake.

"It's true," she whispered. "It's really ... it doesn't hurt you."

What, does she think I'd lie? "It doesn't. I'm sorry."

She shook her head and drew herself up, visibly steeling herself. "I think you should turn on the light. I'm going to unpack, and we're going to have a little talk. Then I'm going to go find Fran—Oh." She cast a quick look over her shoulder. "It's night. Did I sleep all day?"

"You were exhausted." *She has such a pretty voice.* It made even the American accent soft and reasonable instead of nasal and pretentious.

That seemed to earn him a little breathing room. "All right. Turn the light on. Let's see what we're dealing with."

He reached over, his fingers suddenly numb. What would happen when she saw the scars?

Light flooded the room. She blinked owlishly, and his heart turned over inside his chest. Then it fell, because she was staring at him. Her eyes were huge, still smudged with exhaustion, and she was utterly, impossibly beautiful. Just his luck to end up with a witch who was at the "lovely" end of the spectrum. *Now she's going to ask me where I got the scars, and I'm going to have to tell her, and I—*

She swallowed visibly. "Hi. I'm Caro. Thank you for saving my life."

What? "Merrick," he heard himself respond. "No thanks necessary, ma—um, Caro. It's my job."

Something flared behind her eyes, her aura going sharp and lemon-yellow. "Merrick? The Tracker?"

He winced at the nickname. It was a reminder he didn't need. "They call me that. Sometimes."

"I suppose I can't tell you to go away." She folded her arms across her chest defensively, and he saw that her eyes were actually a very dark blue. Indigo, under her dark eyelashes and dark arched eyebrows.

No, you can't. Even if you told me to I'd just Watch you from a distance, little witch. The words rose inside him, were strangled. He contented himself with shaking his head, looking out from under the mussed mess of his hair. If he kept it shaken down, she wouldn't see the scars as much.

Oddly enough, that seemed to spark her anger. "You listen to me, Watcher. I don't want another man dead because of me. As soon as I can schedule a knock-down-drag-out with the Council, I'll have you put back in rotation. You can go commit suicide in front of some other poor witch."

That did it. He didn't precisely glare at her, but his gaze did meet hers. He shook his hair back from his face. "The Council has no jurisdiction over me. You're my witch, I'm not going anywhere." He realized what he was saying just in time. "Look, I'm a Watcher because I'm very good at surviving. You think I can't do my job?"

Her eyes flashed, and he cursed himself for opening his mouth. But instead of taking him to task for disobedience, she simply examined him from head to foot, an appraisal he was half-ashamed to meet. He'd thought he'd stopped caring what he looked like, but now he was acutely aware that his hair was messy and hanging in his face, his scars were plainly visible, and he had barely bothered to rid his coat of the water and dirt from last night. He'd been pulling double shifts for a long time and cleaning up piecemeal when he came in. His T-shirt was threadbare and his jeans worn, his boots scarred. The only thing well-maintained about him was his weapons.

She sighed, closing her eyes as if searching for patience. "I should have known," she muttered. "All right, fine. Okay." Then she snapped her eyes open and met him with a level glare. "I suppose I'm supposed to feel sorry for you?"

He'd never heard a Lightbringer speak so harshly. But it wasn't the harshness of rage. Instead, her eyes were glimmering with unshed tears. Fascinated, he stared as they brimmed over, one crystal drop tracking down her cheek. *If she's so angry, why is she crying?* "Of course not, ma'am. I'm just doing my job."

She whirled away, her aura sparkling. "I've got to get

cleaned up, and I'd better feed both of us at some point. I suppose they've stocked the room?"

Right, then. I am not dealing with this the right way. I don't know if there is *a right way to deal with this. She sounds furious, but she's crying.* His chest twisted oddly. "Of course."

"Then feel free to get yourself a snack in the meantime. Can you cook?" She hefted a duffel bag, selected a suitcase, and started dragging them toward the other door, the one that hid a sparkling blue and white bathroom.

"No." *Not if you want to get any joy from eating, that is.* "Ma'am? Caro? I—" He was about to ask if he could carry the suitcase for her.

"Not until after I've had a shower," she said over her shoulder. The catch in her voice told him she was, indeed, crying. Why? Was she really that upset at finding herself confronted with an ugly, scarred, clumsy Watcher? "Then I'll sort everything out. I'll visit Fran and we'll see what happens."

She lugged the suitcase into the bathroom, slammed the door, and turned the water in the sink on. It was a small sound, and one that wouldn't keep her sobs from ears as sharp as a Watcher's.

Merrick stared at the closed door, and managed to drag his jaw up from the floor after a full minute of puzzlement. He had the distinct feeling he'd just done very badly in the conversation, which wasn't exactly surprising but was worse than he'd imagined.

Where had he gone wrong?

Five

It's not fair. Caro's heels—another pair of black Cubans, since the pair she'd worn last night were still damp—cracked against the hardwood floor as she navigated the safehouse, her wet hair tightly braided and the Watcher a silent drifting presence at her back. *It's absolutely, completely not fair, and I'm not going to stand for it. They can't make me.*

Most safehouses were built along the same general plan, a full city block taken up with apartments on four or five levels, around the main commons and two flanking gardens. This one wasn't any different, which meant Caro didn't get lost as she navigated across to the third floor north wing, where the Council liaison would have her office and living quarters. Fran, as the person responsible for coordinating visiting teachers and healers in Altamira—or at least, this safehouse in Altamira—would be somewhere around here.

It couldn't be put off any longer. She stopped in the middle of the hall and turned halfway, stealing a glance at the Watcher from under her eyelashes.

He was a tall man, of course, wide-shouldered and very graceful. He moved like a cat, all fluidity; his coat sometimes even forgot to make the slight creaking sound leather always made when you moved inside it. The smell of leather—always comforting, for a girl mostly raised in Circle Lightfall—had filled the room she'd awakened in, as well as the ghost of a faint citrusy scent. It was a peculiarly male aroma, and since Watchers didn't believe in cologne she supposed it was natural.

He had green eyes, burning with the peculiar intensity of a man who had been a Watcher for a while, and a messy shock of hair much longer than usual, which he kept shaking down into his face. He probably did it to hide the scars.

He would have been almost pretty, in a masculine way, if not for the ridged tissue; three stripes slanting down the left side of his face as if a big cat had clawed him. One bisected his eyebrow and caught below the socket on his cheekbone, he was lucky he hadn't lost the eye. From one side, he would look like an angel; from the other, the scars marred him. He was quiet even for a Watcher, barely offering a word when she asked him a direct question, and he seemed ... well, sad.

She'd seen that sadness before. It was called "Watcher's despair," a type of fierce sorrow that could kill. There was only so much blood, death, and destruction a Watcher could handle, and the despair, if left untreated, was dangerous. This man had the dark circles under his eyes and the gaunt, almost feral intensity Watchers acquired before they started taking progressively more suicidal chances, courting death with the same intensity they used to protect Lightbringers.

And her skin didn't hurt him. *She* didn't hurt him.

It wasn't fair. The last thing she needed was to be responsible for another Watcher.

He stopped, his hands stuffed as deep in his pockets as they could go, his eyes flicking over the corridor in controlled arcs. He seemed unable to look at her. Well, no wonder. She'd treated him awfully. She hadn't meant to, but waking up in a strange room always unsettled her. It was the bad part of traveling, a holdover from when she was small and at the mercy of the foster care system. A new place meant new rules, and new dangers; even now, decades later and safe in Circle Lightfall, she felt the same breathless anxiety.

She took a deep breath. "I'm sorry," she said finally, when he showed no desire to speak. "I'm a little disarranged. I didn't mean to yell at you."

He shrugged, a supple feline movement. "It's all right. Last night was probably very stressful for you. The office is down on the left, past the statue of Brigid."

Definitely British or Australian, the accent, and he was deliberately trying to speak softly. It just barely worked—the *tanak* would give his voice a harsh growl no matter what he said. But he was making the effort, and Caro supposed the least she could do was meet him halfway.

"Thank you." It was as courteous as she could be, and she set off again, her heels making sharp little frustrated sounds.

Francine Edwardton's office was, as usual, jammed full of books, dusty, and comfortable. And even at this late hour, she had visitors. The tall, blonde, statuesque air witch already had three other women waiting to talk to her. A fourth, a water witch, crossed her arms defensively as her Watcher, a thin intense-looking man with scarred knuckles, curled his hand around her shoulder to steady her. It was obvious they were a bonded pair; the witch leaned back into him, relying on his strength.

Caro's throat went dry. She suppressed a squirming little worm of guilt at what she was about to do.

"I can't tell any more than that, but I thought you should know." The water witch sounded miserable. Her aura was tinted purple with fear and tension.

Caro took her place on the padded bench along one wall, breathing deeply. The other three witches didn't eye her curiously, for which she was grateful. She'd seen only two Watchers waiting out in the hall. A tech witch, her aura glittering and metallic, examined her painted blue nails while balancing a laptop across her knees, her black hair threaded with crimson lacquer beads. *Tech witches. Just like magpies.*

"Thank you for telling me," Francine said, impeccably. She leaned her elbows on her cluttered desk, her entire attention on the water witch. "I'll make a report, and we'll ask the Seers to be very cautious. You're not the only one who's felt this, Corinna. Far from. Why don't you go ask Hildy to give you some valerian?"

The water witch nodded. "I'm glad I'm not the only one. But—I don't know, can't anything be done?"

The other two were a green witch and an air witch, respectively, both in jeans and T-shirts. The air witch stroked a wooden flute, wearing a dreamy expression, as if she was composing music inside her head. The green witch, garden dirt under her fingernails, shifted as she watched the water witch, her clear green aura stretching soothingly toward the other woman's. Green witches, always trying to heal.

Well, I'm always trying to heal the mind. They get the bodies. I wonder which is the easier task.

"Everything that *can* be done, *is* being done." The corners of Francine's eyes crinkled as she smiled. Gray threaded through her hair at her temples, and she was sporting a new hairstyle—a thick braided coronet. *My only real vanity,* she'd noted laughingly several times, *is my hair. Well, that and my copy of Aurelius in Greek.*

Caro found herself wanting to smile. Francine was a rabid booklover even among Lightbringers, always heading off to auctions and poring through catalogs and Internet searches for rare texts. The library here was promising to become one of the best among Circle Lightfall houses, all due to Fran.

Merrick had taken his place out in the hall with the Watchers without demur. Caro was sneakingly glad he wasn't going to be in the room. She was sure he wouldn't like what she was about to do. She shifted restlessly on the bench, wishing she could put this off.

Corinna left, and the tech witch rattled off a few requests, holding her laptop to her chest like a schoolgirl. She wanted the Council to look into some new kind of computer witchery, Francine made a note or two, asked the girl to spell it, and then promised it would be brought up at the next regional meeting.

"The Hollywood image of witches could use a makeover," Frannie had once lamented to Caro. *"I hardly have time for spells and meditation anymore. We're all drowning in paperwork."*

To which Caro replied, *"You know we're out of the Dark Ages when we start choking on bureaucracy."*

It was hard for Caro to remember the Crusade was still such a danger, since they were barred from Santiago City by the Guardians. Of course, even in Saint City they sent in human assassins, but those were no match for the Watchers—at least, most of the time. It was the Brotherhood that was the real problem now, sending in teams of mercenaries to make trouble while they tried to figure out how to slip past the vigilance of the Watchers on patrol and kidnap a few Lightbringers and other psychics to brainwash and sell to the highest bidder as talented slaves. And there were other shadowy organizations, legal and otherwise, that for one reason or another would love to get their hands on a Lightbringer or two.

Caro shivered. Her mood was turning dark again, with the same nameless sorrow that dogged her whenever she left her own comfortable rooms anymore. She wished, with sudden vengeance, that she hadn't left Saint City.

The earth witch simply wanted to go over some garden requisitions. She apparently had big plans for a paving-stone labyrinth in one of the unused garden plots and wanted to see if some of the Watchers would mind helping out. Frannie told her to go to Requisitions and put out a sign-up sheet. "A labyrinth would be a wonderful idea," Fran encouraged, and the earth witch—so shy she stammered, poor girl—almost ran from the room in confusion.

The air witch turned in a sheaf of music for the next sabbat and asked if she could step down from chairing the decorations committee. "I'm swamped with orchestra work. Of course I'll stick around until we find someone else to step in, but I'd *really* like to have some free time."

Frannie had good news: someone else had already applied for the position, and after two weeks of orientation would be happy to take over. The air witch left with a smile and a bounce in her step, and Caro heard a snatch of unearthly flute music begin from the hallway, fading into the distance.

Then Fran's eyes met hers. "Well, hello, stranger. I suppose this isn't going to be pleasant."

"Hi, Fran. Nice to see you too. Can we close your door?" Caro found her palms sweating. Fran always looked so damn *calm*, even during crises.

Fran got up, her silky primrose dress swishing slightly. She wore a light-purple cardigan too, and the smell of Easter lilies followed her around, leaching out from her lemon-yellow aura to trail in eddies along her wake.

She shut her door quietly and crossed her office to drop down on the bench next to Caro with a heavy sigh. "Gods above," she said, staring at her desk. "Seen from over here it looks like a damnable mess."

"No." Caro dredged up a smile. "Just a chaotic organizational system, that's all."

Fran was silent for a moment. "You had me worried, Caro." It was as close to chastisement as she would offer. "Want to tell me what's on *your* mind first?"

"I had an accident because I was out after dark." Caro took a deep breath, wiped her palms on her skirt. *Why am I so nervous?* "I got lost. I'm sorry, and I'm glad the Watcher was there."

Fran said nothing. Caro plunged ahead.

"The thing is, I've been thinking. The Council really has no right to force me to accept a Watcher. I'm too old for curfews too, for God's sake. I agreed to the bargain because I was too young and too scared to know any better. So what I want you to do is take this Watcher—Merrick—and let him go back on patrol or rotation or whatever it is he's supposed to be doing."

There. It's out, it's said. Her hands were shaking. Why? It wasn't like Fran was going to yell at her. Fran rarely raised her voice and was only impatient with what she saw as sloppy work. The older witch was inherently neat and precise; despite the appearance of clutter in her office she could find any document or book in seconds flat. And gods help you if you did a shoddy job on a theory-of-magick assignment while she was teaching.

Besides, Fran had invited Caro out to do some training and take a look at some special cases. She would never be so impolite as to yell at a guest.

The older witch sighed. "Caro, I have to give you some unpleasant news. Unpleasant for you, at least. Merrick made his report. He's no longer under the control of Circle Lightfall. He's your Watcher. I can't do anything about it, and I can't give him any orders to leave you alone. You two are a pair. It's not my jurisdiction."

"But—" Caro began. This was going just as she'd feared.

"I *can't*, Caroline. I'm sorry. And this brings me to another point. This effectively negates the bargain the Council had with you. It's now Merrick's responsibility to look after your safety. You'll have to take it up with him—and please, Caro, *please* be gentle. He's a Watcher."

Be gentle? He's armed, and he outweighs me. Not to mention the fact that I only come up to his shoulder—and barely even that. But she knew what Fran was saying. Merrick was trained to absolute obedience, and Caro could very well do something silly and put him in danger.

She'd promised herself she would never put another Watcher in danger. And she thought she'd avoided the whole problem neatly by only allowing bonded pairs near her when she had to go out at night. Merrick was all but helpless; he had no control over the fact that her aura didn't hurt him. A Watcher couldn't *choose* his witch. The official line was that it was a matter of chemistry, or souls, or just plain chance—not to mention the polite but vocal contingent that insisted the gods had a hand in it. Most bonded witches were firm believers in the gods theory. The Watchers, of course, didn't venture an opinion.

None of that meant a good goddamn. It wasn't Merrick's fault, and unless she could figure something out she was stuck with him.

Caro blew out between pursed lips, almost whistling with frustration. "Well, what's the *good* news?" she finally said. It was a pale attempt at a joke, but Fran didn't laugh.

"That was the good news, sweetie. There's some strange stuff going on, and the healers are getting a little frightened. There's been a spike in the number of cases requiring a Mindhealer—Dark attacks, mentally ill patients, violent traumas, that sort of thing. And there are a couple of . . . troubling

signs. Something's brewing. There are also some . . . some
cases I wanted you to personally look at."

A chill finger traced up her back. It was a routine request,
especially when one was a Mindhealer. But something in the
set of Fran's mouth told her this wasn't at all routine.

Caro shivered. "What kind of trouble are we talking about,
Fran?"

"I don't know. I'd like you to take a look. There's been a
few attacks. We can't bring the victims out, the Mindhealers
we have just aren't powerful enough—and the victims tend to
die before we can really treat him." The Council witch's mouth
compressed. "There's something preying on psychics. And not
just psychics, normals too. We don't know what it is, and neither
do the Watchers."

She flinched. That *was* bad news, and all the more so
because the Watchers had no clue. Dealing with the Dark as
often as they did gave most Watchers an encyclopedic
knowledge of predators. "Really? Preying on *normals*? Is it
Dark, or something else?"

"We don't know. We don't know anything, only that these
people are attacked, and they end up brutally beaten and
catatonic. No Lightbringers yet, but one of the Mindhealers
here—Danica, the one with the long red hair—she tried treating
one of them and got lost. Her heart stopped, and not even her
Watcher could bring her back."

"Gods above." It was a shocked, breathless whisper. There
was always the danger of getting lost inside a patient's mind,
but to have a Mindhealer's heart just *stop* was rare. And
unsettling. Her heart ached at the thought—a Mindhealer, gone.
There were so few of them, and so many patients, so many
people, to heal. "Her heart just stopped?"

"It killed her Watcher too. They were a bonded pair."

Shame welled hot inside Caro's chest. "I would have been
down here sooner, Fran. I'd have come weeks ago without
bothering to finish out the course up north. Why didn't you tell
me this when you called?"

"I didn't want you to hurry, or to be afraid. I still don't. I
just want you to be cautious. Truth be told, I'm almost glad
things have worked out like this. You might need that Watcher
after all, Caro." Fran sounded dead serious. "Please. Even if
you don't like the idea, please just . . . try. All right?"

"Okay." Her breath refused to come back. "Normals too?

Are you *sure*?"

"If I wasn't, would I be risking the famous Robbins Razor-tongue?" But Fran didn't sound upset. Instead, she only sounded tired. "Please, sweetie. Just be careful, and try to be kind to Merrick. It's not his fault."

"I know. It's nobody's fault." *That's the curse of being a Mindhealer. You learn that it really isn't anyone's fault most of the time.* She made it to her feet, swaying as her knees almost declared mutiny. "Thanks. I suppose tomorrow I can start seeing these patients?"

"Absolutely." Fran looked like there was more she wanted to say. "Caro—"

"Thanks, Frannie." She made it to the door, fumbled for the knob. "Tomorrow, we'll have a nice long chat and I'll get to work. Thank you."

The gods were kind and the door opened. She stumbled out into the deserted hall.

Well, mostly deserted. Merrick caught her arm, steadied her. "Are you all right?"

No, I'm not all right. Life's about to get very interesting, and Fran just told me in the nicest way possible that I'm stuck with you.

Another thought, even more terrifying, struck her as she looked up. He had pushed his hair back, and the scars glared against his face. She had no *choice*, Fran had made that clear. She was responsible for him the same way she'd been responsible for Vincent. The one thing she'd tried to avoid had now happened, and she was stuck.

If anything bad happens, he's going to try to stop it. To protect me. Which means he's going to get hurt. Or possibly die. Like Vincent. The vision of Vince, broken and bloody, his sword still in his loosely-clasped hand, rose in front of her. Her knees almost gave out, Merrick caught her by the shoulders. His hands were large and warm. The comforting smell of leather curled around her again.

"Caro?" Now he sounded alarmed instead of concerned. "Caroline?" He pronounced her name oddly, too. She had to hand it to him, though. An English accent made *anyone* sound more educated and reasonable.

"I'm okay," she managed. "Just got some bad news."

"Bad news?" Just like that, he tensed. Ready for the worst, it would seem. *I'm half his size, and he fought off a pack of* koroi *last night, but wouldn't you know, I think he's scared of little old me.*

"It's all right. I just want to unpack and have a nice warm cup of tea, I think." She took a deep breath. Between the reverberations of Darksickness and working herself up for a confrontation with Fran that hadn't happened, she felt like she'd just run a marathon. "Francine tells me you've already made your report."

A long pause. He set her carefully on her feet, made sure she had her balance back, and fell into step beside her as she set off down the hall, her heels clicking. "I have," he said finally, cautiously.

"Don't worry. It looks like you're stuck with me for a little while. Just until I can figure out a solution."

He obviously didn't think that deserved a reply, because he was silent again. Caro hunched her shoulders and wished she hadn't left home. Something attacking both normals and psychis—not all psychics were Lightbringers, and the ones that weren't didn't have the benefit of Watchers looking out for them. Caro could still remember the endless debates in both the regional councils and High Council about whether or not to ask the Watchers to help protect the psychics who weren't Lightbringers. The Watchers would obey, of course, but it wasn't fair to them. There were barely enough Watchers to protect Circle Lightfall—though there had been a recent spike in recruits, Caro remembered hearing.

A mystery, something attacking. Something we don't know if it's Dark or not. Something that can stop a Mindhealer's heart. Her chin lifted, determined, as she stalked down the hall. *Well, I'll figure it out. If it's able to be figured out, that is.*

Six

Morning dawned fresh and clear, thin winter sunlight falling through the windows as Caro stepped into the hospital room. The other Mindhealer—her aura not half as bright as Caro's, but well-disciplined and shielded nonetheless—let out a soft sigh. She was a tall, thin woman with large dreamy blue eyes and fine flaxen hair, her long blue linen skirt fluttering as she moved aside, giving Caro a clear view of the patient.

Saint Crispin's stood on a hill in the south section of Altamira, a tall grim hospital set among quiet tree-lined streets, a graveyard off to one side and the cathedral rising a block and a half away. This hospital had once been run by nuns. Now it was modern, of course, but the walls still held the echoes of female voices chanting in Latin. Merrick's memories of nuns were all from school—the ruler applied to his palms until they bled, reciting gibberish again and again, and the scratchy uniforms. None of which mattered now, but he spared himself a private wince as he followed his witch into the great stone pile.

Caro had pulled her hair back in a loose chignon, long earrings that looked like quivering aspen leaves trembled when she turned her head. She wore a pair of gray slacks and a black silk shirt. Her heels didn't click against the short carpet in the hall but made crisp little sounds when she stepped onto the linoleum. The other Watcher, Avery, exchanged a quiet look with Merrick and took up his post outside the door, his hand resting on a knife hilt. It was, for a Watcher, the equivalent of a nervous tic.

Merrick didn't blame him. The attacks had started a good six months ago, the victims being found mostly on the north side of town, and there was a quiet sense of something-not-right about them that had all the Watchers on edge. Merrick thought sourly that he perhaps should have known that Caro would get tangled up in it. *It couldn't be easy, could it.*

He stepped past her into the room, scanning it once and determining there was no danger. He moved aside, boots whispering over the linoleum floor, and caught a breath of her perfume—a brunette smell, light and spicy. Spice and green tea, the smell that was starting to distract him.

She had, of course, only caught a couple hours' sleep after unpacking. He'd surfaced from a resting trance at dawn to find her already up and making breakfast. She'd presented him with a plate of scrambled eggs and toast, apologizing because she didn't know how he liked his eggs, and he'd been surprised enough to take it. He'd been on patrol so long he had almost forgotten what it was like to have a witch feed him. And especially when the plate was offered with such a grudging, shy smile.

The truce between them was fragile enough that Merrick hadn't protested when she informed him she was heading out to St. Crispin's to take a look at a case. He should have. She was still obviously tired, so pale the circles under her eyes seemed like bruises. But the way she lifted her chin and looked at him, daring him to disagree, had been too much. He'd simply nodded, taking her plate and retreating to wash the dishes from breakfast. The urge to smile had risen when he heard her muttered curse, but he'd banished it. Smiling was beside the point. The important thing was that he'd managed not to annoy her.

Well, at least not much.

"Gods above." Caro sounded pale. "What is—" She took a quick sipping breath, her mouth gapped as if the air was foul. "What on earth is *that?*"

The other Mindhealer nodded. "Awful, isn't it? The Watchers can't smell it, neither can the others. It seems only a Mindhealer can."

"Is that sulfur? It reeks worse than a *gimmerin*." Caro crossed to the bed, her heels marking off each graceful step. "*Gods.*"

The room held only one bed, sunlight picking out the nap of the ripcord blanket and the much-bleached sheets. Settled into the bed's embrace was a human shape, the face puffed and discolored, only the long auburn hair against the pillow marking it as female. "And nobody else can smell it?"

"No."

Merrick filled his lungs, straining to detect anything out of place. He smelled nothing but human pain, disinfectant, the persistent reek of *hospital*, and the breath of lavender from the taller Mindhealer—and Caro's soft spiced perfume, a smell that made his hands want to tighten into fists to keep from touching her. He'd thought it would be awkward, watching over a witch again. It wasn't awkward; it was nerve-wracking. The fact that this was *it*, this was *his* witch, the only chance he had to redeem himself, was enough to make him break out in a cold sweat. Plenty of other Watchers died before they found their witch—died without having a chance to make up for whatever bloody act or series of acts had tortured them into becoming something inhuman to atone for it. He was luckier than he deserved.

And he was finding out that he liked this blue-eyed firecracker, despite her sharp tongue and her obvious ill-temper.

Caro examined the patient, her hands clasped in front of her. He watched the morning sunlight play through her hair, burnish her skin to a matte glow. "How many attacks now?"

"Fourteen that we know of, probably more. Eight of the victims are dead." The taller Mindhealer sounded sad. "All found in the northern section of town, beaten . . . well, you can see. Their bodies just give up. The damage extends so far down, it's incredible."

"And this is the one Danica was lost in." Caro ducked out from under the strap of her large canvas bag, settled it carefully in a vinyl-covered chair. Machines bleeped softly, monitoring pulse and respiration, the EEG showed severely-repressed alpha and beta waves, almost flatline. The delta waves were infinitely small, and very slow.

Merrick took all this in, and his eyes came to rest on Caro again. The other Mindhealer's presence filled his scars with acid, taunted his nerves with pain. He shifted his weight slightly, wishing he dared move closer to Caro and feel her aura brush his again, however briefly.

Caro studied the patient's broken, battered face. "What can you tell me about her?"

"Her name's Colleen Frames. Thirty-four, worked in an ad agency downtown. The last time anyone saw her was three days ago, she was heading to catch the train out to Alta Heights—that's a suburb in the northwest—and just vanished. She was found in an alley six blocks from her apartment, beaten almost to death. One of the trauma nurses in the ER here is a Lightbringer, and she asked Danica to come in and take a look. Danica came in a few hours after Colleen was admitted, worked on her for two or three hours as far as we can tell. Then her heart stopped. Our contact found both her and her Watcher dead in here, and *that* was a mess."

"I don't suppose Danica left any notes." Caro paced to the end of the bed, her eyes unfocused. Merrick could See her aura stretching, gently testing the air around the unconscious woman on the bed.

"You kidding? Danny never slowed down long enough to

take notes." The taller woman's voice broke.

Caro stroked her shoulder, a kind touch. "It's all right, Joanie. Why don't you go get a cup of coffee and head back to the safehouse? Merrick can bring me back. I'll be fine."

He wasn't prepared for the way his heart slammed against his ribs. *Merrick can bring me back.* It sounded as if she had changed her mind about him.

The voice of caution intervened. *Don't count your chickens before they're in the basket, Merrick old man.*

The taller witch glanced at him. "So it's true, you've finally seen reason?"

Caro shrugged. "Fran's asked me to be careful, in light of this ... chain of events." Her tone was carefully neutral. Apparently that sufficed as a warning, because the other woman lifted her hands, taking a step back.

"I was only curious. All right, I'll see you back at the safehouse. Be careful, Caro." Joanie's voice shook.

"I'll be all right. Go on, take care of yourself. Go." Caro shooed her out, then came back to the bed, her heels clicking softly. She stood looking down at the battered mass of humanity, her nose wrinkling. "Gods above," she whispered, and glanced up. Her eyes met Merrick's.

I've been staring at her. He scanned the room again, his attention sweeping the hall—the other Mindhealer and Avery were moving away. Despite the placidity of the room, the air swirled with heavy energy, human pain and desperation. It was a wonder Caro could stand being in a hospital, she was probably so bloody sensitive.

Circle Lightfall had an unofficial understanding with most hospitals. Their healers would work among the sick and traumatized, and everyone would generally look the other way. Most healers had medical training from nurse to doctor to surgeon, plenty of Mindhealers had psych degrees or worked as counselors. But it was still up to the Watchers to make sure everything went smoothly—to keep the interest in the gifted averted, to provide a small *push* where necessary so the Lightbringers could go about doing their work.

"You can't smell that?" Her forehead creased, her eyebrows drawing together. She'd also paled, the color draining slowly but surely out of her face.

I don't like the looks of that. He took a deep breath, closing his eyes. Nothing but disinfectant, pain, and Caro's perfume.

Merrick frowned and inhaled again, this time letting down the walls between him and the crouching thing in the bottom of his mind. Not the *tanak*—that occupied a wholly different space. But this was the part of him that had made being a Watcher possible, inescapable. The hard, cold, ruthless part.

The part of him that tracked a target.

It hit him hard, making his eyes water, a sulfurous stench that wasn't quite physical for all its power. "Bloody *hell*." He tipped his head back, blinking away the sudden stinging in his eyes. His scars lit with sudden, liquid fire, burning into his face; the scars on his shoulder and chest woke up too. "That's what you smell?"

She looked relieved. "You can smell it?"

No, the thing in me that can find a lost child in a shopping mall or a target in the jungle can smell it. Not quite the same thing, love. "Not quite. Feel it, maybe." It was half a lie, but he felt no guilt. She didn't need to know about that part of him, not yet. It was a part he could never allow to touch her. Not this pretty witch with her sharp tongue and her dark-blue eyes. There was no reason for her to know what an animal he was.

She was right next to him, her aura sliding against his. "Are you all right?"

"Fine." His chin came back down, and he shook his head habitually. His hair fell down, curtaining the scars. "It's just . . . it reeks." *And I don't like the thought of you near anything that smells this bad. It smells contagious.* Thankfully, he couldn't smell it anymore. But the sense of a heaviness in the air remained, not like the bell jar effect under Watcher shields. No, it was as if the room itself had become full of a leaden gas.

"Well, she can't help it." Caro turned away so sharply a single curl of her hair popped loose, falling over her shoulder. She dug in the canvas bag she'd brought. "Make sure nobody comes in, all right? I can't have normals poking around while I'm doing this."

"Of course." *What did you do without a Watcher, pretty girl? Took the risk of a normal coming in and disturbing you?* "Caro?"

"Hm?" She looked back over her shoulder, her indigo eyes wide, and Merrick realized he was lost. Now that she was the only Lightbringer in the room, the *tanak* folded itself down at the bottom of his mind, nestled around the cold hard part of him he rarely let out if he wasn't tracking. But it wasn't just the fact that he didn't feel the acid bath of pain as much when she was near, and it wasn't the jolt of agonizing pleasure he'd felt last night. It was the one look, and the realization that she was far more frightened than she would let the other Mindhealer see. Something was very wrong here, something was *off*, and this witch knew it. Still, she was about to do the very same thing that had killed another Mindhealer.

She was terrified, and yet she calmly shooed the other Mindhealer away and set about doing her work.

That kind of quiet, hidden bravery was something to be protected. "How can I help?" *Don't do this,* he thought, but couldn't say it. Not his place to give a witch orders. *Don't risk yourself,* he wanted to say.

He already guessed how well *that* would go over with her.

She drew out a slim shallow bowl, mellow green. It was jade, and the way she handled it told him she loved it, her fingers gentle on the smooth satiny surface. "Just stay near the door and be quiet. I don't suppose I can ask you to wait outside."

You're absolutely right, duck. I'm not letting you out of my sight. It wasn't a direct order, so he simply settled himself next to the door. This room was small and didn't have a bathroom, just a sink. After all, the people in this section of the hospital never left their beds. He watched as she filled the bowl with water from the sink across the room, set it on the small table arching over the bed. She went back to her bag, pulling out a thin silver chain with an amazing teardrop cabochon of amber that could fill her cupped palm set in filigreed silver. Then she removed a long string of jet beads that glowed with Power. Merrick watched, fascinated.

The chunk of amber on its silver chain went down her shirt, and a hot flush worked its way up Merrick's cheeks. She didn't notice, settling the jet beads around her neck and drawing a small glass bottle out of the bag. A few pinches of whatever was in the bottle—probably salt, the great purifier—went into the jade bowl. Then she dragged the vinyl chair to the bedside, and her fingers flashed over the bowl as she stood looking down into the ruined face on the bed.

Power hummed, taut, between her fingers and the water, soaking in. Her lips moved slightly, her aura brightening.

Creature of water, be thou purified. He deciphered the words with no trouble, they were a traditional purification. He had never seen a Mindhealer work this way before.

She sank down, businesslike and graceful, into the chair. She gently, gently, slid her fingers underneath the puffed and mangled hand on the bed, cupping it delicately in both of hers with a tenderness that made Merrick swallow dryly.

"All right, my dear," she said quietly to the ruined face. Her voice was kind now, losing all its sharpness, and Merrick's entire body tightened at the sound of that kindness. "Let's get comfortable with each other and . . ."

She frowned slightly, closed her eyes. Her aura glittered, spun with pinwheels, and he sensed that she had *gone*. The essential part of her had slipped out of her body and was now walking in the corridors of another mind.

Merrick's eyes narrowed. He watched her carefully, every muscle taut and alert. She was so gentle with the hand of a person who in all likelihood couldn't feel it.

He waited, and wondered how frightened she had been, and for how long, to be so good at hiding it.

No more. You're safe now, I promise. For a moment, he wondered why he felt so uncharacteristically . . . involved. She was his witch, she could touch him without dragging acid across his nerves, but that was no reason for him to be feeling so unsettled. Emotional involvement meant he wasn't thinking clearly, and clear thinking was something a Watcher needed desperately. He had watched over many a witch without feeling the urge to shake them and comfort them at the same time.

But how had she become so bloody good at hiding that kind of fear? It wasn't normal. Lightbringers were usually far more transparent.

The water in the jade bowl trembled.

Uneasiness began under Merrick's breastbone. Wrong. This was *wrong*. Was it just his natural inclination to be cautious, or something else? His skin roughened with gooseflesh, and he leaned back against the door, scanning the hall outside. Nothing stirring.

The EEG suddenly blipped into life. High hard alpha waves, beta scrabbling thickly enough to blur, static crawling over the screen. Stink filled the air, heavy and close like the smell of an animal's lair, and Merrick didn't stop to think. He bolted forward, blurring with preternatural speed, *over* the bed, getting her down and away as the *thing* burst like a poisonous flower, snarling in a psychic falsetto that drove through his teeth. Caro let out a short cry, bitten off halfway as Merrick hit her, driving her down.

Landed, hard, twisted so she didn't hit the floor, he barked his elbow a good one and his head smacked the radiator under the window with stunning force. He had her down and *rolled,* covering her body with his as the thing clawed at the air. There was no space, his legs tangled with hers and he pushed himself *up,* knife hilt smacking into his palm. He made it to his feet, facing the thing that rose from the shattered body like a cancerous mushroom. Warmth slid down the side of his neck, wet and coppery. He'd smacked himself a good one in the close quarters between the bed and window.

Red dappled the walls, the runes chased into the black steel of the knife blazing with clear crimson radiance that cut through weak wintery sunlight. Merrick's lips pulled back from his teeth.

The thing squealed again as sunlight pierced it, thin red lines from the blazing runefire bouncing off the walls. The dual assault striped its smoking flesh. A low head, eyes made of unhealthy crimson radioactivity, a clawed paw that swiped at him uselessly as it shredded in the sun falling over his shoulder. The body on the bed twisted and jerked, a fine mist of blood spattering up from broken capillaries in the skin of her face and hands; the machines began to give out warning beeps, boops, and whistles.

Lovely. That will bring everyone running. Dammit.

Caro struggled up to her knees. Merrick kept himself between her and the bed. The jade bowl chattered, water turning to steam, the thing howled again as the steam billowed around it. The smell was insistent, sulfur mixed with a darker tang, and the thing retreated, hopping down from the bed and clumsily splatting on the floor on the other side. He could see it, writhing and melting, and his blood went chill. "Caro?"

"I'm all right." She sounded dazed, and most definitely *not* all right. He was unprepared for the sharp pinch of fear under his skin. He had just touched a Mindhealer during her work. You were *never* supposed to do that lest you disturb the careful balance necessary for them to leave their bodies and walk in other minds. He was damn lucky she was still alive. "Merrick?" Wondering, disoriented.

Thank you, gods. She's alive and conscious. Two to the good, luckier than I have any right to be. "Right here. It's dying, the sunlight hurts it. Get your bowl and your bag, we're leaving."

She shook her head as if dazed, and he was suddenly

possessed of the intense desire to shake her. *Don't ever do that to me again.* He discarded the thought. It wasn't the kind of thing a Watcher could say.

"But—Colleen—"

Who? Then he remembered. The victim. He heard running feet, shouts. The nurses and doctors would be along soon. The thing shrieked again, but fainter. The chaos of noise from the machines splashed through the room, tore at his ears. He shut it out.

Merrick scooped up the jade bowl with his left hand. The water was gone and the stone bowl was hot enough to burn a man's fingers. Thankfully, none of the bloodmist had fouled it. He resheathed the knife—this thing, whatever it was, was losing coherency quickly. Each moment of sunlight made it more insubstantial.

It still might hurt her, so he kept his body between Caro and the thing as he bent down, offered her his free hand. "Come on, love. Best to be on our way."

Her fingers closed over his, but she looked bewildered. Her pupils were so dilated her eyes looked almost black. A bright crimson thread of blood slid down from her nose; Merrick suffered a moment of almost-panic before he remembered it was likely her reaction to the proximity of something Dark.

He pulled her up—*careful, Watcher. She's fragile.* The bolt of pleasure sliding down his arm spurred the *tanak* rather than pacified it, made the scars on his face burn as if they had just been made. Fire slashed down his chest—the other scars. *Don't think about that.*

The jade bowl went back in the bag. He took care not to peer further inside. A Mindhealer's bag was like a Watcher's knives, intensely personal. He got the strap over her head and settled it across her body, trying to avoid touching her through the silk. The back of his knuckles brushed the slope of one breast, he felt lace under the silk—her bra, almost certainly— and he shrilled at himself to *stop being such a bloody idiot and get her OUT of here!*

The door smashed open and he folded her close, pressing her back against the counter that held the sink and cabinets for linens and other things. She bit her lip, wary sharpness returning to her eyes even as his glamour stretched to cover both of them, hard and thick. The medical personnel didn't see him, although one of the doctors, a bright-eyed black woman, looked up and frowned suspiciously. She had a shine to her, almost

Lightbringer, but that wasn't Merrick's problem.

The thing bubbling on the floor—one of the normals, a nurse in thick white shoes and bright dyed-blonde hair, stepped in it and flinched aside, shivering, unaware of why she had felt the chill up her back—squealed again, but weakly. Sunlight was deadly to many forms of Dark, and particularly deadly to whatever this was. It subsided to a bubbling psychic sludge, inert except for its hatefulness and eye-watering smell.

Dark, then. It was Dark, but no kind he'd ever seen before.

Caro shivered, trembling against his chest. He didn't dare speak—sound would break the glamour. Instead, he maneuvered her, step by careful step, toward the door.

Be quiet, love. Please. Just for a few moments. It's past, it's all past, it didn't get you. Let's get you out of this awful bloody room and somewhere nicer. All right? Christ, Merrick, concentrate on your job.

Out in the hall, more chaos. More people pouring through the hall, running for the room. A code. A heart stopped.

Caro shuddered, buried her face against his chest. Merrick was busy keeping the edges of the glamour hard, navigating her through the hall and listening, one hand on a knife hilt. He ducked into the chapel—of course, this was Saint Crispin's, each floor would have a chapel. This was a long narrow room, nondenominational now, a plain cross at the end spotlit with bright white, a few pews, and a great sheaf of lilies and scarlet carnations under the cross. He leaned against the wall just inside the door, felt the years of praying and anguish and misery this place contained lap at his skin, and kept the edges of the glamour hard and impassable. The red-black of a Watcher stained the borders of Caro's aura, a defense against both the emotional atmosphere of the place and possible Darksickness.

He was just glad a *tanak* wouldn't trigger Darksickness in her. That would be awful.

The *tanak* burned, melding the gash in his scalp together, flushing him with Power, ready for combat. He had to breathe deeply. There was nothing to fight here. Yet.

It took maybe ten minutes for Caro to stop shaking. She lifted her head, finally, and he was surprised to find that he didn't want her to. If he could have stayed there forever with his witch leaning against him, her canvas bag at her hip and her hair tangling out of its chignon, he would have been ... what? Happy?

He didn't think he even remembered what *happy* felt like.

"What the hell was that?" she whispered, and that brought him back down to reality. Stray curls fell in her face. He wanted to touch them, smooth them back. Her earrings swung uneasily, delicate wonderful pieces of jewelry he found himself staring at. He tore his eyes away.

"Don't know, love." He touched a knife hilt, then stroked her shoulder under the silk. Reassured himself that she was still alive. "Are you hurt?"

"Me? No, of course not." Her voice shook. "But you . . . you leapt right over the *bed*. Are you all right?"

"Fine." He didn't dare look down. If he looked down he was going to be tempted to do something insane—like maybe shake her until her teeth rattled and tell her to *never* do that again, tell her his heart had stopped, that the thought of that thing tearing at her with its claws still smoking from the touch of sunlight made him afraid in a way he had never been afraid before in his entire *life*.

She wiped at her nose with the back of one hand, irritated. "I hate this. Nosebleeds are so *messy*."

He dug in a pocket, retrieved a crisp white handkerchief. "Use this."

"Just like a Watcher. Always prepared." Her voice shook as she took the cotton cloth and pressed it under her nose, tipping her head back. "What *was* that thing?"

"I don't know." He could finally look down without wanting to shake her. Saw her eyes were wide and dark, the eyes of a haunted child. *But whatever it is, it didn't get you, and I'm going to make sure nothing does. Absolutely nothing is ever going to touch you.*

"You don't . . ." She lost the words as she breathed out harshly, as if she'd been hit. "You're *bleeding*."

"Not anymore, it's closed up. I think I hit the radiator on the way down. It's not bad." Merrick closed his eyes, thinking. Watchers took classes and refresher courses in Dark anatomy and classification. They also shared information informally. There was precious little Dark *someone* didn't know about. But he had never heard of this.

Footsteps approaching. The glamour hardened again, and he pulled her aside into the shadows behind the pews. Her earrings flashed in the mellow gloom.

She appeared not to notice he was all but dragging her around, reaching up as if to touch him. He flinched, and her hand stopped in midair. "But you're bleeding. Let me see."

"It's not bad." *It's already closed up, Caro.* The footsteps passed. He eased his hand away from the knife hilt, hoping she hadn't noticed. "We should go back to the safehouse, make a report."

"The other victims." She swiped the blood away from her face, balled the handkerchief in her fist. "Joanie and the other Mindhealers, we have to warn them . . . warn Fran—. . ."

"Here." He dug into another pocket and retrieved his cell phone. "Use this."

"My, you're useful. I can't carry a cell, my aura drains the batteries. One more thing to love about being a Mindhealer." She gulped, her eyes suddenly huge and luminous in the chapel's dimness. She was not as casual as she wanted him to believe. How many people bought that sharp tough exterior of hers? "Are you sure it's dead?"

"I'm sure." He tried to sound reassuring. "It couldn't stand the sunlight. It's dead, Caro."

"It could have hurt you." She didn't look reassured at all. She looked, in fact, frightened half to death, high hectic color standing in her cheeks. The long gold earrings shivered against her cheeks. He was suddenly intensely jealous of any piece of jewelry allowed to touch her skin.

Settle down, old man. "I'm a *Watcher*." Didn't she understand? He was good at surviving, any Watcher was. He'd just found her, and he wasn't getting himself killed now. A week ago he might have considered it, but not now. "Call in if you want, I'll check the hall. We'd better get out of here."

For a moment he cursed himself—giving a witch orders, was he mad? But she took the phone in her free hand and stared at it, as if trying to remember what to do with such a contraption. He felt his heart actually twist, a painful sensation tinged with fear. It had been so *close*. "Hit redial. Dispatch will know where everyone is."

He slid away from her, not because he wanted to let her go, but because his hands were literally shaking with the urge to touch her again. Just to prove she was alive and unhurt. When he thought of what could have happened—

Not to my witch. Never to my witch.

But he knew, didn't he, what could happen. He'd seen it—Lightbringers in pain, their gentleness horribly abused, screaming as another piece of Dark tried to claw or bite or rend them. He had asked for patrol, damn near begged for it, because he didn't think he could stand to see another Lightbringer in pain.

And her, this beautiful witch with her foolish bravery and sharp tongue, was an accident waiting to happen. No, not just an accident. A *disaster* waiting to happen.

"H-hello?" Her voice shook. "Francine Edwardton, I need to talk to Francine. Now. It's Caroline Robbins, and I need to talk to Fran *right this second*." Her tone firmed, became natural. "No, I'm all right, my Watcher's right here. Get Fran on the phone *now!*" There was a definite snap to her voice now.

My Watcher's right here. He closed his eyes, resting his hand against the chapel door. His awareness swept the hall outside, circled the pews and the altar again, and came to rest on her. She sniffed heavily. The nosebleed had stopped. The slashes of fire that were his Dark-made scars pulsed unevenly, jagged bits of broken pain.

What will I have to do to keep her safe? She wants to get rid of me, and I'm not sure I can obey her if she wants me to go invisible. Duty, honor, obedience. She wants the Council to order me away, the Council wants me to stay on her, and if I don't Watch her closely she's likely to get into trouble.

It was, in short, a situation that could only end badly.

"Frannie? It's Caro. Look, get word to the other Mindhealers. *Don't treat any of the victims!* There's something in them, something Dark, triggered by a third-level touch. Get hold of them however you can and tell them not to treat! Clear?"

She must have heard an affirmative, because her tone softened. "It's bad, Fran. However bad you think it is, it's worse. Do whatever you have to, pull the Mindhealers in so I can talk to them. We're lucky we haven't lost more. I'll be in as soon as I can."

Another pause, then a short sharp sound. "No, I want to visit a few more victims. Whatever this thing is, it has to be stopped."

Merrick's heart splashed down into his guts. *What the hell?*

Caro laughed, but the sound wasn't happy. "Of course I'm serious, Frannie. I'm the most qualified to deal with this, and I'll deal with it. Pull everyone in and I'll talk to them as soon as I can."

She turned the phone off and sighed. "Damn."

"Caro?" It wasn't what he wanted to say. *Please tell me I didn't hear what I think I just heard.* He turned to find her looking at him. Had she been watching his back? The thought sent a rill of something too cold and satisfied to be excitement up his spine.

"Merrick." She flipped the phone closed. "Where are the other victims?"

He felt his jaw clench. "Those things are dangerous. We should go back to the safehouse."

Her chin lifted, and his heart began to hammer. Why? They weren't under attack. "You can go back, if you want. Those things certainly *are* dangerous, and I don't want you hurt. It could have taken your head off."

For a moment he simply stared at her as if she were speaking a foreign language. The thought—*I could just pick her up and sling her over my shoulder, I could drag her back to the safehouse kicking and screaming*—was tempting. Very tempting. Obedience rose under his skin, the harsh training every Watcher received. *The only time a Watcher is allowed to disobey a witch is when her safety is in danger.*

Well, she's certainly in danger now. No Watcher would blame me.

He sighed. A Watcher might not blame him, but Caro certainly would. He decided to try another tack. "I'm *trained* for this, Caro. This is my job. You think I can't do my job?"

She looked very fragile, her eyes shadowed, hugging herself tightly. She held the phone in her white-knuckled right hand. "I lost a Watcher once," she said tonelessly, staring at the floor. "Vincent. He was a good man."

So that's the problem. He folded his arms over his chest, hearing leather creak and small bits of gear shift inside his coat. "Don't worry, I'm not hampered by any decency. I am very, very good at surviving."

Tears glittered in her eyes again. She said nothing.

"I don't know where the other victims are," he finally said. His conscience pricked him, hard. "I could get a list from Dispatch."

Footsteps in the hall again. Merrick listened. They were slowing. He moved closer to her, instinct prickling under his skin.

"Why are you doing this?" The misery in her voice was palpable, and scored him all the way down to the bone. "I won't be the cause of another man's death."

I've already survived more than you can imagine, love. Instinct blurred under his skin, and he stepped close, the glamour closing hard and hot around both of them. She drew in a breath as if to argue, and as the chapel doors opened he clapped his hand over her mouth. Something was wrong—again. He felt it like a discordant note on a pipe organ. The footsteps were lighter than they should be, and purposeful. Merrick smelled cordite and the faint imperceptible odor of bloodlust.

Heat tingled in his palm from the touch of her mouth. Her skin was soft, her lips softer. Creeping velvet fire tingled in Merrick's fingertips. *Don't think about that.*

The man edged into the chapel, a gun held low at his side. His eyes flicked nervously over the interior, and he crossed himself as he walked between the pews. Average height, brown hair clipped close to his skull—and to a Watcher's senses, the faint bloody glow of old, tainted ceremonial magick through his aura shouted what this new visitor was.

What's a Crusade Master doing here during the day? It wasn't like a live Crusade soldier to show up during the day and without any backup. They went out in pairs—mostly to discourage independent thought, the Watchers said.

Caro's eyes widened, irises ringed with white like a frightened animal's. She shook her head, reaching up to grab Merrick's wrist. A bolt of velvet fire slid up his arm, spilled through him. He was suddenly very aware of her pressed against him, his breathing wanting to shorten, his entire body tightening at the *feel* of her, so close, so soft, and so utterly defenseless without him. He had never felt this deeply instinctively *protective* of a woman before, despite all his years of being a Watcher.

His free hand drifted to a knife hilt. He could kill the man quietly. One less fanatic to carry out the war against Lightbringers; one less murderous religionist to control the zombie Knights and Seekers that were the worst weapons of the Crusade's ancient hatred.

Caro blinked. A tear slid down her cheek, touched his hand. He kept the glamour tight, thankful the Crusade didn't train the Masters to detect Watcher glamours. They were, by and large, not psychic enough. No, a Master used the Seekers to find Lightbringers, because the hell-dogs created with ceremonial magick could see the glow of their souls in the landscape of Power. And the Seekers and zombie knights would hunt down Lightbringers like animals, kill them just as they had for hundreds of years.

Except for the one thing that stood between a Lightbringer

and danger.

A Watcher.

His arm tensed as he half-turned, keeping the man in sight. Caro's fingers tightened too, soft against his wrist. Spiked pleasure roiled under his skin, worked in to curl around his bones. And, amazingly enough, it began to have an effect below the belt. *Christ, what a time to get a hard-on. Keep your mind on your work, Merrick old man. Come on now. Get her out of here.*

Thhe Crusade Master spoke, pausing in front of the cross. "Christ is our glory, the earth our dominion," he whispered. "God smiles upon our work."

Fury boiled through Merrick. This man had probably killed Lightbringers before, had probably helped orchestrate the last safehouse attack, and would strangle Caro with his own hands if he could. It would take so little to whip the knife free, send it rocketing through the air, and hear the satisfying *thunk* as it hit home.

Caro shook her head. She hung onto his arm with all her fragile strength, her eyes wide and soft with tears, the trembling spilling through her infecting him. Control clamped down. He was a breath away from either killing the Crusade Master or pulling Caro even closer and maybe, just maybe, doing something a Watcher shouldn't do.

The Master swept the chapel, the gun held ready. Merrick kept still, his body between the danger and his witch. What was a Crusade Master doing *here*? And during the day? They usually hid in their boltholes whispering rosaries during the day, coming out at night to hunt unprotected Lightbringers. His hand tightened around the knife hilt, his knuckles turning white.

No, Caro mouthed against his hand. He had no trouble understanding the faint movements against his cupped palm. *Please. No, Merrick.*

The Master quartered the chapel, crossed himself again, and Merrick almost shook with the urge to kill. The only thing that stopped him was Caro's lips, soft against his callused palm, shaping the word *no*.

Honor. Duty. Obedience. He should kill the man. He *should*. It would make the world a safer place. It would make Caro safer.

She shook her head again, her skin sending shocks of soft hammering pleasure up his arm. The wall was temptingly close, he could push her back against its solidity and press himself against her. *That* opened up new and interesting vistas of contemplation he had no luxury for. *Control. Control, Merrick.*

The Master slowly paced away. The chapel doors closed behind him, softly, reverently.

Merrick waited, heard the footsteps retreat down the hall. *Was he expecting to find her here? Did he see us come in? No, I had her glamoured. What was he doing here? If I didn't have this witch to look after, I could follow him and have a little chat. That would be good, very good . . . but she's here. She needs to be protected.*

His hand fell reluctantly away from her mouth. "Crusade," he whispered, feeling sweat begin to dry on his neck. Caro was dangerous to his self-control, he had *never* been tempted to force a woman before. What the hell was wrong with him? "The bloody Crusade. Now will you listen to reason?"

"You were going to kill him," she whispered back.

"It was a Crusade Master. If he'd seen you, I *would* have killed him." It was hard to make his voice less harsh, hard to keep it pitched low. He could almost *feel* the subliminal click as combat-readiness settled over him again. Ready for anything. *I still might kill him, if I could be sure you wouldn't get into trouble while I did.* "We should go back to the safehouse."

He was prepared for an argument. But, surprisingly, Caro simply held up the cell phone. "Thank the gods this didn't ring," she managed, a little shakily. It actually physically *hurt* to hear the tremor in her voice. A witch this beautiful, this dedicated, shouldn't have to sound so frightened. "I think I've had enough for today. You can call a cab, or we can take the bus."

"Cab." His voice was husky. *See how well I obey you, witch. You have no idea what I almost did.* "Safer for you."

"All right." She dropped her eyes, her shoulders slumping. "All right. You win."

Seven

Caro leaned forward, bracing her hands on the table. Her eyes swept the room.

Six Mindhealers. That was all. And Fran, for once in a matching sweater and dress, both lemony yellow that did wonders for her pale complexion. Six. A bare half-dozen healers capable of walking in shattered minds and restoring peace to the tortured. Only six for how many thousands of people in this city? The familiar feeling of being with others like herself, the touch of other gentle minds, was only barely calming enough to soothe her frayed nerves. Merrick's presence, steady and comforting in its own way, nevertheless reminded her of the horribly-shrieking, vile-smelling thing that had burst out of poor Colleen.

Her hair fell in her eyes, escaping the chignon. She'd barely had a chance to wash her face; her stomach twisted with hunger. Her earrings tapped her cheeks comfortingly as her head moved, and she tried to breathe deeply, forcing down the shaking that threatened to make her hands into trembling claws.

The Watchers were clustered in the back of the meeting room, on the benches—except for Merrick, who stood slightly behind Caro to her right. He had already given a succinct description of the Dark he'd seen, and now it was Caro's turn.

"It was a third-level touch that triggered it," she said, slowly. "I had just soaked through the first few layers and slid in, meaning to make contact just below alpha level, see what the damage was. It was *smoked*, absolutely laid waste in there, as if something had torn out the personality by the roots. It was a good thing I'd used a blessed-water filter, or I'd have been eaten alive." She shivered, remembering the sheer *speed* at which the trap had snapped shut, layer after layer of the psyche exploding as the Dark rocketed up through it, aiming for the shimmer that was Caro's externalized consciousness. "I don't know quite how I triggered it. But it *smelled*, and I wasn't able to elude it. I tried to save Colleen." *Gods, how I tried, but she was already gone.*

Her head still echoed with the last scream of the tortured woman's mind as the Dark burst through her. *If I hadn't tried a third-level touch, would she still be alive?*

"You were able to do a third-level touch through a filter?"

Joanie's wide blue eyes were full of uncomfortable awe. Caro felt her throat threaten to close. "But that's—"

"Eleanor taught me. It's risky, but I wanted to make contact without having to go through the upper waking maze. If I hadn't had the filter we could have two witches dead of a stopped heart." Caro shook her head. "That's not important. The *important* thing is the thing inside was inert and feeding on the victim, like a parasite. And then when it came out, it tore free too quickly and died when it hit sunlight."

"Gods." Lydia, a plump round motherly Mindhealer, folded her hands. Her gold rings flashed, like her aura. Not as brightly as Caro's—*which means she won't be as big a snack for the Dark*, Caro thought. "They're *incubators*. Why didn't we think of that?"

"It gets worse." Caro took a deep breath. "The Crusade might somehow be involved. There was a Crusade Master there, in the chapel. Merrick kept me hidden, but I must have left traces in the room even a halfwit zombie knight would be able to See." *I didn't have much of a chance to clean up after myself. The Crusade Masters aren't psychic, but if he brings back a Seeker after nightfall he might be able to trace me. And, oh gods, if he had some kind of tracking talisman he might have followed us to the chapel and opened fire. Which means I could have gotten Merrick hurt. How could I be so stupid?*

Silence greeted her words. Fran's jaw dropped.

One of the Watchers—Oliver, the Watcher delegate to the regional Council—gained his feet in a single galvanic movement, so quickly his blond mane ruffled. "Begging your pardon, ma'am." His voice turned flinty, blue eyes hard and level. "Why didn't Merrick speak of this?"

"I asked him not to," Caro said smoothly. "If he said anything about it, you would want to question him before I had a chance to talk, and we might lose track of the main thing here—that innocent people are being attacked and hosting some kind of Dark. We don't know that the Crusade is necessarily responsible *or* involved. I want files for all the victims we know of, and I want them brought to the infirmary where we can figure out what they're infested with and how to treat it."

"No." Not only Oliver but Merrick said it, and the air became hot and still. The assembled Watchers—eight of them, one for each Mindhealer, Merrick, and Oliver—tensed, the air going hot and still.

"We can't allow that." Oliver straightened, clasping his hands behind his back. His eyes focused on the floor, but his jaw was set. The air around the seated Watchers swirled with tension and heat, each of them straight-backed and ready.

Fran's voice came like a breath of cool wind, a thread of lily-smell that soothed Caro's nerves. "Allow, Oliver?"

"Under the regs, we can bar a potential danger from the safehouse. What if one of these victims lets loose something Dark to roam inside the wards?" Oliver shook his leonine head. "The infirmary is near the nursery and the children's wing. No."

Caro's hands tightened as she leaned on the table. The whiteboard behind her chattered slightly against the wall, the dry-erase markers clicking in the gutter along its bottom. "We are talking about innocent people here," she said, wishing her teeth didn't want to grit together quite so badly. "I need to examine them, and I need them safe. If the Crusade *is* involved they might kill the incubators."

"The children are innocent," Oliver returned. "The Lightbringers in the infirmary, too. The Watchers cannot agree to this."

"Fourteen victims, nine dead now." Fran's voice almost broke under the sadness of it. The other Mindhealers nodded, their auras turning dark and golden, spangled with grief.

"We need to discuss this." Lydia sighed. "There aren't enough of us."

"How many of the dead held one of these Dark creatures?" Joanie asked.

"We don't know." This from a slim teenaged Mindhealer, a collection of thin chiming gold bracelets falling down her arm as she brushed her dark hair back. "We weren't there when the others died."

"And Danica's death didn't release anything Dark." An ebony-skinned Mindhealer, her hair in several tiny braids tipped with red glass beads, folded her arms, leaning back in her chair. Her large dark eyes were eloquently sad.

"We wouldn't know," Lydia pointed out. "Her Watcher's heart stopped too; they were a bonded pair. Something Dark could have come out and been gone by the time we found them. It smelled *awful* in there, we thought it was just the victim."

"I don't like this," Joanie said darkly. "We don't know enough."

Caro dropped into the chair behind the table, exhaustion closing over her. "We have to stop this." Her voice sliced through the rising murmurs. "If I can't examine the victims, I don't know how I'm supposed to come up with a workable theory *or* figure out how to repair the damage."

Oliver cleared his throat. "Normally, in cases involving a Dark parasite, the victim doesn't survive. Especially when the damage to the physical body is so intense."

"And they were *physically* beaten." The teenage Mindhealer shuddered. "Worked over pretty good. We could be looking at some type of human agency here, even if it isn't Crusade. There are others—the Thains, the Brotherhood."

This sparked a flurry of discussion. "So there's something hunting in the city?"

"Or someone."

"What about the Crusade?"

"How are we going to treat this?"

"The victims die, sooner or later; normals wouldn't see something Dark birthing itself."

"But someone must have felt something, seen something, *heard* something!"

"Gods above—"

"Ladies, gentlemen." Fran raised her hands for silence. Caro slumped in her chair. Merrick moved closer, his aura fringing hers, something she was too tired to work up any energy to be irritated about. "I suggest we get Caro the files as soon as possible and start researching. Someone *has* to have seen this type of Dark before. We'll call some of the other safehouses and ask them to ransack their libraries. And I'll have the tech witches start going through every bit of intel we can pull from the Crusade."

"What about guarding the victims?" Caro felt her chin lifting stubbornly, heard the sharpness in her voice, hated it.

Oliver said nothing, stared at the floor. Caro's heart sank. She'd known, of course . . . but still.

"The Watchers are spread too thin here as it is," Fran said heavily. "Lightbringers are their priority. I'm sorry, Caro."

She sagged further against the chair's back as the meeting broke up. Merrick was completely still beside her. A few of the Mindhealers looked as if they wanted to talk to her, but she closed her eyes and rested her hands on the table until silence rang through the room, telling her she was alone with the Watcher.

He waited quietly. Caro was surprised to find tears rising to her eyes again. "I know she's just doing her job," she whispered. "But *gods*, those poor people. Why would anyone do something like this?"

Merrick seemed to give the question his full attention. "Don't know." His accent clipped the words short. He sounded so calm, so precise; she envied him that calmness. "Lots of reasons. Greed, hate, just plain meanness. Happens a lot, love."

"But *why*?" Her voice broke. *Great, Caro. Show everyone what a blasted coward you are.*

"You're Lightbringer. You won't understand. You're not made that way."

"Oh, and you are?" *Nobody understands these things, do they?*

He was silent for a full sixty seconds. Then, "I'm a Watcher. I have to understand." His aura tightened at the edges of hers, and she felt his attention sweeping the room and the hall beyond, even though they were in a safehouse. Did he ever relax?

No, Watchers never relaxed. Unceasing vigilance was trained into them. It made her tired to even think about. And Caro had to figure out some kind of solution to get him away from her. If the Crusade was involved with this, it was likely to get messy and dangerous. There was nothing the Crusade liked better than killing a Lightbringer, unless it was killing a Watcher. Fran was no help, the Council had washed its hands of the whole problem, and probably breathed a sigh of relief too.

She dropped her head forward into her hands, bracing her elbows on the table. This meeting room was quiet, small, and windowless. Not many Lightbringers would like it in here. Caro's own claustrophobia rose briefly, tore at her throat, retreated a little. "Gods, I'm tired."

"You should rest." A hesitant pause, then he touched her shoulder, his fingers hot through the silk of her shirt. "They'll bring you the files."

"Meanwhile, whoever's out there beating up people and infecting them with Dark parasites is still running around." Her fingers were hot and slick with tears. "I should have been here weeks ago."

"You're here now." His hand closed around her shoulder. "You should rest, love."

"Why are you calling me that?" Exhaustion made the words sharper than she intended.

"It's a habit. Sorry."

Well, now I feel like a bitch. It's not his fault. Probably just some weird British custom, like eating fried fish. "No, I'm just wondering. It's okay. You probably need something to eat, don't you?" *Great, Caro. Feed the Watcher before you let him risk his life hanging around you.*

Did he pause? "I won't say no."

And that, Caro thought as she wiped her eyes, *is exactly the problem.*

* * * *

The dream was always the same, as she tossed and turned in an unfamiliar bed. Again and again, it returned.

Caroline, humming, put her hands in the soapy water and lifted the bowl again. "I don't know. You think it'd work?"

"Theoretically." Vincent leaned against the kitchen counter, his close-cropped blond hair sticking to his skull. He had dark circles under his eyes that never seemed to go away, and the long black leather coat only made him seem paler. Say something to him, *Caro shrieked at her dreaming, oblivious self.* He's falling into a Watcher's despair, you idiot, say something kind!

Dream-Caro sighed. "I wish I could test it for sure without the risk of getting killed."

"You could try it on me. I'm Dark." His voice betrayed no shading of bitterness, but his mouth pulled down at the corners slightly.

"Stuff that works on pure Dark might not work on you," she pointed out, lifting the bowl and rinsing it. The blue ceramic was slick and warm under her fingers. "You're a Watcher, not a Slider or a Seeker."

"True." Now a brief smile. Vincent was by far the most expressive Watcher she'd ever had. They usually changed every six months—the "rotation," so each Watcher had a chance to find his witch. Caro had grown accustomed to silent, grim men. But Vincent was the Watcher who had brought her into Circle Lightfall, who had noticed a foster child with the sparkling aura of a Mindhealer, reported it,

*and been sent to collect her and Trev with Eleanor D'Arcy.
And since then, he had been on the periphery of her life,
always having time for a scabby-kneed, needy foster child
frightened of her gifts and desperate for any sort of
approval.*

*Eleanor helped, of course. She understood Caro's fears,
trained her to overcome them and use her talents effectively.
But Vincent was the closest thing to a father figure Caro
ever had, and she cherished his quiet unconditional
acceptance. "But you never know. I might be able to gauge
the effect on the Dark from what it feels like."*

*"It's a Lightbringer magick." Caro shook her head.
Her hair had been shorter then. "It'll probably hurt you."*

*"In the name of science." Vince's tone was light. The
kitchen, painted a sunny yellow, was suddenly full of the
hot static of his attention.*

*Caro tensed. "What is it?" Her heart began to beat
thinly, rapidly. She didn't feel anything outside the carefully
laid wards on her new house, but her head began to hurt.
A sure sign of something bad about to happen. "Vincent?"*

*"I'll check it out." His dark eyes glittered, and one
hand strayed toward a gun.* It must be bad if he's reaching
for a gun around me, *she thought. He was normally so careful
not to frighten her.*

Run! *she yelled at her dream-self.* Get out of there! Get
him out of there! Get away! It's coming!

*But he crossed to the back door, the wards on the house
sparking and fizzing under his sudden attention. He was
adding last minute bolstering to them, which meant he
probably had an idea of what was outside Caro's first
house—bought with money earned from her job as a social
worker, and helped along by Circle Lightfall's generous
assistance with the mortgage. There were still boxes in the
hall and the bedrooms. She had only been here for two
weeks.*

*"Vincent?" Her fingers clenched on the bowl. She stood
there stupidly, dripping dishwater on the kitchen floor, the
air suddenly thick and close with the nonphysical stench
of evil. Wet warmth trickled down from her nose, a thin
awful sensation. Nosebleed. The Dark. "What?"*

*"Get into your bedroom," he said over his shoulder. "I
mean it, Caro. The shields there should—"*

Then it hit the house, and the bowl leapt from her hand and shattered on the floor.

BANG.

Her room was dark. Caro, bracing herself on her elbows, blinked and swallowed the sour taste of fear as she gulped back her waking scream. The nightlight's glowing edge around the bathroom door did nothing to help. She pulled the hem of the cotton tank top down. It had twisted and rode up under her breasts. Her flannel shorts were twisted too, she must have been tossing for a while.

She always did when she dreamed of Vincent's death.

Something's wrong. What is it?

The Mindhealers were all accounted for, at least, warned of the danger. The files hadn't arrived, but Fran had more than enough to keep her busy late into the evening. Caro had unpacked, made lunch and dinner for herself and Merrick, and fallen wearily into bed at about seven. It was, though she hated to admit it, good to be able to exhaust herself into sleeping. Last night had been a nightmare of insomnia and prowling the suite of pretty rooms.

Caro gained her feet, the bed creaking. The room was utterly silent, but a slight breath told her Merrick was right by the door. She'd almost gotten used to having a Watcher again, he was so quiet. He hadn't spoken much, just silently taken care of things that needed doing—including barring her door when she wanted some peace. He'd even denied entry to a few healers when Caro told him she didn't want to be disturbed. For a Mindhealer used to being barged in on at a moment's notice, the sudden ability to have solitude was overwhelming.

And Merrick's docile, silent obedience was a little creepy, even for a witch used to Watchers.

He hadn't mentioned the Crusade again. Neither had she. The sudden détente was welcome on her part, at least. She had the distinct idea that he could get devastatingly ironic under that proper British façade.

She caught a flash of green—his eyes. Caro stopped, tilting her head. Her cheeks felt naked without her long golden earrings brushing them.

There it is again. She swallowed dryly, heard her throat click.

The receptive surface of her mind rippled, the disturbance

now more pronounced.

"Something's wrong," she whispered. "Merrick?"

She caught a faint flash of movement. He'd nodded. *Dammit, I wish he'd talk, I can't see in the dark like he can.*

She made it to the dresser, pulled out a pair of jeans and some underwear by touch—learning how to unpack so she could find everything even in the dark was a skill she had down cold by now—and hurried to the bathroom. Inside, the light stung her eyes as she changed into the jeans and grabbed a ponytail holder.

When she emerged, pulling her hair back, Merrick had turned the lights on but still stood near the door. He didn't say a word, but one eyebrow arched eloquently. Maybe he had to use body language since he didn't want to talk. He was laconic even for a Watcher.

"If something happens, I want to be dressed," she snapped. She jerked a red cardigan from the pile of neatly folded clothes on the dresser and shrugged it on over her tank top. She felt sandy and crusty, like she usually did waking in the middle of the night. But her heart pounded in her throat and wrists, and her mouth tasted coppery. "I don't like to be—"

She didn't get any further. The safehouse shields shuddered under a stunning impact. Caro cried out and flinched. Merrick tilted his head, listening intently.

There was a breath of silence, then the whole house vibrated with Watcher magick waking up. Caro could *feel* the sudden change—from a sleeping, dreaming safehouse to one under attack. She shook her head, tears starting in her eyes. "No," she whispered. "Gods, please, *no*." *Not again. I hate this.*

"It's all right." Merrick finally spoke. "I don't think it broke the shields. They'll send out a team to clear whatever it is."

Almost nothing could break a safehouse's defenses. The biggest danger in any attack was the confusion and fear it caused inside the walls, not any actual Dark getting inside. The safehouses hadn't been broken since the early 1800s, the time of Molly Grenwine and her Watcher, Harrison. That was why they were called safehouses, nothing Dark could get through the layers of warding applied with painstaking care to every brick, every wall, every nail, every window, every pane of glass or sheet of drywall.

But still, her mouth was dry and the feeling of impending disaster was undeniable.

"No." Premonition trembled under the surface of Caro's thoughts. "Something's really, really wrong. It's about to happen."

Another jolting impact, the shields shivering. The floor groaned. Caro swayed, and he was suddenly right next to her, his arm over her shoulders. He was warm, his heat sinking into her skin. "What are they doing?" she whispered.

"Doesn't matter. This is a safehouse."

The words were barely out of his mouth when something huge hit the shields over her window. She screamed, a thin sound, as the glass groaned and Merrick moved, pushing her behind him. His aura flushed crimson-black, hard and hurtful; the warding laid in the walls tearing and shredding under the pressure of the attack.

There, pressed against the glass, was a heaving snout made of darkness. Two red eyes glowed as it scrabbled for entrance, claws slipping off the sheet of Power that was the defenses gathering, turning hard and slippery as volcanic glass. The teeth were black smoke, frozen and hard, clashing and champing.

No. Please, gods, no.

It slid away, scrabbling. Merrick's back turned hard as iron under the heavy leather coat. He jammed the knife back in its sheath and half-turned, his arm snaking over her shoulders.

"Come on." He pulled her along. Caro stumbled on numb legs, he set her on her feet again. Dragged her out the door as another impact made the walls quiver. The sweet tinkling crash of broken glass echoed as he slammed the door and snapped a single word, laying a quick warding on it to slow the thing down. Her feet barely brushed the ground as he set off down the hall, his boots oddly silent. The walls blurred. He pushed her into the corner at the end of the hall before she could protest. Turning his back to her, the knives slid out of their sheaths as he faced the direction danger would come from—her room.

"Merrick." Her voice cracked. "That was a Seeker. A *Seeker.*"

"Maybe," he said quietly. If he was trying to soothe her, it didn't help. Panic beat inside her chest. "Just stay as still as you can."

"They can kill." She heard her own sobbing breathlessness. Danger pounded in her head, the proximity of the Dark driving glass needles into her temples. *Come on, Caro! Get a spine! Get him out of here, that's a Seeker, it could kill him!* "You have to go. We have to go *right now*." She found herself staring at the middle of his back, the sword bisecting it in a neat diagonal line, the shimmer of glamour to hide his weapons from normals weak and useless while inside the safehouse. "Merrick?"

"Relax, Caro. I've done this before." He sounded so utterly calm she almost believed she might be dreaming. Of course she was dreaming. The Dark couldn't break into the safehouse. It was *impossible.*

A heavy thud, a low snarl from the room. A Seeker. But they couldn't crack into a safehouse. Was it a created Seeker? That would mean the Crusade.

Living in Saint City had spoiled her. They didn't have to worry about the Crusade so much there. Theo and the other Guardians kept those particular fanatics out, though it was a scramble these days with all the other Dark boiling into the city—

Skritch-skritch. Skritch-skritch. A thin, evil scratching came from the door. The ward Merrick had snapped over it started to smoke and pulse. Caro felt a moan rising in her chest, killed it. "We've got to go. Please, Merrick. We have to go right *now*."

"Just stay calm," he whispered back. "Nice and calm, love, I'm here."

Irritation cut through the sinking dread as the glass needles jabbed even more viciously at her head. *You idiot, you could get killed! I promised I'd never let another Watcher die because of me!* She raised her hands, put them flat on his back, and *shoved*. It did no good—it was like pushing a brick wall. He didn't even have the grace to pretend he noticed.

"We have to *go*," she whispered, even as the floorboards groaned. The defenses locked down, sheets of cascading energy snapping into place, any breaches now sealed. The air vibrated— Watchers, sweeping the entire safehouse, teams going out to clear the streets. An unpleasant reminder, as if she needed one, of the danger she'd been born into. "Please, Merrick!"

He might have said something, but the door exploded out in matchwood splinters, peppering the wall opposite with smoking bits. The Dark thing crashed through, skidding, and she screamed.

Merrick moved, blurring as the laws of physics bent. The

knives were reversed along his forearms, black steel glowing with thin crimson-flame runes reacting to the Dark. The blades actually cast dappled red reflections against the walls. *Why are his knives glowing like that?* Caro swallowed the last half of her scream and searched frantically for some way to protect him.

He made no sound as he crashed into the Dark. It snarled and let loose a shattering psychic wail. Caro's hands clapped over her ears, but it did no good—the sound drilled *inside,* scraping, burrowing, twisting. Blood slid down from her nose as her legs gave out and she spilled to the floor, her knees grating against the hardwood.

Then in the dim light of the hallway, another Watcher, a tall brown-haired man, rose up. His face was set and grim, he made one swift movement down with one of his own incandescent knives, twisting as it buried in the Seeker's flesh. There was a *snap!* and the thing slumped, twitching. The reek of it was immense, a psychic sludge of bloodthirsty hatred and feral hunger, with the extra nose-tainting tang of bitter almonds. Caro had smelled that before.

The Crusade. But *how?* Of all the witches the Crusade hated, they hated healers and Mindhealers the most. Had *she* brought it here? Had the Master at Saint Crispin's managed to catch her scent and track her here? But there was another layer to the stench—rotten eggs. Sulfur. She felt her stomach rebel, was glad she hadn't eaten much.

"Caro! *Caroline!*" Fran's voice, high and unsteady. "Let go of me! *Caro!*"

"I'm fine," she heard herself say. "Frannie?"

The air witch slid along the wall, keeping well away from the dead hulk of the Seeker, shaking her gray head and stumbling. Then she ran for Caro.

Caro, on her knees, leaned back against the wall. Her stomach revolved unsteadily. *I think I'm going to throw up. No. Please don't let me throw up.* "Fran." Her eyes were fixed on the slumped shape of the Seeker, already starting to run like a lump of clay in swift water. *It looks wrong. Why does it look wrong? This is all wrong. A Seeker shouldn't be able to break through the wards! Nothing Dark should be able to!*

Merrick rose from the psychic sludge, shaking himself like a cat who has just received an unwelcome shower of rain. It was a fluid, horrible movement, because his face was wet with blood and his left arm was obviously dislocated. A long gash in his jeans, on the left leg, slashing down—*That could have hit an artery,* Caro realized, and a rushing sound filled her ears.

"Caro!" Fran had her shoulders, shook her. "Are you all right?" Her face was chalk-white, her eyes seeming very dark instead of their usual blue.

"Fine." Blood dripped from Caro's top lip, wet and warm, her nose was full of warm liquid copper. Her teeth chattered. "Merrick?"

"He's okay." Fran spared a single look over her shoulder. She wore another long purple sweater over a primrose silk nightgown. Her silvery hair tumbled down past her shoulders. "Look, he's up and walking around."

But his face is all bloody and his sh-shoulder—Caro watched as the Watcher reached up absently with his bleeding left hand, feeling around the dislocated joint, his arm flopping strangely. A shrug, a flare of Power, his fingers turning to iron— and the joint *popped* back into place. Part of a *tanak*'s gift, the ability to heal. If it hurt, his face made no sign of it.

Instead, he stood in quarter-profile, looking down at the Seeker, his body still between the Dark thing and the two witches at the end of the hall. *He's making sure it's dead. Oh, gods.* A fresh jolt of nausea speared through her.

The brown-haired Watcher spread his fingers. Power rose and crackled, cleaning the psychic debris from the air. The Seeker turned to smoke, shredded, and was gone. The stink vanished slowly, leaching away bit by bit. It was a relief.

Then Merrick's shoulders slumped and he made a low hurt noise. He turned sharply, his coat flaring. Not toward her—but toward her door. He was going to make sure another one wasn't lying in wait in her room.

"Let me," the other Watcher said, the knife disappearing into a sheath. "Check them."

Merrick paused, nodded, and turned back. His eyes were glowing, blazing out from under the blood-drenched strings of dark hair sticking to his forehead. He saw her at the end of the hall, and his scarred face froze.

She barely even saw him move before he was kneeling next to Fran, careful not to touch the other witch. He dug in a pocket—not even seeming to notice the blood on his face— and brought out, of all things, another handkerchief, this one pale blue. "Got too close," he murmured, as if to himself, and offered it to her. "Sorry."

He's sorry? He got his shoulder dislocated, and he's all torn up and bleeding and he's sorry? She shook her head, unable to find the right words.

He used the handkerchief to dab at the blood dripping from her nose, exquisitely careful. The contrast between the deadly fighter, moving between her and the Dark, and this gentle scarred man whose green eyes were dark and concerned as he tried to blot the blood from her face, was jarring. She would never get used to this. After decades in Circle Lightfall she was still unprepared.

She found her voice, finally. "I'm fine," she managed, reaching up to take the handkerchief. His fingers brushed hers. She didn't miss the way his eyes narrowed, the sudden sharpening of his attention. "Take care of yourself."

"I'm more worried about you." He looked like he meant it, too. He was staring at her as if he could see nothing else. "Head hurt?"

"A . . . a little." Her voice shook. Behind him, she could sense other Watchers sweeping the halls. The brown-haired Watcher had vanished into her room. Fran grabbed her hand, his fingers sinking in. "It—a *Seeker.* The Crusade—"

"Don't worry." Merrick sounded utterly calm. "You're safe."

"But—" Her eyes jagged over to Fran's face, back to Merrick's.

Merrick's lips firmed and his eyebrows raised slightly. It was maybe the first moment of complete accord she'd had with another person since Eleanor's death. Fran already looked scared half out of her mind, there was no need to make it worse. "My head hurts," Caro settled for saying, in a pale little voice. It wasn't a lie. Her head felt as if demented Christmas elves were smashing the inside of her skull with glass spikes.

The Watcher's fingers hovered less than an inch from her wrist. Warmth slid into her aura, gentler than the usual heat-jolt. Instead of a bolt to the solar plexus, this was a satiny curtain wrapping around her. The curtain tightened, sending a shiver from her toes all the way up to the roots of her hair.

"Don't go into shock," he said quietly, as more Watchers arrived. The air turned electric-hot, prickles racing over her skin. Fran shivered too.

"Brigid's Tears, Caro." The Council witch shook her hand a little, grabbed the handkerchief, and wiped Caro's upper lip, cleaning the blood off and pressing the wad of cloth firmly against her nose. "You and your damn nosebleeds. I swear we could hire you out as a Dark detector, just follow the trail of bloody Kleenex." Fran's voice trembled, humor used to deflect fear but not doing a very good job of it.

Dear gods. A jolting laugh worked its way free. "Would it be better if it was tampons?"

"Caro!" Fran managed to sound scandalized and relieved all at once. "Well, at least now I know you're all right."

Caro's eyes met Merrick's. His jaw was set. A muscle flicked in his cheek. He looked furious.

She swallowed. "How many of these do you have?" She sounded like Elmer Fudd. *How bany of dese do you hab?*

That earned her a flicker of a smile, his incandescent eyes darkening. "Mum was always after me never to go out without a rag." His tone was even, murderously cool.

"Caro, tilt your head back. It will help with the bleeding." Fran was fussing now. She'd be all right. Once Fran hit "fuss" mode, the crisis was over.

Oh, gods, I hope nobody's been hurt. She pushed Fran's hand away, peeled the handkerchief away from her face. "Fine. I'm fine. Go check on everyone else. I'm all right." *I'm lying.* Her stomach did another rolling barrel-dive, she had to swallow hard.

Fran levered herself to her feet and did as she asked. Merrick's fingertips still paused above Caro's wrist, sending another shockwave of warmth through her aura.

She took a deep breath, lifted her hand slightly so her skin met his fingers. He went utterly still, his eyes blazing again. "Thank you," she whispered.

His hand curled around hers, turned it palm-up. His skin was warm and callused. She smelled iron and dark Power and the faint citrusy smell that followed him around.

"For what?" He asked it softly, but his eyes scorched her.

"It's a Seeker," she answered, just as quietly. "The Crusade. You know it is."

He nodded. His hair fell over his eyes, tacky with drying blood. "Or maybe not. It doesn't smell right. But one thing's for certain, it was after you."

The bottom dropped out of her stomach yet again. *I don't*

want to throw up here. Please don't let me throw up here.
"How do you . . ." It was a useless question.

"It came straight for a third-story window in the most
protected part of the safehouse." His face was level and cold.
"And it didn't choose to go the other way, toward the other
Lightbringers. It came this way. For you." His eyes paled,
turning piercing green. "Good thing you have me, witch."

"You could have died." Her eyes burned. Her voice was
so tiny, almost useless. *Stop it, Caro. For God's sake, stop it.*
Grow a spine.

His face went still. "I know what I'm doing." He let go of
her hand, finger by finger. Rising to his feet like a dark wave,
he offered her his hand. "Want to stand up?"

She shook her head, helpless. "I don't think I can yet."
And all the gods help me, but I've got to get you away from
me. I'm too dangerous.

There was the ghost of a smile, and she realized that even
with the scars he was actually quite handsome. "I'll stay with
you then. Until you can."

Eight

"It was similar to a Seeker, but no type we've ever seen before. It came right through the wards." Oliver stared straight ahead, a muscle in his cheek flicking once. "Right through the goddamn wards. And went for your witch."

The Watcher dormitory was a long, low room, the beds marching in even progression down either side. A chest crouched at the foot of each for clothing and weapons, personal effects, and the infrequent cache of ammunition. The windows were privacy-tinted. This was the first floor and the least defensible area of the safehouse. The Watchers gathered at the east end, a half-circle of straight-faced men in long black leather coats, swords riding their shoulders and the hard glitter of Power in their eyes. Power also whisked and slid along the bare white-painted walls, where an occasional movie poster broke the monotony. Most Watchers weren't big into interior decoration. In any case, this was only a room to sleep and occasionally clean and re-consecrate one's weapons in, nothing more. The altar at the west end held a low fluid statue of Mithras holding sword and book, the whip at his belt. Most Watchers adopted a personal god after a while, but Mithras was the god they made communal offerings to before attending the greater ceremonies of the eight Sabbats the witches celebrated.

It seemed to work. The Bull took care of his own. Some of the Watchers visited churches, synagogues, or mosques whenever the need arose; any god a Watcher wanted to pray to was acceptable. But Mithras, worshipped by Watchers since the early 1600s in rites that even at the beginning had taken on a tenor and flavor quite different from the original Roman devotions, seemed to be the one most gravitated to.

"I know." Merrick's shoulder ached. The *tanak* burned inside his bones, healing stretched tendons and melding together sliced flesh. His scars tingled.

Caro was in the infirmary, being checked out over her protests while her room was cleaned and re-shielded, the wall and window repaired. All in all, everyone was taking the first breaking of a safehouse's walls in two hundred years quite calmly. It simply meant more shielding, figuring out how to close up whatever loophole had allowed the thing to smash the window. Panic had been avoided.

Merrick's nose still smarted from the stink of the thing. It smelled like bitter almonds, sulfur, and some other dry noxious scent he couldn't quite place. Almost like the thing that had burst out of Caro's patient and tried to kill Merrick's witch. And yet, Caro hadn't mentioned anything strange about the smell. Nobody else had remarked it either, nobody but Merrick. Which was odd.

Very odd.

He pulled himself back into the present. "There's something else. Whatever *it* is, it smelled almost like that goddamn thing at Saint Crispin's."

A ripple ran through the assembled Watchers. This was an informal meeting, word-of-mouth would pass everything along through the safehouse when they were finished. It was a relief to be among other Watchers. He didn't have to be so bloody *controlled*. Didn't have to hold himself so still and cautious. But still, the *tanak* twisted inside his bones, and all he wanted to do was go back to Caro, reassure himself again that she was all right. Convince himself that she was still alive.

Oliver let out a short, frustrated sound. "A new type of Seeker, maybe? Incubated in normals and psychics instead of built through ceremonial magick?"

Each Watcher mulled this over. Merrick felt a cool bath of dread work its way up his back.

"Fucking awful." This from Ellis, a short tensile Watcher with a brown crew cut and glaring hazel eyes, his thumbs habitually tucked in his belt. "Used to be the best thing, to kill created Seekers. That way the Knight takes the backlash."

A murmur of agreement.

"It could have killed the Mindhealer," Oliver said finally. "Stay close to her, Merrick. Don't let her do anything foolish."

My friend, you might as well ask me to stop a tornado by saying "pretty please." "Keeps threatening to send me back to the Council." He laced the words with casualness.

The Watchers stilled again. They knew, of course, about Caro's refusal to have a Watcher, even if they didn't know the particulars. "She's your witch," Harris Blue said. "Can't send you back to the Council's jurisdiction. Under the regs, you're hers. Lucky bastard, she *can't* send you back."

I know, but I'm not sure how lucky I feel. "Duty. Honor. Obedience." He didn't need to say more, each man in the room understood. If Caro gave Merrick a direct order to leave her unprotected, he would have no choice but to damn himself by disobeying. Leather creaked as they shifted, and most eyes turned to the altar at the other end of the room. A harsh god, a stringent god, who required superhuman restraint and endurance; but they had it to give, didn't they? And the redemption he offered was more than any soul-eaten man believed he deserved.

Oliver's eyes lit with the bleached fury of his own *tanak*. "They don't understand," he said quietly. "It's up to us to protect them. But—" He held up a hand for silence, got it. "They're right. They're better than we are, will *always* be better than we are. Protecting them doesn't mean we can turn into the fucking Crusade. So we fight the good fight. You just stay on that witch and keep her alive, Merrick."

He nodded. *Oh, you'd better believe it.* The thought of anything happening to Caro made his stomach go sour and his fists want to clench. "If you run across another one of these things, remember they're vulnerable to the knives. Damn near explode when touched with consecrated steel. Don't know why the Mindhealers could smell it and why I can now, but . . . I could track one of these buggers if I had to."

"No tracking." Oliver shook his head. "Your responsibility is the Mindhealer."

"Right." Relieved, Merrick straightened. "I'd better get back to the infirmary."

"Good work, Watcher. Honor."

"Duty," Merrick responded, and the meeting began to break up. His shoulders tightened as he ducked out into the hall and took to the stairs, heading for the infirmary on the second floor, below Caro's rooms. In the most protected part of the safehouse.

Why the hell did that thing come straight for her window? And more importantly, why could he smell it? She hadn't mentioned its stink, and Merrick was surprised that apparently nobody else smelled it either. Reeking of sulfur and that other dry horrible smell, enough to make a Watcher's eyes water. Sometimes acute senses were a curse.

Was it because while he'd fought the thing, he had, as always, no time to keep himself separate from the hard cold animal inside his head? The one down at the very bottom, the one that could *track*?

Maybe.

Maybe, hell. Almost certainly. Which means I could find these things. Doesn't take much to find something that stinks that bad.

He reached the infirmary and nodded at the Watcher on duty, a lanky blond with the unlikely moniker of Cougar, and entered the world of the Lightbringers again.

Caro was on a cot at the far end, the statue of Hygieia glimmering soft and alabaster above her. White candles glowed under the statue, and soft murmurs filled the air as the healers on duty moved between the beds. As usual around healers, the air smelled of green growing things and spice, and Caro's bright golden glow was surrounded by the green wash of earth witches.

Her hair glowed, messy and streaked with gold. She pushed a few stray tendrils back and made a short, sharp movement as if annoyed.

His heart leapt. He literally lost all his air. She was beautiful, her dark-blue eyes wide and expressive, her face with its sharp classic lines softening when she thought nobody could see. Even the clear purity of her skin made his breath catch. When she pulled the red cardigan up—she still wore the tank top she'd been sleeping in, a battered cotton number silkscreened with a print of Buddha—over her pale shoulder, buttoning it swiftly and grimacing at the healer who was evidently scolding her, Merrick not only lost his breath but pretty much all of his good sense as well.

If he had to list the worst moments in his life, she was beginning to star in one or two of them. Thinking about her anywhere near something as violently dangerous as the thing they'd just killed—Seeker or not, he still wasn't entirely sure what it was—made something hard and cold rise up inside him, threatening the control that was so bloody necessary for a Watcher to do his job. She was foolhardy enough to give him the cold sweats. If it hadn't been for the other Lightbringers talking some sense into her, she might have gone haring off after the other victims and gotten herself in even more danger. Was he prepared to do what was necessary to keep her safe?

It means direct disobedience if she orders me away. It means betraying the Watcher's oath of obedience, breaking my sworn word. Means going back to what I was before. Do I want to go that far?

He watched as she gave the healer fussing over her a

quick apologetic smile, eyes suddenly sparkling. She still held the bloody handkerchief, and her cheeks were stained with high hectic color. As soon as the healer—a plump, blonde green witch in a long dark-blue dress—turned away to pick up a tray, still shaking her head and evidently not finished with the scolding, Caro's face fell. She closed her eyes and almost swayed.

Merrick's heart stopped. He stalked forward. The healer, used to Watchers, merely glanced up and nodded a greeting. Caro swayed again, and Merrick closed his hand around her shoulder, steadying her.

She looked up, startled, and in that instant he saw the fear lurking in the bottom of her eyes. It tore at him, an unsteady pain somewhere under his sternum. She shouldn't have to be afraid, especially with a Watcher around. She should be as fearless as she wanted everyone to think she was.

Do I want to go back to what I used to be? He let go of her as soon as she was steady, and settled himself to watch as the green witch turned back with a cup of medicinal-smelling herbal tea. "For your nerves, Caroline, and I want you to drink it all."

Do I really want to? Merrick's face tingled as his scars reacted to the green witch's glow, burning with pain. He glared out from under his hair, his hands plunging into his pockets and turning to fists. *You're damn right I do.*

For her, I would. I will.

* * * *

"No." Caro scowled stubbornly, her eyes lighting with a flash of familiar-by-now fire. "I won't cower in a hole. We have to find out what's going on."

The Council witch sighed, clasping her hands together and leaning forward onto her desk. A flood of morning sun fell across her shoulders. Merrick's eyes felt dry and hot. His neck felt as if someone was ramming iron rods down along his cervical spine, his shoulder muscles tight and tense as cables. Caro, once she was checked out at the infirmary, literally hadn't stopped moving since. She stalked the safehouse corridors waiting for morning, and when morning hit she paused only for coffee and a Danish before heading to the Council witch's office. And Merrick privately thought that the Council witch had expected this.

He was beginning to think he should tie Caro up just to make her get some rest. He tried to figure out if there was a way to justify it without running foul of the Watcher vow of obedience.

Francine spoke very slowly and calmly. "You're not doing any good, Caro. I'm simply suggesting that you stay at the safehouse for a couple of days while we get the preliminary investigation out of the way. You've already triggered one Dark parasite coming out of a victim. If you attempt to examine the other victims, you may well trigger another. And if there's a new type of Seeker in the city—if the Crusade is mounting another campaign, you're safer in here than anywhere else. You should get some rest, and you should stop pulling my chain. I am *not* trying to make life difficult for you. I am trying to solve a mystery that could kill more people if we don't go carefully."

"Careful, careful, cautious," Caro chanted, frustration evident in her tone. She paced in front of the Council witch's desk, her arms crossed and her knuckles white as she dug her fingers into her upper arms. "Let me at least go and take a *look* at them. They're patients, for God's sake, I have to do *something*!"

"You want to do something? Quit yelling at me so I can get some work done. Go look after your Watcher, he's still got blood in his hair. Call your brother, so I don't have him breathing down my neck every twenty minutes. Teach a class of Seers how to shield themselves. There's plenty to *do*, Caroline, even for you."

Merrick braced himself for the explosion.

Caro stopped pacing. She stood still for fifteen full seconds, her aura snapping and crackling. Then she dropped into a chair across the desk from the Council witch, who still hadn't moved. "I'm sorry, Frannie." She sounded sorry, too. Merrick's hands began to unclench. "I'm just . . . gods. I'm sorry. I'm being a bitch."

"Mmh." The other witch didn't agree or disagree. "I know how you feel, Caro. I wish there was something useful I could do instead of all this damn paperwork and coordinating. You feel responsible? I do too. I didn't call you, even though I knew I should. I didn't want you to be worried. You have enough to deal with, and I'm sorry I've laid this burden on you. I'm sorry you've come here and had to face this." Her eyes dropped to the paper-choked surface of her desk, Merrick breathed in dust and paper and binding-glue; and the smell of Caro's perfume. "I did what I thought was right, and now another innocent woman is dead and you've been attacked."

"It's not your fault, Fran." Caro leaned forward, her hair glinting in the thin wintery sunlight falling through the window and spangled with dust. "You didn't do anything to poor Colleen. I'm sorry, I'm such a hotheaded—I mean, I just want to help. I don't want anyone else getting hurt."

"Neither do I. Believe me, neither do I. Look, go get some breakfast and take a nap. Do you want a different room?"

Caro shuddered, but her chin lifted. "No. I'll stay in that one. I've already unpacked, I don't want to pack again just to move down the hall. They're not going to scare me that easily."

You should be scared, Caro. You just don't know it. It may be that the Crusade has a new type of Seeker that can pierce a safehouse's walls. Merrick moved slightly, uneasily. He was glad Caro hadn't asked him to wait outside.

Both witches looked up at him. Caro was deathly pale, fever-spots standing out in her cheeks. Francine looked far older than she ever had, her mouth pulled into a tight line.

"What do you think, Merrick?" Caro's gaze was worried and hopeful. She bit her lower lip as soon as she said his name.

I think you're entirely too brave for your own good, love. And I think you should be tied up and locked in a basement with me standing guard until we can figure this thing out. He cleared his throat, acutely conscious of the dried blood still in his hair and the bloody stain of his aura. "When we were at Saint Crispin's, you asked me if I could smell it. Smell the thing. I did, for a few moments. And that thing that attacked you smelled almost the same to me. For my money, it's all part of the same bloody puzzle, and the Crusade is mixed up in it somehow. I think you should get some rest, and we should be very, very careful. Whatever this is has been brewing for a while. We've all been a little off. The Watchers, I mean." Then he shut his mouth, aware of having said far more than he'd intended.

The fever-spots drained out of Caro's cheeks. "I thought it smelled like that too." The tiny, breathless voice she used tore at his chest. "You're sure?"

He made himself nod. "Could be my subconscious playing tricks," he admitted, without any real hope. "It *looked* like the thing at Crispin's. Smooth instead of with a Seeker's pelt, red eyes, and four claws instead of three on each foot. No tail."

Memory rose under his skin, knowing he was the only defense between the thing and his witch, the knives glowing in his hands and adrenaline pouring through his blood. "Also, knives hurt it more than the average Dark. They seem to react to blessed steel, for some reason. It's remarkably vulnerable to Watcher combat-magick."

Francine let out a short sigh. "That will teach me to overlook a Watcher at the scene," she remarked to thin air. "Anything else, Merrick?"

He mentally replayed the footage again. "No ma'am. I reported to Oliver. He was going to bring you a summary as soon as he finished interviewing some of the others."

The Council witch nodded. "Go get some sleep, Caro. You look about ready to fall over. Merrick, thank you."

Summarily dismissed. He tried not to feel happy about it. Caro pushed herself wearily up out of the chair.

"I'm sorry, Frannie. Why don't you smack me when I get like this?" She sounded genuinely contrite, her soft voice easing some of the pain in Merrick's tense shoulders.

"Are you kidding?" Fran waved a hand. "It's best to just let you blow yourself out, like a hurricane. Never lasts very long. Anyway, if I laid a hand on you, your Watcher might object." She dredged up a laugh, pulling a file folder across the desk and opening it. "I'll have the files brought up to you later. Go, get some rest."

Caro nodded. Her shoulders slumped, and—wonder of wonders—she reached out blindly, as if for support. Merrick moved closer, let her slide her hand into the crook of his leather-clad arm. "All right, all right. I'll try to get some rest. Shouldn't be too hard."

Fran didn't reply, apparently absorbed in the file folder. Caro sighed and led Merrick from the room.

The hall outside was dim and silent, the safehouse just beginning to wake up. Caro walked with her head down, Merrick navigating them through the halls. He had almost worked up the courage to speak when she beat him to it.

"That thing could have killed you," she said, so quietly he almost had to strain to hear her.

He shrugged. *If you only knew what I was before, maybe you wouldn't worry.* But he couldn't tell her. "It didn't."

"But it could have," she persisted.

"So could a car wreck or a plane crash." *Though it would*

have to be a hell of an event to even dent me. He didn't mean to sound sharp, but the sentence came to a clipped, abrupt end. *Or getting deep into enemy territory and realizing I'm being tracked and my support's gone. Or coming back to base and realizing I've been sold out, or even any mission I went on thanks to the bloody Army or the mercenary field. At least here my worthless life's spent protecting something worth fighting for.*

"Listen to me." She stopped, and after a quick check of the hall Merrick did too, automatically moving between her and the stairwell door. "Vincent was my Watcher. He was the one that noticed me in a foster home and got me and my brother out. And I repaid him by getting him killed. A *belrakan* broke into my house and killed him, coming for me. I'd only been in the damn house two weeks. If I hadn't moved out of the safehouse, if I hadn't had Vince with me . . . he wouldn't have died." She wasn't looking at him; she was staring at the floor.

Merrick swallowed his response. Waited.

"I won't have another Watcher die because of me," she whispered. "I *won't*. Vincent was a good man, and he saved me. You're a good man too, and I won't have you die because of me."

It was such an exotic statement his jaw almost dropped in sheer amazement. A faint tingling rushed up his throat, and his face began to burn with a heat that wasn't the agony of his scars. Him? A *good* man? Christ, he'd joined the Watchers to *atone*. No good man needed atonement.

She seemed to expect an answer, and Merrick cast frantically about for one. *Think quickly, old man.* "I don't know about your Vincent. But if there's one thing I'm not, Caro, it's *good*. I'm a Watcher, I know what I'm doing, and I'm going to keep you alive."

He would have said more, but the words—*and that's all you need to think about, witch. Calm down and just let me do my bloody job, will you? I want to stay near you, I'm* going *to stay near you, and if I have to break my oath as a Watcher and turn in my knives to do it I will*—wouldn't come. He settled for taking a deep breath, wondering what it was about this fragile-looking witch with her sharp tongue that could drive him to the brink of his carefully trained control. He hadn't felt this unsettled since his first night in sniper training. Then, marginally calmer, he tried one last time.

"Your Watcher knew the risks. We all know the risks. You're my witch, and if you want me to go invisible, you say the word. But I am *not leaving you.* Is that clear enough even for you, Caroline?"

He knew it was a mistake as soon as it left his mouth. No Watcher should ever say such a thing, especially to his witch. But the damn woman was so bloody stubborn it was a wonder he hadn't shaken some sense into her yet. His hands ached, his scars tingled, and the frustration mixed with the overpowering need to touch her again, to feel that velvet-wrapped spike of pleasure flooding up his arm and jolting through the rest of his body. Tangled, tattered, and exhausted, she was still beautiful.

And he was in trouble, because she looked up, tears glittering in her indigo eyes again. The red cardigan slipped off her shoulder, she impatiently yanked it back up. She said nothing, but blinked furiously and owlishly, her chin lifting just a little.

Christ, Merrick, good one. She's been attacked twice in twenty-four hours, the last thing she needs is you arguing with her and acting like an idiot.

"I'm not like you." His throat ached with the words. "I'm good at survival, you have no idea *how* good. Just trust me, love. All right?"

Her shoulders slumped even further. "I'm tired," she answered, in a tiny voice that hurt him to hear. "I just want to sleep."

"Right then." He took an experimental step, then another, and she followed. He led her through the halls, vaguely unsettled. *That didn't go well. And she's being too bloody docile now. I don't trust this.*

But as they navigated the morning hush, she laid her head against his shoulder and leaned into him, and Merrick realized he wasn't just in deep water, he had already drowned. There was no going back.

Nine

She thought she'd have trouble sleeping during the day, but as soon as her head hit the pillow she was out. She only woke up six hours later because a familiar voice was raised, almost breaking.

A young male voice, perhaps the only person who could call her up out of a dead sleep. "What the—who the hell are you? She's my sister, and I'll wake her up if I damn well *want* to!"

Caro groaned, turning over, and buried her head in the pillow.

Merrick's voice, instantly recognizable, his accent making the words crisp and no-nonsense. "She's sleeping. She's exhausted, sir, I can't—"

"Best to just let him." Yet another male voice, also familiar. She tried to remember where she'd heard it before, lost in the muzzy hinterland of sleep. "Or you'll get the sharp tongue from both sides."

"I could do without that. She's tired, be careful."

Someone jumped on the bed and Caro gasped, slamming into full wakefulness. Her hands jerked up to defend herself, a childhood reflex. Trev grabbed her, shook her by her shoulders, and proceeded to give her a sloppy, wet kiss on the cheek.

"That's for scaring me," he said promptly. "Good morning, you're in bed early. Where'd you get the Watcher from? Why didn't you call me? Dammit, Caro, you're getting flighty in your old age. I had to cancel a gig to come down here, I hope you know. Elise is furious."

"Elise is always furious," Caro mumbled. "Go 'way." She shook off her brother's hands and turned away, grabbing the pillow again and dragging it over her head.

"No way, baby. I'm here, and I'm not going anywhere until you tell me *everything*. Have you eaten yet? You probably haven't. Hey, Keenan! Turn the lights on and bring the groceries in. I'm gonna make you an omelet, Caro. Spinach, mushroom, Havarti, and dill. Your favorite."

"Go *away*," Caro moaned. "Or I'll order Keenan to make you."

Keenan—it must have been him, since Trev was still on the bed—opened the drapes. Pearly light flooded in, the cold late-afternoon glow of a winter storm moving in. "This window was just repaired," he remarked quietly, his pleasant light tenor harsh with the undertone of a *tanak*'s rumble.

"I called in and got Fran, and she promised to have you call me." Trev nudged Caro none too gently. "You didn't. Care to tell me how the Miata got all smashed up and you got a Watcher?"

"It's not my fault," Caro groaned into the pillow. "Leave me *alone* or make me some coffee."

"Coffee. You hear that, Keen? She wants *coffee*." Trev was probably rolling his eyes theatrically.

"Enough said." Keenan retreated to the kitchenette. There was the rustle of paper bags and a low baritone—Merrick, asking a question. Keenan laughed, a short sharp sound.

Caro cracked an eyelid and saw her brother's face, less than four inches from hers, his hazel eyes sparkling. "Get *up*," Trev said. "I'm going to kick your ass for making me worry, Caro. I was *scared*."

She blinked, yawned, and shook him away. "I got some wires crossed, maybe some bad directions, and ended up on the wrong side of a pack of *koroi*. Then I went to examine a patient and got attacked by something. It's been a bit busy here." She blinked again, pushed herself up on her elbows. The tank top was twisted uncomfortably, and her flannel shorts were rucked up too. She wished for her own room and her own bed back in Saint City with a vengeance that suddenly surprised her. "I'm sorry, sweetie. I promised I'd call, and I didn't."

Trev's hair stuck up in an artful crow's nest; he wore an *Angelcake Devilshake* T-shirt and the familiar leather cuff around his right wrist. A small gold hoop glinted in his ear. He had a tiny leather bag on a thong around his neck that pulsed with a soft golden glow—probably Anya Harris's work, it had the faint tracery of silver that meant a Guardian magick was attached. It was a protection, bolstering Caro's own work on his shields, and she felt a sudden burst of gratefulness for the Guardians. At least in Saint City she wouldn't have to worry about the Crusade, because of them.

Trev studied her closely. "Who's the hunk?" He tipped his head back to indicate the kitchenette. "He tried to stop me from coming in, typical overprotective Watcher."

"Merrick," she said. "Don't mess with him, he's a nice

guy."

Trev's eyebrows nested in his artistically-mussed hair. The gold earring winked mischievously.

"He thinks I'm his witch," Caro whispered.

Trev's eyes were as big as dinner plates. He let out a strangled whoop of laughter and keeled over onto the bed. Caro, never one to let an opportunity pass, curled up to her knees and began to tickle him, unmercifully.

It took ten minutes to reduce him to giggling tears and begging for mercy. She threw her hair back, dug her fingertips in, and got him right under the ribs until he was gasping and pleading. He tried to get her back, but she trapped his wrist under her knee and considered giving him an Indian rope-burn just for good measure. She decided against it, but kept tickling until his face turned an alarming shade of crimson. Finally, breathless, she let him up and glared at him as he lay curled against the covers, giggling in a squeaky little-boy whisper. She hadn't heard him laugh like this for months.

I wish I could remember being so happy. "That will teach you," she announced, and scrambled off the bed before he could mount a counterattack. "I hope you've learned something, young man."

Then she bolted to the bathroom and made it just in time, locking the door and listening to him curse. He pounded on the door, but she took her time, brushing her teeth, washing her face, combing her hair, using the toilet. By the time she peeked out, he was in fine fettle.

"Dammit, Caro!" He barged past her, she grinned and edged out, closing the door. Trev always had to pee after she tickled him.

Humming to herself, she tucked her hair behind her ears and stalked across the room to the dresser. Jeans, underwear, a red sweater, and a nice thick pair of wool socks—that would do just fine. She scratched on the bathroom door, pushed it open, and proceeded to stick her tongue out at her brother. "Works every time," she said, loftily.

"I'm going to get you."

Caro struggled out of her tank top, pulled her sweater on, settling the V-neck just right. Then she proceeded to get dressed, ignoring Trev as he ignored her. He flushed, then shouldered her aside to wash his hands.

"Will you please put the lid down?"

"Oh, for Christ's sake, Caro. You're a nag."

"I'll tickle you again."

"And I'll get you back. I might even give you a noogie."

"Ungrateful little twerp."

"You like him?"

"Who?"

"The *Watcher*, Caro. He's not bad."

He's scarred. But Caro realized that she barely saw the scars, except to wonder where he'd gotten them. "Thought you were straight," she said lightly, avoiding the question.

Besides, it wasn't Merrick's scars she thought of when she saw him. It was his voice, calm and crisp, saying *You're safe.* That, and the gentleness in his hands.

That was it. She did feel safe. Seeing him go after the Seeker had given her a healthy respect for just how dangerous Merrick was likely to be. But hand-in-hand with that feeling of safety was an edge of fear. If something happened to him, she would be responsible.

She didn't want another Watcher dying because of her.

"I have an eye for quality." Trev dried his hands, folded the towel, and smacked her gently on the arm with it. "Come on, Caro. Give it up."

I'm blushing. Heat rose to her cheeks, a blast-furnace of embarrassment. *Why am I blushing?* "What's to give? He thinks I'm his witch. Apparently I don't give him the burn when I touch him."

"How often have you touched him?" Trev's hazel eyes all but sparkled.

"Oh, shut *up.*"

"It will be a great relief to me," he intoned pompously, "to know that I can relax, safe in the knowledge that you're being watched over by such a big, strong—*urp!*"

Caro hefted the water glass in her hand. "Go on, Trev. Say it again, I dare you."

He had to use the pretty blue hand towel to dry his face off, his gelled hair dripping. "Testy, testy." But he was grinning. "You haven't done that since fourth grade."

"Eighth," Caro reminded him. "Didn't you mention an omelet?"

"Didn't you mention *koroi* and being attacked? What the hell's going on?"

The weight of being the responsible one settled again on

Caro's shoulders. "Coffee, and I'll explain everything. Or maybe you should ask Merrick, since nobody seems inclined to want *my* opinion."

"I want your opinion." Trev sounded uncharacteristically serious. "I always want your opinion, Sis. Whether I admit it or not."

Caro closed her eyes, leaning against the counter. She said nothing. He stepped close and hugged her, his birdlike slenderness more fashionable than hers. His belt dug into her stomach. Everyone was taller than her.

It's okay. I more than make up for it in cussedness. As an attempt for humor, it barely worked.

"Jeez, I'm sorry, sweetie." Her brother smelled, as usual, like Drakkar Noir and the faint tinge of cigarette smoke and beer from playing in bars. And under that, he still smelled like the same little boy she had taken care of all her remembered life, a smell of salt and heat and youth she suspected would never fade. Trev would be a little boy until he died. He was one of those people who never seemed to get any older, and he'd be irrepressible and buoyant to the end. She breathed him in, her brother, and he ruffled her hair affectionately like he always did.

"Coffee." He managed to sound rueful and impatient all at once. "And an omelet. If I know you, you've been living on toast and orange juice. And then I'll bug you for what's going on. Fran sounded not at all like her usual sunny self."

"And well she shouldn't." *You should have stayed in Saint City, Trev, and I'm going to send you back ASAP.* "You shouldn't have come, Trev."

"How could I stay away if I think my sister's in trouble?" He made a little scoffing sound. "Come on and you can tell me all about it. Ten to one says it's not as bad as you think."

* * * *

Afternoon sun slanted down as Caro shivered, wrapping her scarf around her neck. She was beginning to get a little bit of cabin fever, and a walk through the central commons was safer, since Trev insisted on going with her. The Crusade, after all, were perfectly prepared to utilize mundane weapons as well as magickal. They had been known to use grenades, and assault rifles.

The thought sent a chill down her back.

Admit it, Caro. You're worried about your own safety

too, and Merrick's. How long is it going to be before you retreat into the safehouse for good like some of the Seers? You won't be able to go out and see your patients, and you might as well rot in here.

The thought that she would be afraid to go outside, even with a Watcher standing guard, taunted her. She pushed her hands into the pockets of her hooded jacket and looked down at her sneakers, carrying her over the flagstones. Here in Altamira, the paths winding through the commons between plots of herbs, ornamental flowers, and shrubbery were stone, not white gravel like in Saint City. She'd been to a safehouse in Florida that had white crushed shell walks; there was one in the Cascades that had glassy obsidian paving. Caro was suddenly grateful for the gardens, for the safety and beauty that closed around her each time she stepped inside a safehouse. She'd seen enough ugliness to last her a lifetime, she was glad she didn't have to live in it.

Keenan and Merrick tactfully waited at the edge of the common under an oak tree that stretched its bare branches to the sky. The wide rectangle of green lay inside the four walls of the safehouse, flanked by the two smaller gardens. A familiar pattern of green and quiet, lying under a winter sky beginning to crowd with thick dark rainclouds in the north. The light had begun to take on the weird look of sun coming under clouds while the sky was dark.

Trev fussed with his corduroy jacket. It was too cold for him to be out with just that on, but she didn't have the heart to nag him, for once.

"You're awful quiet." He stuffed his hands deep in his pockets, his bony freckled face lit by kind light. He looked almost handsome with the raw chill bringing out a blush in his cheeks and turning his freckles to gold. "Whatcha thinkin', Lincoln?"

"Nothing very comfortable," Caro admitted. "These things—they're showing up just as the Crusade does, and those poor people. I don't like thinking it's connected."

"Don't blame you. What does your gut say?" As usual, Trev asked the right question. She often thought he was far more intuitive than his weakly-glowing aura said he should be. Or maybe it was only because he shared that most important of bonds with her, shared parentage and the almost-telepathy that came from depending only on each other in the foster system.

She dropped her head and looked at the flagstones, fitting together so perfectly. Lavender grew on either side of the path, and the low hedges of rosemary breathed out a pale scent nowhere near its summer robustness. Low stone benches, a willow tree at the west end of the garden—she glanced back over her shoulder instinctively to see the two dark shapes of the Watchers under the oak tree. Merrick was slightly taller, his hands in his pockets and his green eyes glittering through his untidy hair shaken down over his face.

She should have been ashamed of herself for finding that so comforting. "I think it's connected." The wind touched her hair, a gentle, chilly benediction. A few curls had come free and were stubbornly falling in her face again. "If only because Merrick said it smelled the same."

"Jeez." Trev blew out between his teeth, a low, not-quite whistle. "Where do you think he comes from?"

What? "What? Who?"

"Merrick. Where's that accent from?"

"England, I think. Trev, this is serious. That thing broke through the wards and came into the safehouse. It could have killed someone."

"Merrick said it was vulnerable to the knives. Really vulnerable." Trev looked thoughtful, matching his pace to hers and not fidgeting with impatience as he usually did. "He's really nice, Caro. I think he's a good one."

She gave him a look that could have peeled paint. Chill, rain-heavy wind teased at her hair, made her shiver. The light was changing, clouds drifting over the sun. "What are you on about? For God's sake, Trev, I'm talking about people *dying*, and you're nattering on about a Watcher."

"He's nice, and he's obviously very professional. Keenan worked with him in Delhi and in Arizona, says he's a good Watcher. They say he tracks *belrakan*." Trev's voice dropped to a confidential whisper.

"Trevor." Caro's tone was a warning. Irritation sparked through her aura, and she took a deep breath. Decided to change the subject. "So when are you heading back home?"

He shrugged. "When this is all over, I guess."

Oh, gods, please. Give me patience. "Trev. This isn't safe for you. I'll feel better if I know you're back in Saint City and—"

"Gee, this sounds familiar. Only I'm used to saying it to you." Trev's hazel eyes danced with mischief. He executed a happy little dance step, his gold earring winking in suddenly-liquid sunlight. "I can't wait to get started on gloating and saying *I told you so*. Oooh, that's number one. *I told you so*. Two."

Caro rolled her eyes. "Trevor Dodge Robbins, you little punk, shut up and listen to me."

"Caroline Ame—"

"Don't you *dare*." She longed to grab him and tickle him again, or maybe give him a wet willie. The breeze, turning cold, slanted against her back. Her cheeks felt scraped under the cold wet wind. "Seriously, Trevor. People are dying, and each hour that goes by—"

Trevor stopped and turned to face her, his pale face uncharacteristically grave. "Vincent would approve," he said quietly.

Caro stopped dead. Hearing him say Vince's name gave her a queer uncomfortable feeling, as if she'd been hit in the stomach and lost all her air.

He folded his arms. "He would have been the first to tell you that you were being ridiculous about the Watchers. It would have hurt him to think of you without any protection."

How strange. I should be angry at him, and probably will be. Once this lump in my throat goes away. "He would understand," she managed, through a mouth suddenly gone dry. "He always understood."

Trevor shook his head. "He would have told you to stop being a ridiculous little prig. He'd be right, too."

Her voice was a strangled whisper. "I am not going to discuss this with you."

"Someone has to tell you. You're making a mistake. You're going to put that Watcher in danger if you don't start acting like a responsible adult instead of a weepy little tweener, you dig? All the rest of us deal with seeing Watchers get hurt, too. You're not the only one." He nodded smartly, his dark gel-spiked hair frozen in place against the wind. "So snap out of it, okay?"

I don't know whether to laugh or cry, or call him something a lady should never say. She settled for taking a long, deep breath and nodding. He was only trying to help. "Thank you for caring." *I sound like I'm about to cry. I will not cry.* "But I'd really like to talk about something else now.

Like when you're going back to Saint City where it's relatively safer."

Trevor laughed. The sound caroled over the still, quiet gardens; nobody was out on this raw day, not even any of the green witches. The entire safehouse hunched under the rapidly darkening sky, as if expecting trouble.

Preparing for another attack.

"I'm not going to leave my big sister out here facing down the Crusade and gods-only-know what. Tough noogies, Caro. I'm staying. And if I have to nag you to get you to treat your Watcher a little better, I will. Heaven knows he can't do it."

That managed to nettle her. She glared at him. "I've been nothing but polite!" she flared, and realized it was a lie. She *had* treated Merrick dreadfully.

She glanced over her shoulder again, nervously. They were still there, the two broad-shouldered men in dark coats with slim sword hilts sticking up over their right shoulders. The unwilling feeling of comfort returned, so strong she almost shivered again.

Trev gave an inelegant snort. "Since when?" But there was no rancor in it. "I wouldn't tell you this if I didn't honestly believe it to be true, Sis."

Caro nodded, just as she heard the sharp sound of a door slamming shut. Then footsteps, hard and hurried.

She whirled and saw Fran across the common, wearing a purple sweater and an acid-green knee-length dress. Fran was running, and a few strands of her gray-threaded hair had come loose.

Caro's heart sank, splashing into the omelet she'd eaten at Trev's urging. *That's the problem with being a witch, you always know when the worst is just going to keep getting worse.*

Fran finally skidded to a stop. "Thank the Lady I've found you," she gasped. "Horrible news, Caro. There's been another attack. And this time it's a Lightbringer."

The clouds slid over the sun, plunging the commons into shadow, and the cold wind touched Caro's cheek again.

Ten

"Gods above." Caro's voice was muffled by her fingers, pressed hard against her mouth. She stepped back blindly, instinctively flinching, and collided with Merrick. His hands automatically closed around her shoulders, he sank his feet into the floor and made himself a rock for her. Her hair brushed the back of his hands, a silky caress. She actually leaned back into him, as if her legs wouldn't hold her up. His scars tingled with her nearness, and he was faintly, nastily glad that he was there to steady her. "Oh, my God."

The Lightbringer on the cot was unrecognizable except for her hair, a sheaf of rich glossy chestnut matted with blood. Merrick swallowed, hard. She'd been beaten, badly; the kind of damage that was meant not to kill but to maim and disfigure. Her aura, not as bright as Caro's but well-disciplined nonetheless, was the deep blue of a water witch, ragged and torn. Whatever had attacked her had done so both physically and psychically.

Here in the infirmary, the wards resonated thickly with distress. The curtains around this bed were drawn, but every witch, patient or healer in here could *feel* the waves of pain pulsing out from this little enclosure. Two healers—both nurses in the outside world—spoke in low frantic voices at the station near the door to the main hall, the other healers, doctors and nurses both, went about their business with set faces, often glancing in the direction of this bed.

Merrick swallowed hard. They had cleaned her up as much as they could. Two healers hovered at the bedside, one in pale-blue scrubs and the no-nonsense manner of a professional nurse, the other holding a willow wand with a quartz crystal set in the tip, humming with Power.

The first healer checked the battered Lightbringer's pulse and blood pressure again, then closed her eyes and concentrated, *scanning* the body lying on the bed. She looked definitely nauseated. The second murmured to herself and touched the quartz gently to the battered body's forehead, sending a pulse of earth-flavored Power down through the wounded aura. An IV pole stood next to the bed, and an abalone shell full of sea salt sat on a small table on the other side.

"Who is it?" Caro asked so gently Merrick almost didn't recognize her voice. His entire body leapt at the sound.

Christ, if she ever talked to me *that way I'd . . . what? Probably die and go straight to heaven.* His scars gave a burst of tearing liquid pain as the wounded witch's aura pulsed. Caro's presence soothed the scoring across his nerves, but didn't erase it.

"It's Nicolette Jansen." The Council witch was equally hushed. "Her Watcher is—well, he's not expected to live. He must have put up quite a fight." She hugged herself, and Merrick thought she must be unaware of doing so. Her eyes were the wide, haunted hollows of a frightened child.

"Were they a bonded pair?"

"No. He was on guard duty."

Poor bugger, Merrick thought. If he survived, the agony of losing a Lightbringer—of *failure*—would torture him.

"Where was she attacked?"

"The last place she was seen was at Seventh and Iroquois. She was on a shopping trip yesterday."

The location showed up on Merrick's mental map, terrain considered tactically out of old habit. *Seventh and Iroquois, that's the north edge of downtown. Whatever this is, it's spreading from the north.*

"Files, Fran. Get me those files on all the victims and a map of the locations. Where's the Watcher?" Caro's voice was gentle but inflexible. Yet her shoulders shook under Merrick's gentle hands. She was trembling. He stroked with his thumbs, gently, soothing her. Sent a thin trickle of Power through her aura, a wire of heat that would keep her from shock. His aura fringed hers, thickening reflexively against the danger breathing through the air.

She shouldn't have to deal with this. No Lightbringer should. The woman on the bed had a face so puffed and bruised it was a wonder anyone had been able to identify her. Her ragged breathing was painful to hear. Merrick felt the familiar sick rage rise in him. Why? Why would the gods make them so gifted, so gentle, and then allow them to suffer like this?

Gods are all very well, but it's up to a Watcher to make sure.

"The Watcher's in their dormitory. The off-duty Watchers are trying to help him." The Council witch swallowed audibly.

Merrick blinked. He felt the subliminal *click* as the walls inside his head—between him and the hard, cold animal who had shared his thoughts since childhood—slid down. The smell roiled around him then, a thick reek of sulfur and that other smell . . . What was it? Dry and terrible, whatever it was, a stench mixed with blood and offal.

It's the same bloody thing, and it's attacking Lightbringers now. Gods help us all. Panic wormed under his breastbone, was shoved down with training. His witch needed him right now, even if she thought she didn't.

The feel of her soft slenderness leaning against him was another distraction, one he couldn't shelve and would have to just live through. Caro took a deep breath, her shoulders rising slightly under his hands. He felt the shiver that went through her, a high-voltage shock against his own nerves. Her hair still smelled like the cold, fresh wind outside. "Trev, my bag. Can you get it for me?"

"Aye, aye, Captain." The beaky-nosed boy didn't argue.

It was a good thing. Merrick had almost grabbed him by the scruff and hauled him away from Caro's bed earlier. *Set too high, that's me, wound too tight. Almost hurt a Lightbringer.* Keenan followed the boy out at a dead run, his booted feet soundlessly echoing the boy's pounding sneakers.

"I wonder if she was attacked during the day, or during the night?" Caro's voice was soft, thoughtful. She stepped away from Merrick's hands. "Frannie, I need those files. Please?"

The Council witch nodded. Her cheeks were cheese-pale and her graying hair tumbled in disarray. From the look on her face, she was probably blaming herself. *Enough guilt to go round, why do they always think they have to take it?* He shook that thought away, tried to tear his gaze from the bloody mat of chestnut hair on the crisp white pillow. She was probably missing teeth, and it looked like her cheekbone had been shattered. That kind of force, that kind of calculated *damage*, made his gorge rise briefly and pointlessly, made the *tanak* snarl inside his bones, a spike of pain not eased by his witch's presence.

Caro slid out of her coat and scarf, handed both to Merrick without looking. He cherished the inattention, it meant she was beginning to take his presence for granted. He laid them carefully over a forgotten chair right inside the curtain that closed this space off from the rest of the infirmary.

"Okay. You two, wait outside. Merrick, keep your eyes open. If one of those *things* starts to come out, I'll try to keep her alive while you take care of it. All right?"

What?

Fran squeaked, and Caro threw her an indecipherable glance. "The *files*, Frannie! Go. You don't want to see this."

What the hell did you just say? Merrick found his voice. "Caro, it smells the same as—"

It was his turn to get a look that threatened to stop his heart. She blew a long sandy curl out of her face and her eyebrows pulled together. "I *know*, Merrick! Get another Watcher down here if you're worried about being unable to kill it. She can't hold on much longer." Caro took Fran's shoulders, gently pushed her outside the enclosure. "Go."

Wonder of wonders, the woman went.

Merrick slowly drew a knife, steel whispering out of the sheath, with a silent apology to the gods he might be offending. This was a holy place, a place of healing. Not a place for a Watcher with naked steel. The runes chased into the knifeblade twisted uneasily, thin crimson lines of flame.

The healer in the blue scrubs stared at him, her brown eyes wide. "You're not serious?" Her voice was a low, pleasant Southern drawl that dragged pain through his nerves. He wished, suddenly and totally, for the narcotic jolt of pleasure from his witch's skin. Discarded the wish, it would serve no purpose.

Who's not serious? Does she mean me, or Caro?

"Go outside so I can tend to this patient properly." Merrick's witch stepped up to the bedside, reached down, and threaded her fingers gently through the mangled hand lying on the tan cotton bedspread. Then she did a strange thing—she leaned over, her face inches from the ruin on the pillow, and inhaled deeply.

Merrick's stomach cramped briefly with nausea; he discarded it. The thought of his witch so close to that foul smell made the back of his neck prickle. He moved, trying to calculate the best angle to defend her.

Her lips pursed, and she blew out over the battered face.

Merrick almost gasped. The two healers *did* gasp. A heavy pungent scent filled the air. He sniffed cautiously and identified it. White copal, as if she was burning incense. It was a nose-stinging scent, but a cleansing one, almost antiseptic. Power threaded through the air, a simple Lightbringer charm meant to purify the space she was working in.

Caro closed her eyes. Her body seemed to sag, barely

able to hold up its own weight. "Nicolette," she breathed, and that strange purifying scent cut through the thick reek of sulfur, slicing it out of the air. "Just hang on, sweetheart. I'm coming."

And then . . . she *left*.

Merrick cursed to himself. *Caro, Caro, be careful. Be careful, love. Don't do anything rash.*

He might as well ask the sun not to shine. She sagged even further, her aura surging with golden pinwheels. The two healers stood frozen in place. It was unheard of for a Mindhealer to attempt this without proper purification and fail-safes. Walking in someone else's mind could go so very wrong if you didn't use the time-honored methods. In other areas of magick, experimentation was allowed and encouraged; in Mindhealing, experimentation was almost frowned upon unless it was under rigidly controlled circumstances. There was just too much that could go wrong. A Mindhealer could be trapped in another's psyche, or her heart could go into arrest because of the shock of dislocation if she exited a mind too quickly. Worst of all, the madness or damage in the patient could *communicate* itself to the healer, driving her mad or leaving her damaged as well. It was a delicate, finicky branch of magick, like the Seers.

The two healers stared. "Have you ever—" the one in blue scrubs asked.

"No," the other replied, in a shocked whisper. "What if . . ." But she let the question lie unfinished, dying in the air.

Get out, he wanted to say. *Didn't you hear her? Get the hell out of here like she told you. If one of those things . . .*

If one of those things came out, he had to kill it before it could reach her. There was no room for error. The fact that there were other witches—and Lightbringer children—who would be helpless against another one of those things was secondary. All Merrick cared about was the Mindhealer, her face absent and drained of personality as her consciousness walked through the wounded Lightbringer's mind.

Caro's slumped body stiffened, swaying. Merrick tensed, muscle by muscle, becoming a coiled spring. *Just my luck. I find my witch and she's determined to take suicidal chances. Lovely. It's my job to take those chances, Caro, not yours.*

He had only a split second of warning. The shock hit him in the chest, right where he'd felt the insistent tugging call that led him to his witch. A heavy squeezing pain, similar to a cardiac arrest, tore against his nerves like the *tanak* but without the brutal burning of the Dark symbiote. With the pain came comprehension—this was the pain of a Watcher whose witch was dying, going elsewhere, *leaving*.

CARO!

The knife's black blade woke in a blaze of thin crimson, the glow from spidery runes chased into its surface dappling the curtains around the bed, cloth rippling uneasily. Merrick pitched forward, his hand blurring out just as the nauseating stench boiled over, his heart squeezing and his breath suddenly torn out of his chest. Caro went to her knees, hard, slid bonelessly to the floor. He had no time to worry about that because the battered body on the bed convulsed, bones cracking as it contorted into an arching hoop, and the *thing* boiled free in a noisome stream, psychic fibers becoming physical, blood splashing out in a fine mist as capillaries burst. It screeched, its hairless head lowering; Merrick moved without thought, blurring between the creature and Caro.

The two healers screamed, their voices rising in an odd harmony that might have been funny if it hadn't been so deadly-terrifying.

Impact. He felt ribs shatter as the thing took compact weight and smashed into him. The knife blurred forward as his hand closed on its suddenly substantial neck, fingers squeezing against black smoke, his simultaneous psychic grasp sinking, slipping—and *catching*. Held.

The knife made a sound like an ax sinking into wood, and the thing howled, a falsetto screech that spiraled out of the audible and into the psychic. The healers screamed again, their voices less harmonic and more raggedly breathless. Merrick's head hit the floor with stunning force, the curtain ripped off its pole and descending in a swathe of bleached fabric, whispering against the sudden current of bloodlust in the air.

He twisted the knife with both mind and hand, agony grinding in his chest. *Caro. Christ don't tell me she's hurt, please, oh gods please—*

Then, miracle of miracles, he heard her voice. Shaky and hoarse, but indisputably hers. "Help him. *Help him!* And you, get over here and anchor her! *Move, dammit!*"

She could give a battlefield general shouting lessons, he thought hazily, the pain ebbing out of his chest. She was alive. Alive.

Then why does it still hurt?

"Merrick?" A well-camouflaged note of panic in her beautiful voice. Sounded like her nose was full, because she pronounced it *Merrig.* "Merrick, are you all right?"

The thing slumped atop him, psychic sludge, its claws dissolving inside the bloody rips and rents in Merrick's skin. He had three broken ribs, and he was sure he'd done something to his leg. His skull rang with pain, and the monstrous, dry smell of the thing threatened to invade his nose and turn his stomach inside out.

"Just . . . fine," he rasped. *She's alive.* Relief burst inside him.

"Pull her back! Pull her back!" Caro's voice broke. "Everyone! Everything you have, *now!*"

A great swelling orchestra note of Lightbringer magick struck the air just as the ripped curtain was pushed aside and a hand closed around Merrick's, dragging him to his feet. The *tanak* roared with pain, converting it to Power along with the psychic fuel of the Dark thing's death. His ribs twitched and crackled, the breaks messily fused together. A spike of blackness twisted in his right leg, high on the inside of the thigh. A claw had caught him, could have opened the femoral artery there.

His breath came harsh and ragged. *Still alive. Did I ever think I wanted to die? I don't. Not now.*

First things first. The Watcher who pulled him up—Oliver himself, his eyes blazing blue—was spared only a single nod of thanks before Merrick looked over his shoulder, his eyes searching the sudden crowd of Lightbringers, whose collective presence rubbed vinegar salt into his wounds. They clustered around the bed, soft faces and bright eyes, their glow swirling and becoming brighter as more of them dropped into a trance and directed their energies toward saving one of their own.

Oliver was flanked by Keenan and Ellis. Other Watchers arrived. Someone set to work clearing the sludge of the Seeker-thing from the air. Merrick shook like a cat, ridding himself of its stench. Thankfully, once the wall between him and the tracker inside him slammed up he could no longer smell the sulfur reek.

"God*dam*mit," Oliver rumbled, staring down at the writhing sludge on the floor. Venomous red-black Power crackled, cleansing the air. "What the *hell* is going on?"

Merrick shrugged. With this many Watchers, the thing didn't stand a chance; its reek vanished, replaced by the smoky fragrance of Watcher magick. He tried to peer through the gathered Lightbringers, looking for Caro. "One of those things was in a Lightbringer. Caro's trying to save her."

Oliver tipped his head back, his jaw working as his hair brushed the sword hilt protruding over his shoulder. Merrick understood. How were the Watchers supposed to protect witches if they kept taking suicidal chances and behaving illogically? He dragged a breath in, two, suddenly very glad he could breathe. The world took on new color and weight, from the torn curtain to the clothes the Lightbringers wore, light melding and flowing around them. He saw Caro's brother, his eyes closed and his beaky face alight, his aura soaking into the glow around him, offering his limited strength without reserve.

Merrick was almost beginning to believe he was alive. His lungs worked. The *tanak* twisted painfully inside his marrow. His heart was still beating, and the awful dragging agony drained out of his chest. He was alive, Caro was alive, the thing hadn't killed anyone else. He'd done his job.

It wasn't as comforting as he expected it to be.

The soft, bright Power in the air slid away like the tide along a sandy beach. "No," someone whispered. "Oh, no."

One by one, the Lightbringers took on individual shapes again, instead of the massive glow of a spell. They held each other, arms over shoulders, some turning their faces away. There was a soft confusion and Caro appeared, stalking through them. Her face was deadly white, her eyes flashing, and the only thing worse than the anger crackling through her aura was the devouring sorrow laid underneath, tinting the golden pinwheels of her aura a deep purple.

Her eyes flicked over Merrick. He pulled himself up straighter, wishing he wasn't covered in blood. There was a creaking sound as the *tanak* started working on his ribs, smoothing out the messy fusions it had done as an emergency measure. Merrick flinched slightly, his scars turning into dry whips of flame across his face and down his shoulder.

"She's dead." Her tone was flat, and terribly, terribly sad. "Where's the Watcher?"

What Watcher? I'm right here. "Caro?" His voice had gone hoarse. Fire drilled through his ribs, his leg straightened. Blood trickled wet and warm until the symbiote closed the rips in his skin.

She stepped close to him, reached out, and closed her fingers around his wrist again. "I'm sorry." She sounded more than sorry. She sounded, in fact, as if her heart was broken. "How badly are you hurt? Are you all right?"

Oh, Christ. The thought was tinged with deep-red desperation. Pleasure rolled up his arm, spread through his chest, and smashed at his control, leaving him with only the thinnest margin. He felt more than saw the other Watchers drop their eyes, felt more than heard the murmur that went through them. And he barely felt that because his entire world narrowed to one thing—the witch who stood in front of him, deathly pale, a smear of bright blood trickling down from her nose. Her eyes were bloodshot too, and her aura held the sparkling luminescence of pain. But the curve of her cheekbone cried out for his fingers to touch it, the gold-streaked curls falling in her face begged for him to brush them back, and the rest of her—Well, what he *wanted* to do didn't bear thinking about.

He swallowed, roughly. Invoked control. *Duty. Honor. Obedience.* But even those watchwords, drilled into him with harsh exactitude, had a hard time getting through the shell of velvet-covered, iron-spiked desire that slammed through him, spun around his skin, and jolted home again. His scars throbbed, his bones ached sweetly, and he had the irresistible urge to slide his hand around her nape and pull her close, feel her soft slenderness fitted against him. He wanted her, dammit, and she wasn't making it any easier by being so completely, infuriatingly stubborn—or so absolutely vulnerable it made his heart ache, a pain he had never felt before, a pain her touch soothed and made worse at the same time.

Her soft fingers dropped away. He didn't dare move. If he moved so much as a muscle, he was going to take her face in his hands and do the unthinkable in front of everyone.

"I'm so sorry," she whispered. "Are you all right?"

Behind her, the other Lightbringers began talking in low voices, matching the thunderous murmurs of the Watchers.

"Fine," he managed through the obstruction in his throat. "Just fine. Bloody brill. What about you?"

She used the cuff of her red sweater to dab at the blood under her nose. "Headache. Feel like I could sleep for a week."

You probably should. He dragged in another sharp breath, invoked thread-thin control. "I could carry you back to your room."

As soon as he said it, he regretted it. Levity was the wrong thing in this situation, it was rude and thoughtless.

Amazingly, though, a ghost of a smile touched her lips. "Barbarian. And here I thought you were so English and civilized."

"It's a thin veneer." He watched her face, carefully. Her mouth trembled, firmed. There was a suspicious brightness in her eyes.

Tears.

"Caro." Her brother appeared, put a protective arm over her shoulders. "Come on. The healers will take care of her. You did everything you could."

"No, I didn't." Her shoulders sagged, and she dropped her eyes. "I should have brought her out."

"Don't. Don't hurt yourself." Trevor's arm tightened, and Merrick was surprised by a thick green flash of jealousy. She leaned into her brother, accepting comfort, for just a moment. *Lucky boy, he gets to touch her whenever he wants to.*

Then she straightened. "Go get some rest, Trev. You're drained. Merrick, where's the other Watcher?"

What other Watcher? I'm the only one you have, witch, and it's going to stay that way. He swallowed the words, wondering at the sudden flare of possessive anger. "Which one?"

"The one that was on guard duty," she said impatiently, all but tapping her foot. She swiped at the blood under her nose again, and her bloodshot eyes were so sad they threatened to stop his heart. Sad—but also determined, a steely glint to the indigo that warned him not to argue with her.

"Dormitory, they said. First floor." He took a deep breath. *Duty. Honor. Obedience.* "I'll show you."

She nodded. "Let's go." And she brushed past him, leaving both him and her brother staring at each other, her brother's face transparent with disbelief, Merrick hoping his own feelings weren't showing.

Caro's brother examined him for a few seconds. "Better get going. She means business."

So do I, young one. "Sir." He turned on his heel, ignoring the mutters and the whispers. Set off after his witch, whose shoulders hunched as if warding off a blow.

She's alive. She's alive, that means I haven't failed yet.

But oh, God, he had almost broken. Almost done something

unconscionable, and it hadn't been the pain or the Seeker forcing him to it. It had been *her*.

* * * *

"He's thrashing around. It isn't pretty." The Watcher on guard at the dormitory door shook his head. Merrick dug in his memory for the man's name—Jasper. He was a scarecrow, lean where most Watchers were bulky with muscle, but with a tensile speed that made him very dangerous indeed. His dark eyes glittered as he looked down at Merrick's witch, who barely seemed to notice.

"Are you disobeying a direct order?" she asked, softly, and Merrick winced. One solitary Watcher was no match for her when she was this determined.

Jasper's eyes caught Merrick's. An unspoken question crossed his face. *Is she serious? And are you going to let her do this?*

"I'll look after her." Merrick's hand curled loosely around a knife hilt. "There's a dead Lightbringer upstairs. It's an emergency."

The guard paled and stepped aside, his coat whispering. Merrick pushed the heavy iron-bound door open, reaching over Caro's shoulder. She was so bloody *small*, it was a shock to realize she only reached his collarbone. The glittering anger and terrible sadness sparking through her aura made her seem much taller and indomitable. *What are you going to do, Caro? Whatever it is, I'm sure it's going to be a parade of heart-stopping excitement. I should tie you up and have your brother sit on you.*

That's an excellent, wonderful idea. I wonder if he'd go for it.

She stalked into the dormitory, sparing a single glance at the privacy-tinted windows. Night was well on its way to falling, helped along by heavy clouds coming in from the sea. More rain. A miserable night for the Watchers out on patrol, especially with this new danger to make things lively.

It was immediately obvious where the wounded Watcher was. Several tall men in long black leather trenchcoats clustered around a bed halfway down the long room on the left side. The subsonic painful humming of Watcher magick rattled the air and the floorboards. Mithras stood at the far end, his gaze fixed into eternity; the shadows around the altar were full of thrumming force. It was like being under fire in the army again, the sense of camaraderie and high-octane adrenaline fear. One of their own was in jeopardy, and the others face-to-face with what could be their own fate.

Caro swept down the aisle between the beds, head held high, Merrick drifting in her wake.

A scream cut the air, an agonized howl of flesh pushed past endurance. Caro's aura sparked, and the Watchers suddenly, collectively, became aware of her presence and parted automatically to let her through. Merrick caught up with her, his bootheels clicking on the floor. Closed his hand around her shoulder. "Let me take a look. Safer."

She nodded, peering through the screen of black leather-clad backs. Each of the Watchers was armed to the teeth. It wasn't likely she would be harmed . . . but still.

Merrick slid between Ellis and Tanner, took one glance down at the Watcher on the bed, and his gorge rose briefly, pointlessly. He pushed the sensation of nausea down. *No. Don't let her look at this. Dear God.*

The Lightbringer had been terribly beaten, the kind of beating meant to damage and disfigure. The Watcher had been *ravaged*. He would have been dead if not for the *tanak* smoking and pulling at all available Power to try to hold the shattered body to life. It looked like several of his bones had been reduced to almost-powder, blood boiling out from skin continually renewing itself as he convulsed, screaming again. They had taken his weapons and his coat, not that he could have used a weapon with hands so broken and twisted.

Caro appeared next to him. "Oh, gods." The soft thread of her voice cut through the sound of the Watcher's screams.

Amazingly, the Watcher fell silent. His battered body, barely recognizable as human, stilled as she approached. Merrick felt a shudder creep under his spine—to be that badly hurt, and feel the acid pain of a Lightbringer's aura soaking into your wounds, didn't bear thinking about.

"Be careful," Ellis managed. "He's been thrashing, could do something without knowing it."

Merrick nodded and moved closer to the bed. How was this man still alive after all the damage done to him? Why couldn't the *tanak* heal the injuries?

Caro reached down, but didn't take the Watcher's hand. Instead, her fingers hovered just above his. "I'm going to go in," she announced.

Every Watcher present stilled. Merrick finally found his voice.

"Caro, he's a *Watcher*." He sounded shocked even to himself. *You can't go inside his head, he's a one of us. He probably has things in there that will drive you mad. It's never been done before. Mindhealers don't heal Watchers; they don't go in when a* tanak *has been bonded. It's too bloody dangerous.*

"Something's re-injuring him so fast the *tanak* can't heal him." She looked up, and the tears spilling down her cheeks tore at his chest. "Do you know how to anchor a witch?"

He nodded. His throat was full of sand, and blood still matted his shirt and jeans. It was drying rapidly, a crackling pulling sensation against newly-healed skin. *Don't. Don't do this. You're already exhausted. You can't take this, Caro. He's a Watcher, he's tough. He'll survive. Or not. It might be a mercy if you let him go.* "I know how."

"Then anchor me. Don't pull me out unless I go into cardiac arrest, is that clear?"

His jaw set. *Duty. Honor. Obedience.* "Yes, ma'am."

She held out her other hand. Merrick's pulse skyrocketed. His fingers slid through hers, sugared heat slamming up his arm and detonating in his chest. *Christ, I can't take much more of this, my heart's going to give out.* He couldn't look away from the salt water on her cheeks, shining in the light from the overhead lamps. The edges of her aura meshed with his, a thin gossamer link that would allow him to monitor her heartbeat and theoretically allow him to draw her back if she lost her way in the wilds of another mind.

Theoretically.

"Don't *ma'am* me." She swallowed hard, her pretty throat moving, and he had the sudden intense urge to lean forward and press his lips to the soft spot where the pulse beat. Fear slammed through him, sharp and total, he might have done something unforgivable—like yanking her away and tossing her over his shoulder, carrying her up to her room—if she hadn't hurriedly looked away, down at the bleeding, moaning shape on the bed. "What's his name?"

"Asher," someone answered harshly. "Asher Green."

She nodded, and bent down. Tendrils of her hair fell forward, almost brushing the bloody mess. The shape on the bed twisted and moaned again, but didn't scream. Caro's presence seemed to tranquilize it, even though every Watcher in the room must be acutely aware of the pain of a Lightbringer so close and wincing in sympathy.

She breathed out, and the smell of white copal and spice cut through the reeking air. Merrick watched. If the body on the bed started to thrash again, she could get hurt.

"Asher," she whispered, as if he was a lover. Another sharp twist of jealousy bit at Merrick's chest. "Just hold on, I'm on my way." Her fingers tensed, descended onto the blood-drenched piece of meat that was the wounded Watcher's wrist.

Then, again, she was *gone*, and a sharp collective gasp of wonder went through the assembled Watchers. They had never seen a Mindhealer do this before.

"Dear gods," Ellis whispered. "Have you ever—"

"No." This from Nevin, whose harsh bass voice was soft with wonder. "Look at that. She's doing that for one of *us*."

"Watch." Someone obviously didn't trust the sudden tranquility. "Wait."

Seconds ticked by. Merrick was vaguely aware of more Watchers arriving, of a heated, whispered discussion. Someone objecting, or being brought up to speed on what was happening—

Arcing through the contact of his fingers in hers, the agony was so sudden and intense Merrick let out a short, sharp sound, then clamped his teeth together and dug his heels in. *No. Caro, you shouldn't feel this. Don't feel this.*

The pain rolled under the surface of his awareness, sinking in, bones shattered and muscles torn, his eyes burning. He took it, buried it in the same place he had buried every other dark emotion, the place of cold self-sufficiency that allowed him to *track*. Didn't have time to wonder whose pain it was. Caro's hand in his was the only thing that made the agony bearable, and he focused on the feel of her skin, the way her fingers tightened, the light of her aura brushing his—

Caro stiffened. Her back arched, and her hand suddenly clamped down in his. His heart pulsed once, twice, stuttered under the strain, something black and supple rising with snakelike speed, a trap waiting to snap closed. For one blinding second Merrick felt the full brunt of agony from the body on the bed, an unfiltered raw jolt that peeled his skin back and doused him in fire. He strained to *move*, to tear her away from the danger rising from the shattered Watcher, to pull her back.

Mental muscles tore as the tenuous link between their fingers slipped, strained . . . and, thank the gods, *held*.

Confusion. Watchers shouting. Caro let out a short, horrible scream, her voice breaking. Merrick's entire body turned to caustic sand, blind, only the pale shimmer that was part of her waking consciousness locked against his visible to his staring eyes. Time slowed, stretching like taffy, and snapped forward.

He half-fell, his knees turned to mud. Someone caught him, strong hands at his shoulders; Caro's fingers still tangled in his. More motion, a cacophony of yells and harsh oaths, the sound of steel sliding back into the sheath. A long, exhaled breath, and Merrick found his balance again, shaking away whoever had caught him. *Caro. Where is she?*

His vision cleared, painful light striking his eyes. He pulled on her hand, and Caro fell against him, Ellis letting go of her arm as soon as Merrick had her. She was breathing, but her head lolled strangely and her eyes were closed. Her nose was bleeding again. Unconscious. Her pulse thundered; he could *hear* it even as his fingers found it beating in her slim wrist.

The last vestige of hurt left, new strength roaring through him as the *tanak* converted pain to Power. He found himself holding the deadweight of his witch with an arm around her back, under her arms, her head cradled against his shoulder as if she was hiding her eyes.

On the bed, the shattered Watcher lay sleeping now. His skin was knitting together, faint crackles pulsing underneath as the *tanak* mended shattered bones and burst organs. He'd taken a lot of damage, but he wasn't being reinjured again and again. He would live.

Something flopped weakly on the floor, emitting a faint, whistling psychic scream as three Watchers methodically set about ripping it to pieces with pure Power. It looked like a tattered snake, blunt teeth in an eyeless head snapping as it quested blindly, thrashing against the iron hold of the Watchers. Merrick's skin prickled with recognition. No wonder Asher had been unable to heal himself. The Crusade had beaten him to a pulp and infected him with something. The *tanak* might have healed him, given enough time; after all, it was in him of his own volition. The Watcher's consent gave the *tanak* a psychic hold greater than any other infestation.

But it would have been very, very painful.

Merrick let out a soft breath. His ribs creaked, settled.

Caro was utterly unmoving except for the flicker of her breathing, the birdlike rattle of her pulse. She was still alive, and the *contact* between them saved him from the awful dragging agony of a Watcher whose witch was leaving. And yet, she was curiously *absent*.

Nobody saw him ease back, handling her slight weight effortlessly. They were so focused on killing the snake-thing, and the sudden influx of other Lightbringers—how had he missed the amount of people suddenly crowding in here?— that he was able to make it out the door and past Jasper, who carefully looked away. Tactful as always, with the kind of politeness only another Watcher would think of. Caro's sneakers brushed the floor until Merrick paused, tucked aside in a little-used hall, and picked her up like a child, her head against his shoulder, her hair springing out of its confinement and brushing his jaw, her legs dangling.

She didn't stir as he carried her into her room, his eyes adapting to the darkness as he laid her carefully on the bed, keeping the contact between them with a simple pressure against her aura. The edges of their minds still meshed, but it was like a live telephone line into an empty house; she was elsewhere. She breathed deeply, the fever-flush in her cheeks fading. He managed to unlace her sneakers and pull them off before the shakes hit him.

Merrick paused, his head dropping, his fingers suddenly numb. *She just went walking in a Watcher's mind and triggered something. A trap? Likely. Possible. Probable. I could have lost her.*

The thought wouldn't go away. He stayed nailed in place, barely noticing that he hadn't closed her door. *I could have lost her. Lost the only witch who can touch me.*

She was so heartbreakingly, misguidedly brave, flinging herself into danger. He would have thought her suicidal if he didn't know it was pure determination. She was, like every Lightbringer, trying to save the world. But who was looking after her? She'd even convinced the High Council to keep the Watchers away from her. To *protect* them.

No more of this. Christ in Heaven, I almost bloody well lost her. If I hadn't been anchoring her, that . . . thing . . . would have eaten her alive. No more. I swore obedience, not idiocy.

He pulled the covers up over her and made his legs work,

carrying him over to the door. Shut it, locked it, and leaned against it, his breath coming harsh and tearing. The echoes of agony from whatever had been done to Asher still scraped against his nerves. To think of her suffering that pain strained at his already battered control.

"No more," he whispered, bracing his back against the door and sliding down. He was going to sleep, couldn't help himself. He was too tired, had stretched himself past the ends of even a Watcher's endurance. Mindhealing was draining work. He had given everything he had and was grateful it was enough. She was still alive, his witch.

And Merrick was going to see she stayed that way.

Eleven

It was not so surprising, really. Eleanor had warned her of this.

Caro wandered through the labyrinth, featureless doors set in the stone, none of them looking familiar. This was the space-between, the place of boundaries between two minds. As always, here she wore a long white dress, its hem dragging the floor and its tattered sleeves bound with silk ribbons. She carried the small silver globe in her left hand, memory and light rolled into a compact form for carrying. Something had happened, but it was difficult to see clearly here. There was always the danger of becoming lost in another's mind, of the heart stuttering if the healer pulled away too quickly, of catching the viral sickness some minds carried. It was a danger she had always accepted—after all, the world itself was a garden full of peril. She had learned early and well that there was no safety, not for someone with her gifts. If the insanity of a mortal mind didn't get her, the Dark would.

Tracing through the labyrinth, she reached out, trailed her fingers along the stone and the smooth wooden surfaces of the doors. She had gone into a mind, and something had happened. She was now trapped in the space-between, the shock of disengaging from the other mind knocking her into this space. Dangerous, especially if they tried pouring Power into her. This was not like astral travel, where the silver cord would hold the consciousness to the body. No, this was something different, something only another Mindhealer would understand.

Fuzzy voices twisted through the walls as she passed a low arch twined with ivy. Through it, she caught sight of a clear reflecting pool, lipped with stone, and with a stone bench beside it. Hanging over the pool was a tree watching its own reflection with bloodshot eyes. The leaves were bloodshot too, dripping; the plink of every crimson drop hitting the rippling surface of the pool was loud through the sound of faraway, radio-static voices. Soft voices, whispering voices.

Female voices.

"How long has she—"

"Since the . . . since Nicolette. The Mindhealers say not to touch, not to disturb her."

"Her poor Watcher. Look at him."

"Shh, he'll hear you."

"He hasn't moved. Won't let anyone help him, won't let anyone—"

"Shh."

Then she moved, because the pool had begun to bulge and ripple, and she did not want to see what would birth itself from that bleeding reflection.

Walking. Barefoot. Chill stone against her feet. Her fingers were growing numb, and that was a bad sign. She was lost. She could not find her way.

Stop, *she whispered to herself.* Doubt is useless here. Be quiet, and walk. You'll find the way soon enough.

But she had nothing to guide her. She had gone into the mind—whose mind? Someone's. And she had gone without preparation, without setting her landmarks, gone in a terrible hurry. Why? It must have been important. If she could only remember.

She looked down as she walked, at the silver sphere. It pulsed reassuringly. A memory was locked inside, a memory not of her making. She would have to carry it out and scry it in a bowl of water. Or a globe of malachite or granite. Anything less would shatter under the force of recollection. She knew that. How she knew, she could not guess.

Walking. The mist began, rising like the numbness, clouding her vision. Mindhealing was really mostly about seeing, *about being able to see what was right in front of you. To obscure oneself, that was death.*

Voices, again. Weirdly directionless through the mist.

"She's fading." *An agonized, gentle voice.* "We can't do anything for fear of hurting her."

"Let him try." *A young boy's voice, hoarse as if he had been crying. Why was it so familiar?* "For God's sake, let him try."

Mist, rising. She should have been afraid, but instead she felt a strange relief. She saw the archway ahead, through the mist. The bleeding tree was there, and if she looked into the pool she would forget all this.

Caro. *The world echoed strangely, as if through a weight of air different than anything found on earth.* **Where**

are you?

I wish I knew, *she thought in reply.* I wish I knew.

The mist began to billow. Caroline froze. She felt . . . something.

Her hand lifted, thought becoming action, and the mist retreated. A strange sensation, as if heat was folding around her, a rope wrapped around her middle, drawing her.

I'll find you. *Male. A familiar voice, but older. Who? She couldn't think, it was too hard. Keeping herself whole and complete in this space took so much attention, so much concentrated effort.* **Pull.**

Pull what? But she knew. She looked down and saw a thick rope around her waist. It was a line, meant to draw her out of the labyrinth. It spiraled along the floor in a pattern like three lines drawn on a face, then soared up beyond the walls of the labyrinth. And for the first time since coming to this place, she saw a flash of blue sky.

It was such a long, long way away. And the archway was getting closer. She heard the plinking of water dripping. Plink, plonk. They grew heavier—thud, thud, thud.

Footfalls? A heartbeat? Who knew?

Caro wrapped her free hand around the rope. It tautened, and another warm wave of strength poured into her.

She cast one longing look at the archway. There was a bench there, looking over the pool, and she could rest.

Rest forever, until her feet grew into the floor and her fingers split into bleeding leaves, until her bloodshot eyes could not look away from whatever spectacle awaited in the water's depths.

She dug her heels in, tightening her fingers around the rope, and threw herself back, *inertia combining with effort and intent, the rope suddenly a stretched-thin, thread-thin, too-thin* link. *A connection, snapped taut, letting him know she was there, that she heard him, that she wanted out.*

Images. A hot, steaming place where water dripped from every leaf, crouching in the mud as the leeches novocained his skin, the crosshairs settling perfectly over the target, not even a human shape, merely the taste of consummation in his mouth as he pulled the trigger—

Don't look at that. *He pulled her away, closing that set of mental doors. Pulled against the rope, his hands slippery with blood, his eyes dry and grainy, his shoulders aching and his legs frozen from kneeling.* **That's not good, don't go there. This way. Here.**

And one last convulsive effort, pulling, his eyes rolling back into his head and the hard cold part of him roaring with satisfaction, he had tracked her. He had tracked her, caught her, and brought her up, up, spiraling into the blue, wind whipping her hair, every nerve alive and then . . .

CRASH—

—ing through the glass ceiling and into the land of the living again.

Caro slammed back into her body and screamed, thrashing. Pain smashed through her, the pain of a mind gone too long and forced back into the cloak of the body, confined to a shape that altered slower than the lightning speed of thought. It passed, only a brief second of the agony of being trapped inside her own shell again. Then it was comforting to feel the weight of flesh once more and she sagged, except for her wrist, braceleted in hot iron. She fell back into softness, light striking her eyes hard and harsh.

That's why newborns scream, she thought with dazed wonder, and squeezed her eyes closed. Heard herself whispering, the shapeless speech of a dreamer. Her body was asleep, safe now that she was back inside it, like a hand inside a glove.

"Caro." Hoarse. He sounded like hell. That was the first surprise, his usually calm voice so ragged she almost didn't recognize it.

The second surprise? He wasn't Trev. She would have thought Trev would be the one to bring her out.

And the last surprise, almost mundane in its depth, was the fact that she needed only the single word to know who it was and feel completely, utterly relieved. Safe.

Merrick?

"You're safe now," he whispered, and his fingers eased on her wrist. "Tracked you. Just rest."

Then a sliding, heavy sound. He'd passed out.

Darkness closed over her, the clean familiar darkness of slumber. Caro fought it as hard as she could, only winning a few seconds before it swallowed her whole.

* * * *

The coffeemaker gurgled as she stared blearily at it. Caro pushed her hair back, tucking vagrant curls behind her ears, and yawned again. She didn't know how long she'd slept, and she was still tired. Wandering around in the space-between was dangerous and draining. It couldn't have been more than a couple of hours, could it? She wouldn't have lasted much longer in that unphysical realm.

Merrick was asleep on the floor; a human sleep instead of the deep trance the Watchers sometimes used to skip the need for human unconsciousness. He must have been utterly exhausted. She'd covered him with the down quilt from her bed and thought about trying to ease a pillow under his head, but he was too heavy for her to lift and she might wake him. Guilt bit at her—after all, he'd somehow performed the miracle of reaching into the space-between and pulling her out.

How he'd done it was another mystery, one she was going to have to solve soon. Even another Mindhealer wouldn't risk a *touch* when she was in the space-between. It was dangerous, so dangerous she was tempted to wake him up and scold him.

But that simply raised another cascade of questions—why did she recognize his voice? Why had she felt so goddamn breathless, when she'd awakened suddenly in the pale pearly light of a rainy winter morning that was still falling through the windows, automatically glancing over to the door as if she would see him there?

And why, oh why, had she felt disturbed when he wasn't there, and ridiculously relieved when she found him collapsed on the floor by her bed, lying on his coat, his weapons piled neatly aside, so deeply asleep he was barely breathing? Why had she wanted to touch him to make sure he was still alive, and why had she hung over the side of the bed peering at him like an idiot, watching the way the light fell over his scarred face? Asleep, he didn't look nearly as solemn. But she missed the gleam of his eyes and the slight movements at the corners of his mouth that clued her in to what he was thinking. She even missed that dry, ironic sense of humor he sometimes displayed, when he spoke at all.

Caro frowned at the coffeemaker. As soon as it had squeezed out enough brew for a cup she grabbed the pot, slopping the liquid around in her hurry, and poured it into a handy mug. She wished, with sudden vengeance, for her own red Fiestaware coffee mugs. And since Trev was here, her ferns were probably withering, unless he'd remembered to make them someone else's problem.

She was so tired of waking up in strange places, always feeling the shock of disorientation, always feeling like a guest and never like she was at home. Her one attempt at owning a home had only lasted two weeks before Vincent—

Caro sighed, jammed the coffeepot back in, and was grateful it was one of the ones that didn't make you wait until it stopped brewing. She was, like most witches in the western hemisphere, addicted to caffeine. Some tried to make do with tea, but most of them just gave up and started drinking java, at least in the mornings. Rare indeed was the witch who didn't like a decent cuppa joe. Eastern witches liked tea better, but you could always find good coffee in their safehouses just in case. Like the safehouse in Beijing with its exquisite gardens and the fresh-ground Kona beans, or the one in Paris. Paris was her favorite, for all that she'd made Saint City her home. She'd trained in Paris for two years with Eleanor, and still remembered the thick stone walls of the Rue de Jeanette safehouse, drenched with Power; remembered visiting Notre Dame while Eleanor's cane tapped the ancient floor and her teacher pointed out ancient pagan ideas frozen in the cathedral's stone. They had moved back to New York after that, and spent time in Florida, too, examining cases, Eleanor's softly-accented voice a counterpoint to Caro's. Eleanor never raised her voice, but her tone could slice through granite when necessary.

Thinking about Eleanor was tinted with sadness. She missed her teacher's quiet confidence and even temper. Just like she missed Vincent's calm and ironic patience. *I wish both of them were here. Eleanor would have an idea of how to treat the victims and Vincent would have an idea of what to do about Merrick.*

Caro let out another sigh, leaning back against the counter as she cupped her hands around her mug. *Tired. Headache. My arms hurt. So does my back, come to think of it. But all in all, I'm feeling far better than I should be. Why? I should be almost blind with the headache, and sick to boot. I should feel terrible.*

Instead, she felt a little muzzy, and a little sore. Dehydrated, certainly, and very, very hungry. Nothing like she would expect.

As soon as the coffee cooled, she took a cautious sip and

grimaced at how strong she'd made it. But, acidic or not, it was the best bet to give her a jolt so she could start in on making sure nobody else was hurt by whatever the Crusade was doing. Circle Lightfall no longer had Eleanor, Caro would have to do her best.

Once she'd some toast made to take the edge of hunger off, she paced through the dining room into the main room, taking care to move quietly. There was a stack of file folders on top of the dresser—Fran's doing, probably. Caro took another scorching gulp of coffee and glanced over at the bed. Merrick was behind it, hidden from view, and she struggled briefly with the impulse to check on him. He was sleeping, he would be all right.

Are you sure?

Of course she was sure. She wouldn't be much of a witch if she couldn't tell the difference between sleep and the space-between. Besides, his aura was strong and disciplined instead of pale and thready, a red-black pulsing that resonated inside the room. He'd set Watcher defenses inside the standard warding in the walls, probably after the room had been invaded. And even now, while he was dead asleep, he was unconsciously checking those defenses, making sure they were intact. She was willing to bet that if anything hit those shields, he would be awake instantly and ready to fight it.

It was comforting having a Watcher around again, she decided, but also frightening. Like every Lightbringer, she didn't understand why the Watchers did what they did. Well, maybe some of the bonded ones; ever since she was ten years old she'd seen the devotion and care between witch and Watcher. It was part of the reason why she'd never been afraid of them. Kids weren't stupid, and a child used to learning the rules by inference at each new foster home was usually more than acute enough to see below the screen of falsity adults put up.

Especially a child gifted with the abilities of a Mindhealer. It had taken her exactly ten minutes to decide that Vincent, though scary and armed to the teeth, meant her no harm. Oddly enough, she had trusted him before trusting Eleanor. The Mindhealer had not been very fond of children, though always gentle and supportive of Caro's talents and fears.

She decided to take a peek at Merrick, just to reassure herself. Padded to the foot of the bed and looked.

He was still asleep under the blanket, his hair pushed back

and the scarred side of his face clearly visible. She wondered again where he'd gotten the scars. Watchers didn't usually scar unless it was a mortal wound, one that could have killed them if they didn't have the *tanak*. Even then, the scars tended to fade after a while.

She realized she was biting her lower lip, almost chewing on it. *I promised myself I would never endanger another Watcher. He could have been killed; I've almost gotten him killed twice now since the* koroi. *I don't want anything to happen to him.*

And, of course, if she truly *was* his witch, he was incapable of going back to guard duty over some other poor witch. Or going back out on patrol. He was going to be in danger no matter what she did.

That doesn't absolve me from trying. What can I do? Every impossible problem has a solution, Eleanor always used to say that. Somehow, some way, I have to get him away from me.

As long as she was a Lightbringer, the Dark was going to be drawn to her. She had people to heal, patients to help, and work to do. The Dark was a danger she would just have to live with, like car accidents or airplane crashes.

He looked so peaceful, even with his tangled hair and scarred face and scuffed boots. He hadn't even taken his boots off.

Caro's heart gave a twisting leap behind her ribs. *Oh, damn.*

Why did he have to be so . . . so *British*? It was the best word she could come up with. She shook her head, ignoring the tangles in her hair for a little while longer, and shuffled back to the dresser. The neat stack of file folders eyed her balefully. Each one represented a victim.

Let's just make sure the stack doesn't get any bigger. Do some reading while you drink your coffee, then get yourself ready for the day. You can scry this afternoon to see what you brought out of that Watcher's mind. It must have been something very important for you to bring it out that way.

Decisively, Caro scooped up the file folders and carried them to the kitchenette table, laying them next to her plate of toast. She sat down, took another gulp of coffee, and began to read.

* * * *

Early afternoon came before she finally took a shower. It was heavenly to get into a long, green silk skirt—a gift from Theo back in Saint City—and a black sweater, she was feeling cold and slightly sick from going through the files. The careful recitation of each victim's statistics and the bloodless collation of information about the attacks and deaths were chilling, to say the least. She'd only made it about halfway through, stopping to breathe deeply each time she felt nauseous. She would go over them again, making notes the second time. Eleanor had taught her to read carefully and thoroughly, and to read everything about a case twice. It was good practice, even if the information made her feel sick. She was guiltily glad there were no pictures; she didn't think she could have handled the pictures without throwing up.

As it was, she saw Colleen's broken face, Nicolette's blood-soaked hair, and Asher Green's unrecognizably battered body. Impossible not to think of them while she read of other damage, of bones broken and organs failing, of saline and morphine drips to ease the victims' pain, their psyches crying out in a chorus only a Mindhealer could hear.

The warm water helped, and while she scrubbed she used the deep breathing and mind-clearing Eleanor had taught her. Every Mindhealer needed an organized, clearheaded space in which to work. It was a little eerie, because she felt far too good to have spent very long in the space-between. She should have been blind with backlash. Instead, she was feeling much better. The caffeine and a little bit of breakfast helped, and the shower completed the job.

As soon as she opened the bathroom door, scrubbing at her hair with a towel, she knew Merrick was awake; his attention crackled through the room like static electricity. Her conscience rose. She had to get him new boots, maybe a haircut, and more clothes. She'd shopped for Vincent for years, even dragged him through outlet stores trying to get him to loosen up and wear a blue T-shirt instead of unrelieved black. Once she'd even tried to convince him to get his ear pierced, *that* had been one hell of an event.

For the first time, the memory didn't send a bolt of pain through her. Instead, it was a sweet ache, remembering how kind he had been. She glanced around the room, feeling the slow static of a Watcher's conscious attention brush the walls and come to rest on her.

Merrick leaned against the wall by the door, in his usual spot; his hair was shaken down over his face and wildly mussed. His eyes glittered, peering out from under the shelf of darkness, and he looked, quite frankly, like hell. He was back in his weapons harness, the sword hilt riding his right shoulder; it was habit with the Watchers to take their weapons everywhere. At least he wasn't wearing his coat. Still, the smell of leather was faint in the air, and that citrus scent, too. He'd been in here for a while, and the smell was . . . comforting.

Caro let the door drift half closed while she hung the towel up and rescued her comb. "Bathroom's yours," she said, finally, emerging into the main room. Her skirt swirled around her ankles; Theo always got them a little too big. *It's that aura of yours that makes it difficult to tell your size,* the green witch would say with a wry smile. *Your mouth makes you seem taller than you are,* Elise had piped up. "I'll make you something to eat, you must be star—"

He barely seemed to move before he was in front of her, his hands curling around her upper arms. "Are you all right? Why didn't you wake me up? Are you hurt? What happened? Are you *hurt?*"

He was *shaking.* It was the most emotion she'd seen from him, and the rapid-fire questions were so utterly unlike the laconic Watcher she had begun to know her jaw threatened to drop. *"Merrick!"*

She hadn't meant to yell, but gods above, he looked furious. His eyes blazed and he looked like he was developing a tic in his scarred cheek. He shut up, but he didn't let go of her arms. His grasp didn't hurt, but it was uncomfortably tight. He twitched, as if he wanted to shake her. There was a shadow of stubble on his cheeks, even the scarred one, and she wondered how long he'd been at her bedside.

I haven't done right by him. He's a Watcher, he's all but helpless. If something happens he's going to be in terrible danger.

It was ridiculous to think of him as helpless, but feeling him shake through his hard grip on her arms convinced her. He was in a dangerous mood, anger fueled by frustration and fear, the worst kind of tangle for a Watcher to get himself into. Once, Vincent had been driven to anger by something she'd done, something idiotic, and he'd trembled like this. In the middle of the swirling haze of emotion, she felt a curious comfort.

Caro took a deep breath. He was locked down so tight she could almost feel the air hardening around him. Despite that, a complex welter of dark fury and anguish she shuddered to feel trickled out, staining the edges of his aura. "Calm down," she whispered, looking up at him. "Just calm down."

"Calm down? *Calm down?*" His green eyes were incandescent, and she wondered if she was going to be the first witch in the history of Circle Lightfall to be burned by a Watcher's eyes.

That's ridiculous. He wouldn't hurt me. "Yes." Her voice shook. "Please. Just calm down." She did the only thing she *could* do, simply reached up and laid her fingertips against his cheek. He didn't stop her, but his hands didn't loosen either.

He went still, so motionless he seemed to have turned to a statue. She was touching his scarred cheek, the smoothness of long-healed tissue under her fingertips, He felt feverish. Watchers usually ran warm, their metabolisms higher than normals, but he was so hot she had a sudden uncomfortable mental image of smoke threading up from his clothes.

Her practical side reasserted itself with a vengeance. *Give him something else to think about, a question to answer. Keep him talking. He won't hurt me, but he's upset, and a Watcher in this state is dangerous. Not to me, maybe, but to himself.*

"You brought me out. How long was I gone?" She heard the snap of command in her voice, winced against it. *Do you have to be so bossy, Caro?*

Oddly enough, that seemed to defuse the tension. His hands relaxed still further, though he didn't let her go. Even his face softened slightly. "Four days." A slight rippling shudder went through him. "You were *gone*, Caro. Your brother finally persuaded them to let me track you."

Her eyes widened. She could feel them practically start out from her head, a prickling cold fear touching her nape, her hair trying to rise. "Four *days?*" It was a shocked whisper. "But—gods above, I shouldn't have lasted more than six hours." *And I should be half dead with backlash!*

Merrick's throat worked as he swallowed. A deep rumbling growl lifted from him, his cheek turning to iron under her touch, muscle standing out under his T-shirt. *Well, that was probably the wrong thing to say to him,* she thought, and felt a lunatic desire to giggle rise up in her and fall away.

"Merrick." She used her schoolteacher voice, the one that could stop a giggling group of young witches in their tracks and return them to a boring theory lesson. "Stop it. I'm right here, I'm all right, and you're not going to do any good by going all overprotective on me."

His eyes found hers, and Caro swallowed dryly. He didn't look merely grim. No, his eyes burned, his scars flushed, and he looked *lethal*.

He leaned down, shaking free of her fingers on his face, and Caro only had time to take a short shocked breath before his mouth descended on hers. He kissed her, his breath flavored with male and the spice-taste of city night, neon, and cold wind.

Fire. Liquid heat slid down her skin, slammed into her belly, crackled between her nerves. Her hips tilted forward, her hands tangling in his hair, and she drowned in the wave of velvet-spiked oil until he took a little pity on her and broke free. Her lips felt bruised, almost swollen, and she was suddenly extremely aware that he was taller than her, still holding her shoulders, and she had her fingers twisted in the rough tangled darkness of his hair.

What the—

She couldn't seem to catch her breath. She wasn't inexperienced—one of the good things about learning to control her abilities was the opportunity to carry on a semi-relationship with a normal man, especially once she had refused to have a Watcher. Unfortunately, a relationship with a psychic wasn't something most men could handle. It was hard to be affectionate toward a woman who could read your mind and had to be home by dusk, not to mention one who sometimes disappeared at the drop of a hat for an emergency. Even casual encounters had been a little difficult. And none of them had ever, *ever* felt like this, drowning in fire, her nerves torn apart with heat. She was damn near ready to pull his head back down and find out if he could do it again.

Caro! The short, sharp voice of her conscience jolted her. She untangled her fingers from his hair, let her hands drop. *For God's sake, control yourself. This is no time for hormones. You have work to do. And your first task is calming him down.*

He pulled her forward, wrapping his arms around her, and said something she couldn't hear because it was muffled by her hair. He was still shaking, a knife hilt jabbed her right in the ribs, and he smelled like leather. She was suddenly, incredibly, acutely aware that her hair was wet and she probably had coffee breath because she'd taken the cup into the bathroom with her.

Great, Caro. Lovely. What the hell is wrong with you?

But she knew, didn't she. Witch and Watcher, they were a bonded pair. It was the most natural thing in the world for her to . . . *react* to him. Did other witches feel this way too? They should have told her. Someone should have warned her.

This is going to make everything even more difficult. Wow. Where did he learn how to kiss like that?

Quit it. You shouldn't be thinking about that. You should be thinking about getting the rest of the files memorized and looking for a connection, any connection, anything.

Sure. In a minute. I'll get right on that.

His heartbeat thudded under her cheek. One of the straps of his weapons-harness pressed into her chin. Her own heart was racing, pounding in her throat, racketing against her ribs. He took a deep shuddering breath, and the tension in him drained away.

He raised his head a little. "Take my knives if you want," he said harshly, as if he was being strangled by the words.

What? If she could have, she would have tried to look up, see his face. As it was, she wasn't likely to be going anywhere. His arms were still gently but definitely around her, and she knew how strong a Watcher was. She settled for sliding her own arms around him, felt him stiffen reflexively. The hard edge of one of his guns pressed into her hip. "What the hell are you talking about? Why don't you use teensy words and go real slow so I can follow you? I'm not feeling up to my usual speed, you know."

A few moments of silence stretched around them. The safehouse hummed to itself, the walls singing their slow song of protection, and she felt the unease swirling through the halls. Had she really been out for four days, walking in the space-between? Why wasn't she more backlashed?

"Duty." Merrick shivered. "Honor. *Obedience.* You're *my* witch, Caroline. *Mine.* And I'm bloody well going to make sure nothing happens to you. If I have to violate my oath of obedience, so be it. I will not lose you. You will never, ever, *ever* do anything like that ever again, do you hear me? If I have to hold you down or sit on you to keep you out of trouble,

I will."

She'd never heard a Watcher say anything remotely like this. "I'm all right," she soothed. "We're both alive. Why don't we just have a—"

"I mean it, Caro. If you want to take my knives and shun me, do it now. *Right* now. But even if you do, I'm not leaving you. I will *not* let you put yourself in danger again. If I have to damn myself to protect you, I will."

Oh, for heaven's sake, I need more coffee before I can handle this. Caro took a deep breath, felt the high voltage running through him. He was serious. Taking a Watcher's knives meant that the Watcher had lost his chance for redemption, had done something so awful the Lightbringers had cast him out. In all the history of Circle Lightfall, it had only happened twice, and one of those times had only been temporary. It was the worst thing that could happen to a Watcher, and if Merrick thought she was going to do that he might well work himself into a frenzy and hurt himself.

"Nobody's going to take your knives." *I wish Theo was here. She can calm anyone down. I've never been known to be soothing except with a patient.* "You haven't done anything wrong."

"I'm about to." But the dangerous staticky sense of a thunderstorm about to strike lessened. Caro was aware of sudden stasis—was the entire safehouse holding its breath? No, just her. "Never, *ever* do anything like that again, Caro."

A Watcher telling me what to do. Yeah, like I haven't heard that before. But even Vincent never said it quite that way, like a command instead of a request. Her chin would have lifted stubbornly if she hadn't had her face buried against his chest. "I did what I had to. You'd have done the same thing."

"I'm a Watcher, Caro. I'm *supposed* to do the foolish, suicidal—" He was working himself up again. The way he said her name—the faint possessive inflection stronger now, the vowels shaped differently through his accent—made her heart pound again, as if she'd just run a marathon. *I won't have to take aerobics if this keeps up. I'll get all my exercise just listening to him talk.*

"Shut up." And miraculously, he did. His heartbeat settled, his aura closed around hers, and she closed her eyes, breathing him in. "Listen to me."

He was quiet. She moved slightly, pushing a knife hilt aside to get more comfortable. Finally, he drew in a deep shuddering breath. "I'm listening," he whispered.

All right, I've got his attention. "You're my Watcher," she said carefully. "If you'll be careful, I'll be careful. I don't want you hurt—"

"It's my *job*," he interrupted, again. *All this time he says almost nothing, and now I can't get a word in edgewise.* "How would you like it if someone told you not to Mindheal because it was too *dangerous*?"

That stopped her. Damn the man, he had a valid point. "But—"

"I am *perfectly* capable of taking care of myself," he hissed out between clenched teeth. "You don't know *how* capable. The only thing that's going to get me killed is if you keep making it harder for me to do my bloody fucking *job*!"

She had nothing to say to that. What if he was right? "What do you want me to do?" Her voice wavered on the edge of tears. *Good one, Caro. Show how tough you are by being a weepy little whiner. Damn it, why can't you ever learn to buck up and be strong?*

"Just let me do what I'm meant to," he whispered. "Everything's going to be all right, Caro. I promise, I will protect you. I *swear* it, on my Name and my knives."

That made the tears spill over, she could feel them soaking into his shirt. It was the most solemn oath a Watcher could swear, the most binding. There was nothing else to say. The room ticked and sang its slow song of wood and drywall heating up and expanding for the day, even on such a gray and rainy day as this. He gradually stopped shaking, simply held her, the smell of leather and male enclosing her. She had never been able to lean into someone like this, feel someone else providing a little shelter. Even Vincent had never touched her. For all her life, Caro had been the strong one, never letting down her guard, never letting Trev or anyone else see her indecision, her fear.

She could have stayed there far longer, but a sudden knock at the door made her jump, half-guiltily. Merrick's arms fell away, he looked down at her. The tension of half a dozen things she wanted to say to him stretched between them, just like a rope knotted around her waist.

"I promise," he repeated, then went past her, leaving only the guilty heat in her cheeks and the bruised feeling in her lips, and the smell of leather and a very big, very careful man who had pulled her—how?—out of the space-between.

"Caro?" Trev's voice, muffled by the door. "Caro? Is that you? Open up!"

Oh, God, she thought, feeling her cheeks burn with heat, *what next? Please, not another crisis. Not now.*

Twelve

"Two days," the boy said, watching his sister's face. "Then you slept for another two while we all took turns shoving Power into you, which is probably why you're not feeling backlashed." He pushed the plate toward her. "You need to eat. Look, it's my famous curry chicken. I've turned your kitchen into a disaster area again."

"Mh. Look at this. Most of the attacks have a seventy-two hour cycle. The—yes, the normals, not the psychics. Now why would it be seventy-two hours for the normals and—"

Merrick's witch chewed her lower lip, frowning as she stared at the papers spread out over the table. There were no pictures, for which Merrick was grateful. He didn't want her to see dead, brutalized bodies. Quite frankly, he'd had enough of Caro seeing awful things. A tendril of chestnut hair streaked with gold fell in her face, she blew it back irritably and his heart leapt, throbbed in his wrists and other places, too. He should have taken an ice bath. She was dangerous to his self-control, and he'd had just about enough of the *look don't touch*, no matter how damn thoroughly he didn't deserve her.

He'd had enough of her rushing headlong into danger, too. There was a long list of things he'd had enough of, and if he wasn't careful he would end up doing something indefensible and being cast out. It made him wonder what would happen if Caro took his knives and he still stayed around to protect her. Would the other Watchers become his enemies? Would they exterminate him as just another piece of Dark, without the obedience and honor that made a Watcher one of the good guys?

I don't care. Merrick leaned back against the wall, his heartbeat finally slowing down. He had forced himself on her, but he couldn't have stopped himself even if he'd wanted to. Just the remembered feel of her in his arms was enough to make his pulse spike again. It was a feedback loop, her skin against his and her mouth opening shyly to him. He'd tasted morning coffee and the flavor of *her*, salt and spice and something too sweet to be called bitterness but too bitter to be truly sweet—his own failure. He'd broken the central law of being a Watcher, and nobody had realized it yet. The next time Caro tried to throw herself into peril, he was going to handcuff her if he had to and keep her locked up in the safest corner he could find. His heart couldn't take this.

"A seventy-two hour cycle?" Trev dropped into the chair to her right, slanting the Watchers a meaningful, indecipherable look. "Keenan, Merrick, get your plates. This won't stay hot forever."

Merrick, startled, scraped himself off the wall near the door. He was getting very used to the way the pretty blue room looked from that angle. It was better than kneeling at the side of Caro's bed and fighting to track her through a shifting waste of mist and weird internal ballrooms while his chest felt like it was being torn in half. He now understood why a bonded Watcher didn't survive his witch's death. How could a man survive when his heart and soul were torn out and carried away? It wasn't possible.

Christ, he'd never even known he *had* a soul until she had stood up, clutching her car door, and demanded just who the hell he was. Never even dreamed he had one. And if he had a heart left, it was sitting at the table, murmuring to herself as she paged through another file and made a notation with a precisely sharpened sun-yellow pencil.

Keenan handed him a plate as soon as he made it into the kitchenette, but the younger Watcher didn't let go when Merrick tried to take it.

"Got a second?" Keenan's tone was a warning in and of itself. The kitchenette was tucked behind a half-wall, and there was precious little space to hide them, but Trev was chattering at Caro far enough away that a private conversation was possible.

Merrick was hard-pressed to stop a guilty start. Had he been found out somehow? He'd learned to keep his face impassive, and the scars helped, but even his breathing might have given him away. "What's on your mind, mate?"

"Had a chat with Oliver." Keenan's eyes turned even darker, his pupils fading into the irises and giving his gaze a Watcher's intensity. "Asher Green woke up and started talking." He took a deep breath as if steeling himself, his coat creaking slightly. "The Crusade caught him and the witch. They beat them both, and Asher fought as hard as he could—poor bastard, says it wasn't enough. You know."

Merrick nodded, taking his plate. He did, indeed, know. The specter of failure would haunt Asher, would torture his every waking moment. He'd lost a Lightbringer.

"There were ten or twelve of them, and fifteen Seekers. They had a hideous number of zombies, too. They put the witch out of commission first and moved in on Asher while he was trying to get her to safety. They talked while they were working him over and sinking the filthy Dark into the Lightbringer. He says they're trying to create Watchers of their own, looking for a Dark parasite that'll give them the benefits of a *tanak*. They want something that can withstand Lightbringer magicks, so they've been trying to trap psychics and Lightbringers, infect them with these things—testing some kind of Seeker hybrid that they'll eventually put into their version of *us*."

Merrick's entire body went cold. He heard Caro's voice, a faint distracted murmur, and her brother trying to make her laugh, telling her some humorous story. A faint breath of her green tea perfume reached him. And his shirt smelled like her shampoo now, since her hair had been damp while he held her. "Christ in Heaven." His scars began to pulse with fire, a sharp reminder of the Dark.

Keenan nodded, his sharply handsome face drawn and pale. "Yeah. Oliver said to give you a message—do *not* pass this on to your witch. We sent a detail out to take a look at some of the other victims, each one of them was dead except one that burst with one of those *things* while the Watchers were there. There aren't any survivors, and your witch can't treat the patients. The Council liaison'll take care of breaking the news to her. We're supposed to take her and her brother back to Saint City as soon as she's well enough to travel. The Crusade's targeted Mindhealers as priority-one terminations; something about them possibly being able to treat the infection."

Oh, good God, this just keeps getting worse. "Fucking hell," he whispered, and tightened his fingers on the plate.

"Whatever was in Asher was supposed to kill him. And whatever they put in the Lightbringer was supposed to birth itself, come out, and run riot in the safehouse before it escaped and made its way back to them. They were counting on the Lightbringer being brought in." Keenan's paleness wasn't fear. It was tightly controlled rage, allowed to surface only because he was fairly sure neither Lightbringer in the other room was paying attention. "It gets worse."

How could it get any worse? Merrick didn't ask, simply waited.

"The Crusade's hooked up with another organization, one that calls itself Dominion. We don't know anything about them yet. The tech witches are working 'round the clock to find out. But the important thing is this. Do *not*, under any circumstances, let the Mindhealer out of your sight. Try to convince her to stay in the safehouse. If you absolutely can't stop her, bring her back well before nightfall. Oliver said to tell you that certain . . . leeway . . . is permitted to Watchers in cases like this. It's a goddamn emergency."

Merrick's throat was dry. He looked down at his plate, the chicken curry, the salad, the neat double-slice of fresh bread. Caro's brother was a good cook, and he seemed to be the only person who could make her see reason. "Her brother?" The question was only half articulated.

He got the idea Keenan might have laughed out loud, if it hadn't been so important to be quiet. "Understands, but he's not sanguine. As he puts it, *it's like beating your head on a brick wall, only Caro wins against the wall almost every time.* Time for 'act first and apologize later,' Merrick."

Keenan was deadly serious. The urge to laugh rose under Merrick's skin. It was repressed with a savagery that made his plate tremble slightly. *This has got to be a first. I am getting permission to do what I'd already made up my mind to do anyway. The gods have a sense of humor, at least.* "Understood."

The other Watcher raised a single eyebrow. "You're not going to have any trouble?"

Bloody hell, I'm going to have more trouble than even I know how to deal with. She's going to be extremely unhappy about this. "Doesn't matter. She's my witch. I'm not about to let the Crusade or anyone else get their filthy fucking hands on her. Right, mate?"

"Right." Keenan looked a lot more relieved. It was probably unpleasant for him to break this news to Merrick, not knowing how a newly-bonded Watcher might react to the threat to his witch.

"Hey." Caro's brother, his voice a cheerful ribbon of brightness, called from the table. "You guys die in there, or is my cooking so good you're standing up and scarfing?"

Caro laughed. It was a tired, strained, but beautiful sound that tightened every muscle in Merrick's body, curled through him like smoke and made him remember her fingers in his hair, the brush of her skin against his scars making them burn with an intensely pleasurable agony. Remember? No, he'd been thinking of her the whole time. No matter what thought crawled through his head, she was always underneath it now.

"If either of you has a spare hand, I could do with a glass of water," she called, and Merrick automatically cast around for a glass.

"I'll bring it." Keenan's voice dropped further. "Just be careful. You're a good Watcher, I'd hate to mourn you."

"Honor," Merrick mumbled.

"Duty," Keenan said just as softly. Then, louder, "We're on our way. You need anything, Trevor?"

"Just a crowbar to separate Caro from these papers."

Merrick paced to the round oak table, a move that prompted Caro's frantic scrambling to clear places for him and Keenan. She still looked tired, but two days' worth of sleep and Power had done quite a bit to erase the dark circles under her eyes and the slight trembling in her hands. She'd bounced back remarkably well.

I shouldn't have lasted six hours, her voice echoed, and he didn't even try to squelch the flare of possessiveness that went through him. What a fine, ironic twist. He'd all but been given permission to drag Caro kicking and screaming up north, to where the Guardians kept the streets clear of the Crusade even if other Dark swarmed in.

His conscience gave one last stinging twinge as he set his plate down and lowered himself into the chair, checking to make sure his coat was still lying across the foot of her bed. It was habit, keeping track of an important piece of gear. His attention touched Caro's aura for a few moments, reassuring himself. She paused, stacking the file folders to one side, and gave him a shy smile that made her dark blue eyes light up and the persistent shadow of worry flee for just a moment. Her long earrings—a delicate cascade of tiny amber beads on thin gold wires—glittered in her ears. The vulnerable curve of her throat and the thinness of her shoulders made her look even more fragile.

That gave his conscience even more to work with. *You don't belong to Circle Lightfall. You belong to her, Merrick. You were so insistent on that fact a few days ago, weren't you? They've asked you to hide something from her, admittedly just so the Council liaison can try to make her see reason, but still. She's your witch, you owe her your loyalty. You owe her your duty, your honor, and your obedience, remember? The Watcher's watchwords. If she finds out you knew about this and didn't tell her, you'll lose her trust. She trusts you.*

He rallied as the other Watcher brought a glass of water, setting it down carefully as he leaned across the table.

"Couldn't find a crowbar," Keenan said pleasantly, and Trevor laughed. But the boy's laughter had an edge, and his eyes held a question, one the Watcher answered with a slight shrug as Caro's head was down as she shuffled through the file folders again, murmuring to herself.

Listen, Merrick told himself. *You joined the Watchers because you almost killed a Lightbringer for cash. Now is not the time to be telling yourself that you have a problem with being a total bastard. Your government tried to use you, each client you pulled the trigger for tried to use you, and the Crusade tried to use you. She's the only person in your miserable life who's tried to protect you, and you want to start second-guessing yourself and possibly let her get hurt or, God forbid, killed? Keep your mouth shut and do what you have to do, Merrick. It's your only hope.*

"Caro, quit looking through those and eat. It'll get cold, and you know how bad you feel when you let the curry get cold." Her brother reached over and firmly subtracted the files from her unresisting hands. Amazingly enough, she didn't give him a single sharp word. Instead, she looked at Merrick, and the softness in her wide, beautiful eyes was another kind of exquisite torture.

"So I've been *sleeping* for two days, and you've been pouring Power into me." She nodded a thank-you to Keenan. Then her gaze returned to Merrick's, and he had the sudden uncomfortable idea that if she kept looking at him that way he was going to spill every secret he'd ever thought of keeping. "No wonder I don't feel as backlashed as I should. You brought me out."

He dropped his eyes to his plate and couldn't for the life of him remember what he was supposed to be eating. His scars tingled with pain from her brother's weak light, but Caro's aura glowed reassuringly.

"How did you do it?" she persisted. "It's dangerous to touch a Mindhealer, physically or mentally, while they're in the space-between. How did you do it?"

"They weren't going to let him," her brother volunteered. "But—I mean, it was either that or watch you fade, and we really had . . ." He looked down at his plate, a sudden flush rising in his cheeks. "I thought we were going to lose you."

"You didn't lose me." Her smile rewarded them, but there was a glimmer of uneasiness to it. The glimmer, however, was fainter than it should have been. "I'm right here. It was a bit frightening, but it all worked out in the end."

He would never get used to their faith in the goodness of the world. Just like a Lightbringer, so bloody optimistic, everything worked out, didn't it?

Not all the time, love. Merrick's scars throbbed with heat. He knew how close it had been. He still had precious little idea of what he'd done to bring her out of wherever she'd been. He hadn't cared where she was, just that he was supposed to follow. Even if she went down into the dark dry land of death.

"Merrick?"

She was looking at him. He felt the words rising—*Caro, listen to me. There's nothing more you can do here. I'm taking you back to Saint City and standing guard at your door until I'm sure it's safe enough to let you out. That place you were in was no different than a jungle, sweetheart, and I tracked you because that's what I do. I find targets and eliminate them. Only I brought you back.*

The hard, cold animal in the bottom of Merrick's mind agreed with a snarl. She was *his*, his witch, it was that simple. Of *course* he'd brought her back. There was no other option.

He swallowed, wished he had a mouthful of food or something that would give him an excuse not to talk. "Hm?"

"How did you do it?" There was a line between her perfectly arched eyebrows. "If I knew how you did it, I might be able to help the victims. If I could pull them *out*, and get rid of the infection—"

"No," Merrick heard himself say. His voice rattled the plates on the table, made the wood groan, and Trevor looked up, his hazel eyes wide and warning. He pursed his lips and shook his head a little.

And Caro saw him.

"What?" She laid her fork down and folded her hands. Then she smiled, but it was the private smile of a schoolteacher who has suddenly caught her students out. "What's going on?"

Silence. Merrick's heart gave another guilty leap, started to pound. He stared at his plate, not even daring to steal a small glance at her out of the corner of his eye. He felt her gaze pass over him, across the table, and finally come to rest on her brother.

"Trev?" Soft, but irresistible. If she spoke like that all the time, Merrick would find himself doing anything she asked, danger or not. "Anything you want to tell me?"

"You should talk to Fran." It was the first time Merrick had ever heard the boy sound repentant and uncertain, his buoyancy gone. "She'll tell you."

"Tell me *what*?" Caro's tone was dangerously quiet. More silence. Then Merrick felt her eyes come to rest on him. "Merrick?"

He'd thought he was prepared for anything, even for this. *Oh, Christ. How can I lie to her? I can't.* He managed to look up, met her eyes, and the suspicion he saw there only sharpened the knife in his chest. *Say something, Merrick. Something, anything.* "The victims are all dead, Caro."

Her eyes darkened even further. "There's sure to be more. We don't know what the Crusade's plan is, just that they're involved somehow. They might be . . . Merrick? You're going to break the plate if you keep stabbing it with your fork like that. Trevor, where's your milk? Keenan, would you like something to drink?"

The change in tempo was so abrupt he almost opened his mouth and spilled everything. But her eyes passed away from him. She seemed to dismiss her own suspicion and his objection at the same time. He was grateful for that, but Trevor suddenly looked far more apprehensive. His aura abruptly turned the acrid lemon-yellow of worry even as Keenan shook his head, staring at his plate.

"No ma'am." The younger Watcher seemed to be pulling into himself, as if preparing for an explosion.

She took a bite, closed her eyes briefly in appreciation, and smiled at her brother. But her eyes were suspiciously bright and far too sharp for Merrick's liking. "Trevor? Your milk. You need it."

"I'm not four years old, Caro." But he got up, his chair scraping against the laminate flooring, and headed for the kitchenette. His back was tight under his T-shirt, his belt—a loop of chain, of all things—glinting in the warm light from the overhead fixtures.

"Merrick? Want to tell me what's going on?" Again, that soft irresistible tone. Her hair, drying, lay in gold-streaked waves against her shoulders and made his fingers tingle with the need to touch her again.

Good God, she was relentless. "I don't know much," he hedged. "The Council liaison wants to see you. If I gave you what I had, it would just muddy the issue."

She examined him for a long moment, long enough that he almost started to sweat. *Forgive me, love, I'm doing the best I know how. I can't lie to you, but I don't want to try to convince you to stay under cover while we go after the Crusade and make them wish they had never been born.*

"All right. I'll be a good little girl. All of them are dead?" The sudden sadness in her voice was almost too much to stand.

He nodded. *Don't worry. I'm going to make sure you don't end up the same way.*

"And Fran wants to talk to me." She searched his face, and he was glad he'd shaken his hair down habitually. His scars burned with shame and Dark-laced pain.

Another nod. His neck was too tight, and the movement felt uncoordinated.

Caro didn't say another word, but applied herself to her lunch. The silence turned impenetrable. Her brother came back, and by the time his plate was clean he looked miserable. Keenan was tense too, trying like hell to make himself invisible without thickening his glamour, and Merrick was beginning to feel a little uneasy. He had never before thought that a Lightbringer's silence could feel so much like a punishment. Caro's quiet seemed designed to accentuate the guilty way his heart was pounding.

Caro vanished into the bathroom once the meal was over, and Merrick caught Keenan's eye.

The younger Watcher shrugged, and Merrick cursed inwardly as he carried the plates into the kitchenette.

He didn't like the looks of this.

* * * *

Caro shooed her brother out gently but inexorably. "I'll see Fran in an hour or so, after I've finished my research. Thank you for lunch, you make the most wonderful things. No, Trev, I mean it. I'll be just fine. Merrick's here. We get along just splendidly. Go on, now, tell Fran I'll be along. No, no, I'll be okay."

After about ten minutes, Trevor gave up, leaving Merrick facing a witch whose indigo eyes were beginning to glow dangerously.

Still, she didn't quiz him. Instead, she paced for one of the chairs in front of the fireplace, the one that held her canvas bag. The skirt she wore made a soft, sweet sound as she moved, barefoot and with her hair tangling softly and streaked with gold. She looked more like a witch than her usual polished, professional veneer would have him believe was possible. Digging in the bag for a moment brought out her amber necklace and the slim, shallow jade bowl. She fastened and dropped the necklace down her shirt again before carrying the bowl into the kitchen, her footfalls still soft when the carpet changed to laminate underfoot.

I don't like the looks of this. Merrick leaned against the wall and made himself a statue, so still he felt his lungs cry out for breath.

Caro brought the jade bowl and set it carefully on the carpeted floor. "Lock the door, please, Merrick. You can wait outside if you want to."

Was that an order, or just telling me I can? He decided to err on the side of misinterpretation and locked the door, moving slowly just in case she decided to notice him further. She was stalking around the room, trailed by nothing more than green tea perfume and the burned candle-wax smell of— what was it? Anger? He hoped not. The food he'd managed to eat turned into a cold lump in his stomach. If he had to sit through another long silence like the one Caro had subjected them all to, he might well swear off food altogether.

She tied her hair back with an elastic band. Opening her canvas bag again, she brought out a thick, white candle and a little Ziploc bag full of something dried, as well as a small brass incense burner. This being a safehouse, she found a charcoal tab and candleholder in the kitchen, and obviously settled down to work some magick.

She shouldn't be doing this, she might get a serious case of backlash. Is she insane? What's she doing?

"Open the window a little, will you, please?" Her voice was careful and neutral, but the bald edge of anger was beneath it. He'd miscalculated. "And when you're done, you can come over here and sit down. I won't bite."

"Yes ma'am." He moved to obey, cursing himself. What was she about to do now? She wasn't leaving the safehouse, and she wasn't in any *obvious* danger; but how was he going to stop her?

"It's not *mum*. It's *Caro*." Now she sounded arch. "While you're at it, you can tell me what you know. I'm going to find out anyway, so you might as well make it easy on yourself."

He stole a glance at her. She sat cross-legged on the blue carpet, the bowl in front of her and her quick fingers sinking the candle into its holder and setting it upright. With her hair pulled back but still wildly curling and her mouth just slightly pursed, she looked like a pre-Raphaelite Ophelia, her skirt pooling on the floor around her. Her aura ran with golden pinwheels, a glow that should have hurt him. He didn't deserve to touch this beautiful woman. She was far braver than any Watcher. A Watcher had the benefit of weapons and predatory instincts. She only had her faith in the inherent goodness of the world to protect her.

And her Watcher. That had to be worth something, didn't it?

Conscience struggled with obedience, both of them on the same side in some ways. It was the original no-win situation.

"You won't listen." He cringed. *Did that really come out of my mouth? Good one, Merrick. Dammit, you've held your tongue in worse places than this, just shut up!*

He opened the window slightly, smelled the chill of winter rain. The room looked in on the commons and the gardens, drenched green cut with wet supple stone paths. The quivering in the wards reminded him that this room had already been broken into once by a new Seeker, incubated in a helpless victim. The other Lightbringer infected with the *thing* had died, even with a safehouse full of Lightbringers seeking to heal her.

"I'll listen," she said quietly. "*Please*, Merrick."

He stared unseeing out the window. *Duty. Honor. Obedience. I am a Watcher. I protect, I defend—do I even protect her from herself?*

Christ. I've been infected with that damn honor complex. That was the trouble with being a Watcher—you ended up believing in it, holding yourself to a standard bound to cause you grief. "The Crusade's found another partner to play with. They're trying to breed their own version of Watchers, probably since zombies aren't enough anymore. They want the things immune to Lightbringer magick, so they picked psychics and a Lightbringer to test-incubate them. That's all I know." His hands curled into fists. "I'm warning you, Caro. If you try to go running off to get yourself in trouble, I'll do what I have to." *Even if it makes you hate me.*

Silence. He felt more than heard the snap and sudden intense flare of Power as a candle flame guttered into life. Then the charcoal began to spark, the saltpeter in it igniting, and he smelled something familiar.

Mugwort. She was burning dried mugwort.

He whirled away from the window, finding his witch cross-legged on the floor, her eyes closed, the charcoal burning in the incense holder and a pile of dried mugwort fuming on top of it. The candle was white, and the sparkle of Power shimmering around it told him she'd done this before.

"What the bloody hell are you *doing*?" He tried not to sound flabbergasted.

"I brought something out of the Watcher. Asher," she said calmly, her eyes closed. A tendril of golden hair fell in her face. "A Mindhealer can do that, especially if the patient is unable to face whatever traumatized him or her. The best way to deal with it is to scry what happened so you know how to help the patient."

"Caro." The table in the small dining space rattled, the Cezanne print over the fireplace moved uneasily against the wall. *Good gods above. Why does she have to find the worst, absolutely most dangerous thing to do wherever she is?* "You're courting backlash. And if the Watcher couldn't face it—"

"Are you going to come over here and anchor me, or are you going to stand there and glare?" She took a deep lungful of the smoke, it was a time-honored way to sharpen the psychic senses and induce clairvoyance. Unfortunately, its use could also tip a witch into backlash by tempting her to go too far, especially when she had already exerted herself. Caro needed a few days of rest before she tried anything this difficult.

Merrick tipped his head back and felt his scars burn as his jaw worked. What was it about this witch that could drive him to the very brink of his control? He had never in all his life been so tempted to grab a woman and *shake* her.

When he was sure he could speak without snarling, he filled his lungs and tried one last time. "Caro, this is dangerous.

Please, wait. Just a couple of days, until you're stronger."

"I can't *wait*, someone else may be attacked," she returned, in that soft inflexible voice. "I'm here in the safehouse. Nothing's going to happen to me. That's what you wanted— me locked up inside the safehouse all safe and sound, right? The longer I hold onto this, the more concentrated the jolt will be when I finally scry it. This is the less dangerous route. And if you're anchoring me, you'll be able to pull me back, won't you? You did last time."

You don't bloody well understand. You almost died, Caro. And I almost died with you. I thought I was ready to die, but I know I'm not ready to lose you.

But it was too late. He could feel the Power trembling around her, swirling, readying itself; a Lightbringer magick that should have run hot acid into his marrow. Instead, it wrapped around him with all the soothing comfort of a warm blanket.

He found himself pacing across the room, his boots making no sound against the carpet. Merrick sank down behind her, breathing in the fumes of burning mugwort. Spice, green tea, and the smoke of incense. He laid his hands flat against her supple sweater-covered back. "I'll anchor you." His voice sounded harsh even to himself. "Just . . . be careful." *And if I feel the slightest twinge, I'm going to drag you back.*

It was too late. She had fallen into a trance, her aura dilating, golden pinwheels racing through its glow. Merrick watched as the pinwheels covered his own hands, sliding through the crimson-black blaze that covered a Watcher, and felt a slow creeping fire of velvet pleasure slide up his veins to his shoulder. *Do other Watchers bonded to Mindhealers feel this?* The borders of his mind meshed with hers, the link suddenly full-blown and raw. He caught a flash of fading anger before the schooled tranquility of magick folded over her.

He felt her attention curve forward, the water in the jade bowl soft and receptive, touched faintly with the salt she'd sprinkled to purify it. Then the *shift*, as if something foreign had been introduced, a ball she juggled from mental hand to mental hand with a sure, deft touch. *What the hell is that?*

Something she'd taken, she said. From the Watcher. Something even a Watcher wasn't able to face? Or something she didn't know if the Watcher would survive to tell?

I don't like this. Helpless, Merrick's fingers tensed against her back. He felt the fragility of her spine, the muscle over her ribs, her bones so delicate under his broad, callused hands. *She just woke up. Why is she doing this?*

She stiffened, the water in the jade bowl rippling. Merrick felt it again, the complex transferal of Power. Caro's touch was light and definite, a memory that wasn't hers rippling and unfolding in the water before her, tiny figures moving through a dark alley, voices heard in another room . . .

Merrick's eyes drifted closed. He *heard*.

"—kill them."

"Christ is our glory, God smiles upon our work."

"The witch?"

"Eliminated. She might be able to affect the process. It should be triggered as they try to heal this abomination."

"They will suspect."

"They may suspect all they like. We will still overpower them, with God's grace."

"Here. The picture—."

Burst of static like a radio dial twisted to the blank space between stations. Maddening, the bursts of words, coming too quickly to make sense.

"Success. All it requires . . ."

'But . . . true . . . no . . ."

" . . . woman . . ."

Then Caro broke away and slumped, shaking, against his hands as the smoke swirled into almost recognizable patterns. The smell of burned candle-wax brushed the air under the herbal rush of mugwort; the candle had snuffed itself and water trembled in the jade bowl. Shudders poured through her, peaked, were driven back as heat rushed through Merrick's palms, an instinctive burst of Power to bring her out of shock and keep her warm.

He had to catch her as she slumped again, and found himself pulling her onto his lap. It was the only way to make sure she didn't fall over and hit the floor, but he still felt a guilty twinge. "Caro?"

"I'm all right," she murmured, in the sleepy, slurred tones of a witch in shock. He sent another heatflush through her, this one less gentle and more powerful, watching it explode through her suddenly thinning aura. "Just—whoa. Wow."

"Are you all right, then?" He was suddenly, critically, aware of the difference between his voice and hers. Even mumbling, her voice was beautiful, a soft restful bell; his was inordinately harsh and crisp. "Talk to me, Caro."

"Fine." She settled against him, curled into his lap with her head on his shoulder, and Merrick swallowed dryly. *I'm not made of stone, I can't—it's been a rough patch for us all. Just let her get her bearings. Stay under control.* "I should go . . . talk to—" She sighed, closing her eyes.

"Stay with me." He sent another slamming tingle of heat through her, relieved when her eyes drifted open and she gave him an irritated glance.

"I'm fine." Her aura thinned out further, and a bright red trickle of blood slid down her upper lip. Her nose was bleeding again. He pressed his palm to her cheek, the touch of her skin sending a shock of liquid fire up his arm. Her eyes rolled back into her head and her aura drained almost to transparency.

"Caro!" Another heatflush, but this one did no good, and his chest began to ache. It was a preliminary, a warning. He'd felt this pain before. Pain like a tearing spike through his ribs. Pain like half of him being torn away. "*Caro!*"

She didn't answer. She was sliding into shock, and the heatflushes weren't working. An aura force wouldn't work either. It would just jolt her body with the equivalent of several cups of coffee and overload her, sending her paradoxically further into shock.

Christ. Dear gods. No, please, no.

He found himself on his feet, Caro cradled in his arms. Her hair fluttered as he dumped her on the bed. His coat slid off the end of the bed, little bits of metal gear inside clanking as it hit the floor. She was in shock, had stretched herself too far, and now he was going to have to bring her out the traditional way.

Skin on skin.

The gods are kinder to me than I deserve, he thought, and unbuckled his weapons harness.

Thirteen

She was cold, so cold. Her fingers were numb, and she felt tingling prickles flooding her arms and ice dragging behind them. Lassitude swamped her, weighted her entire body, heavy and sluggish, going numb, going down, sinking.

Drowning. Water closing over her head. Falling. Going down into darkness, into a softness that was icy and yet comforting, no more struggle, no more striving, no more pain.

Knowledge beat under her skin—she had to wake up. She had to warn Fran. She had to . . .

What? What did she have to tell Fran? It was too hard. She couldn't care. Her skin was made of lead. She felt someone's hand against the side of her face, hot as a live brand, scorching so badly she cried out, weakly. Someone's voice, ragged and pleading.

Heat, painful and stabbing, tore against her chest. It scorched through the cotton wool surrounding her, the foggy sense of something not quite right. Sudden tearing, as if her sweater had stuck to her skin and was being ripped off an inch at a time. She heard a muttered curse, cloth moving—sheets? Clothes? What was happening?

More warmth, stealing painfully into her arms and legs, stabbing needles as if the nerves were waking back up. *Did my entire body fall asleep? What happened?*

"Caro," he whispered into her hair. "Caroline."

Her head hurt, with a fuzzy far-off pain that intensified, as if demonic Christmas elves were pounding against the inside of her skull, sending waves of twisting, piercing needles down her neck, down her back, up her arms from her fingers, up her legs from her toes. She almost convulsed, the pain was that bad. It crested, thousands of tiny electrified pins stabbing into her skin, retreating, then stabbing and shocking her again.

The pains receded, bit by bit. Warmth crept after, stole in, she was beginning to feel more like flesh than insensate stone now. Beginning to wake up from the slow, creeping languidness of shock. Warm hardness against her, a different texture than cloth, an insistent probing against the outside of her hip. Felt familiar. Where had she felt this before?

The last time I felt this warm, I was in bed and—

Her eyes flew open and saw the white ceiling with its

brilliant reflective speckles embedded in the paint. Even the thin layer of paint on the walls and ceiling had a protection laid over it, and she wearily wondered what it was like to live with no idea of danger, no need for a Watcher to boss you around or stay so harmfully, constantly alert. Caro found herself on her back, her bones aching as the shaking pain of shock receded in fits and starts, flushed out by Power and the unrelenting drenching warmth that penetrated down to her aching bones, sealing her back in her body. Warmth coming from the body that curved against hers, his arm laid over her, his aura melded tightly to hers.

Merrick lay next to her, his eyes closed, rainy afternoon light picking out the fine charcoal fans of his eyelashes, the flush along the edges of his scars. The shape of his lips, his mouth set and grim.

And he was completely, utterly unclothed.

So, for that matter, was she. Well, except for her amber necklace, lying warm and forgiving against her breastbone.

Shock. I went into shock, and he had to bring me out. Oh, dear gods.

Knowing this was the traditional way of bringing a witch out of the dangerous languor of shock and having it applied to *her* were two very, very different things. Nowadays, Watchers didn't use this method unless they were bonded, or unless the situation was an extreme emergency. The heatflush and aura force usually worked, especially since the Watchers had grown more skilled and powerful at applying them. A witch had to be nearly dead and in extreme peril before a Watcher would try skin-on-skin.

Witches were generally very easy in their bodies, especially those raised by Circle Lightfall—but still. A flush began at her collarbone and crept up to stain her cheeks. She lay unmoving, heat pulsing on her face, and thought two different things.

First, *I'm warm. I haven't felt this warm and safe since . . . oh, since that affair with the poet. Even then I didn't feel this safe.*

And second, *He's beautiful. He's really, really beautiful, and he's my Watcher. Mine.*

And judging by the insistent poking against her hip, he was more than interested in her. She could *feel*, like a haze over hot pavement, the intensity of the pleasure striking home through his nervous system. No wonder she'd all but drowned in it when he'd kissed her. They were *linked*. Somehow, pulling her out of the space-between had tied him to her on a psychic level as well as a physical one, made her sensitive to him. Mindhealers were exquisitely sensitive to Watchers anyway, but she had never thought a Watcher felt *this*. It was a subject of whispered excitement among teenage witches, what exactly a Watcher felt when the right witch touched him. Now Caro knew those hurried, giggling conferences really had no way of approaching the truth. It was a sheer miracle he managed to stay so impassive, if *that* was what he was feeling.

She moved slightly, bumping her hip against him, and almost gasped at the flood of sensation that caused. His face didn't move. *Damn.*

"Merrick?" The whisper died in her throat. She could feel the fine humming voltage of arousal going through him. He was actually sweating. He smelled really good, male with the darker note of leather over the top of it—clean and healthy, with a slight spice of city night and cold wind and the citrus note that followed him around. It was a comforting scent, she decided, and snuggled a bit closer to him. His throat worked as he swallowed, but he didn't move.

Why won't he look at me? I haven't been nice to him, true. Maybe he doesn't like feeling this way. He doesn't have any control over it; it might scare him.

The thought of Merrick being scared of *anything* made a laugh catch in her throat. She lifted her left hand, sliding the covers away. He'd obviously stripped her down and gotten her into the bed, then set about warming her up. Which had succeeded very nicely.

Now Caro had to figure out what to do with this infuriatingly British hunk of Watcher in her bed.

He didn't move when she reached across to brush his hair back. "Merrick?" Her breath caught, saying his name. "Hey, you alive in there?"

She could feel that he was most *definitely* alive. Her own pulse was skyrocketing. It had been a long time, as the saying went, and a witch had needs.

But he's a Watcher. He doesn't have any control over it. Caro, for God's sake, you have to be the responsible one, and you have to remember—

Caro clapped a lid on the voice of her conscience, something she had no idea, until that very moment, she could do. Then, decisively, she touched Merrick's unscarred cheek with her fingertips, slowly and soft. Her arm felt heavy, not obeying like it usually did. She would be a little slow until her body shook off the lingering effects of shock.

It could have killed her. That deep languor had been her bodily systems shutting down one by one, literally losing the will to live. Like hypothermia, the dangerous sleep of a woman caught in a snowstorm. She could have *died*.

His eyes drifted open, caught hers, and Caro lost her breath. She had never noticed before how his bleached, intense irises had a thin darker border, or how they seemed to speak with a single glance. She'd never gotten close enough to see that two of the scars extended up under his hair, or that his stubble was charcoal like his eyelashes, and that despite the scarring, and maybe because of it, he was extremely attractive. He would have been too pretty before. Now he looked beautiful in the way anything complex and deadly was beautiful, the pattern of scales on a cobra's back or the rigging of a clipper ship.

"You were in shock," he said, his voice husky, uncertain. "I'm sorry."

The immediate apology hurt her, actually physically *hurt,* like someone squeezing her heart in bony fingers. Caro's throat was dry, but she touched his bare shoulder, her fingers meeting muscle hard as tile under skin with a different texture than her own. Then her arm tensed, and she struggled slowly onto her side, facing him, deliberately sliding her leg up over his hip.

Let's see you get out of this, she thought, holding his eyes, her heart skipping beats, as if it was going to throw itself out of her chest and beat in two places at once. She barely managed to get in enough breath to talk. "Don't be sorry," she whispered. Her necklace slid against her skin, fell down toward the pillow. "You don't have to be sorry anymore."

The color drained from his face, leaving his scars vivid stripes against his flesh. She could see more, across his shoulder and spilling down his chest, whatever it was had clawed him relentlessly. Marked him. She tucked her heavy right arm under her head and let her fingers roam in a gentle looping pattern across his shoulder, feeling the deltoid muscle under the skin, the edge of his clavicle, touching the vulnerable hollow in his unshaven throat where the pulse beat. He *was* shaking. It didn't matter because she was too. Whether it was the aftermath of shock or just the insistent throbbing low in her belly, she couldn't tell and didn't care. Now she felt the hard tip of his phallus against the softness of her inner thigh, and she wondered just what she was going to have to do to get him a little more interested in using it.

"Merrick?" The way he was staring at her made her begin to wonder if he was trying to figure out a polite way to tell her he wasn't interested. After all, she'd been sharp and rude to him, and insisted she was going to get rid of him, not to mention she'd run him all over the safehouse going from one crisis to the next and—

He muttered something that definitely wasn't polite to say in front of a lady, skimming his right hand up her arm and curving it around her nape. Then he pulled her forward gently, his skin scorching hers, and their mouths met again.

This wasn't a nice kiss, or a soft one. He kissed her as if he wanted to drown in her, as if he wanted to drink her breath and her in the same inhale. And he obviously didn't believe in foreplay either, because it was only a short time before Caro locked her ankles together at the small of his back and closed her eyes, feeling muscle flex in his back as he drove his body into hers. Fire crackled between her nerves, and she sank into the pleasure he felt, a feedback loop of her skin on his, tension released, skidding across the surface of a dark snarling reality before crisis took him and his entire body, stiffening, seemed to explode. She held him, comforting, his face buried against her throat, and felt the fringes of the borderland between their minds unravel, binding together.

The Watchers know all about bonding, but nobody ever tells the witches we're just as bound.

He kissed her throat, his stubble rasping against her skin, and murmured her name in a desperate, broken voice. The afternoon light had taken on a different cast—winter sunlight sliding into darkness. Night was falling.

Merrick's mouth found hers again, and Caro lost herself in the backlash of his pleasure. It was the absolute antithesis to the grinding pain of having a *tanak* welded into his body.

Does he really even like me, or is it just the fact that it feels good?

"Christ," he whispered against her mouth, his accent making the word sharper, crisper. "Caroline."

"Merrick," she whispered back. He kissed her cheek, her chin, bracing himself on his elbows.

"Are you all right?" It was touching, actually, the concern in his voice.

Caro nodded, her eyes still closed. "Fine."

He slid away, off to the side, reluctantly. Took her in his arms. His skin was feverish-warm against hers, a few moments of rearranging ended up with her head on his scarred shoulder, exhaustion weighing her body down. She had to think, had to remember something very important—whatever she'd brought out of the other Watcher and seen in the trembling water of the jade bowl was rising through the layers of shock-draped fuzz in her mind. Now she felt like she *could* think, like she was finally in a place where she had a few moments to rest and consider everything. Safe.

She felt safe.

Caro yawned, settling herself against him. He was warm, and he stroked her hair gently, smoothing down the rebellious mass. He started to speak, once or twice, ended up just shaking his head. She could hear his hair rasping against the pillow.

Her sense of duty returned. "I have to go talk to Fran," she said, softly, her cheek pressed against his shoulder, sweat-damp hair tangling against her neck and over his arm. "Once I remember what I brought out. I feel a little strange."

"Mh." It was a companionable sound, showing he heard her. "Just rest, love."

There was another question that needed to be answered, first. "—feeling for real?" She finished her sentence through a yawn that threatened to let her tonsils out.

"What?"

"I said, how does a Watcher know what he's feeling is real? How does he *know* . . ." It was getting more and more difficult to talk. She was tired, a clean sleepiness instead of the dragging gray cloud of shock. *Next time I'll insist on a little foreplay,* she thought, and felt a twinge from her buried conscience.

If there was a next time.

Merrick seemed to consider this question. Then he sighed. "I have never met a woman I felt more like shaking some sense into." His fingers wound into her hair, tightening. "We know, Caro. We have to. You're my witch, and there's no way you're getting rid of me. Just go to sleep." A pause while he untangled his fingers, stroked her temple soothingly. "You're the only thing in this goddamn world worth fighting for." This time his tone was private, as if he was talking to himself. "So no more heroics, witch. You hear me?"

Caro didn't reply. She was, after all, falling asleep.

* * * *

She woke up confused, because the entire safehouse rocked on its foundations. Merrick swore, already moving, untangling himself gently from her and disappearing from the bed's warm cocoon. Another thumping crash, and Caro pushed herself up on her elbows, blinking against the darkness. Night, again. And something was happening, because—

A third thump, faraway but still rattling the Cezanne print against the wall. She flinched, *feeling* the impact against the safehouse shields, the ripple of fear and confusion spreading through the halls. And the sudden intense swirl of readiness and fury that was the Watchers. "What's going on?"

Merrick shrugged into his coat. "Don't know yet. Stay put." He seemed almost to flicker through space as he strode for the window, eerily silent, the sword hilt poking above his right shoulder and the faint gleam from his eyes barely visible.

Caro struggled out of the bed, taking the sheet with her. She wrapped it around herself as she started looking for her clothes. She found her sweater on the floor and was casting around for her skirt by the time she heard Merrick make a small sound of annoyance. "Thought I told you to stay there."

She found her skirt. "With an attack this big, there's going to be a lot of frightened witches in the infirmary and the nursery. Better go see what I can do to calm them down. And the *last* time we heard anything like this, something broke my window. This may not be the safest place to be." She pulled her skirt up over her hips and ran her fingers back through her tangled hair with a grimace. "Anyway, I don't like cowering in a bed while something bad—"

Another shuddering, jolting impact. Caro winced. Merrick suddenly went still, his eyes flaming brilliant green under the darkness of his hair. "Bloody hell," he whispered. "Get your shoes and a coat, Caro. Quickly."

"What is it?" she whispered back, frozen in place.

"Machine gun fire." Now he sounded like himself, cool and ironic. "Sounds like the north wing, the Watcher dormitories maybe. They can handle it, but best to be prepared."

Caro swallowed dryly. She felt sticky and sore in some very tender places, but her head was clear. She remembered now, without the tolling of shock inside her head. "I've got to find Fran." Her heart suddenly pounded thinly against the wall of her chest. "Merrick?"

He had gone still, looking out the window. "Get your shoes, love. Please."

Mechanically, she moved to obey. A pair of sandals were in the closet by the door to the hall. She slipped them on, suddenly hoping she wouldn't have to leave the safehouse. These strappy little numbers looked great, but they wouldn't hold up to the chill outside. *I haven't worn proper shoes or clothes for two days, just jeans and T-shirts. I feel like a slob.* "Why my shoes? What's going on?"

He shrugged, a fluid catlike movement, and reached up for his sword hilt. "There's one of those things down in the garden, Caro." His voice was calm and thoughtful, and she felt a curling, sweet heat low and deep in her belly. *It shouldn't be legal for him to sound that good. I was never one for men with accents, but he could change all that.* "It looks like it's looking for someone. Best to have your shoes just in case."

The steel sang free, glinting in the faint glow from the nightlight in the bathroom, and his aura turned hard and hurtful, Power rising as combat-readiness folded around him. "Grab a coat, too, love. Don't want you catching a chill."

A chill? One of those things *is down there in the goddamn garden, and he doesn't want me to catch a chill?* She had to strangle the urge to laugh. "What else is down there?"

She reached up blindly, found a long sweater-coat with a tie belt. *My hair. I probably look hideous, why am I worrying about my hair at a time like this? Get a grip, Caro!* "Trev," she heard herself say breathlessly. "We have to find Trev."

"He's got a Watcher." The sword blade finished a neat half-circle and ended up poised and slanting down, the hilt held loosely and professionally, ready to be brought up, acquire momentum, and slash across anything Dark, banishing with steel. "Stay there, Caro."

I don't want to. She wanted to cross to the window, to see with her own eyes the thing in the garden. Shivers trickled up her back. Merrick took two steps away from the window, utterly silent. His silence became almost a living thing, heavy liquid in the air. Caro heard her own breathing, insistent against that thick hush.

"It's down there in the garden?" *How utterly typical. I sound scared to death.*

What a coincidence. I am scared to death.

He nodded, the movement barely visible. "Stay back," he mouthed, a breath of sound in the vast awful quiet seeming to spread from him in waves. "Don't worry."

Of all the absurdities, that was surely the worst. Caro shivered, and another massive impact shook the safehouse. *What are they doing? Who is it? The Crusade? I've never heard of them attacking like this, not for decades, not since the twenties and the Dark War.*

The window shattered inward again, sharp glass flying silver-deadly. Caro screamed, a pointless sound, cowering back between the closet and the door to the hall. Merrick moved, engaging the low hulking shape with a fatal whistling sound as steel clove air. Crimson light flamed. *He's drawn his knives, or one knife, at least.* Her knees gave and she spilled down to the floor, her back sliding against the wall. Another thudding impact, the wall disintegrating around the window.

Oh, gods, there's TWO of them! The stench, sudden and intense, coated the back of her throat and made her eyes prickle. Caro struggled to get to her feet, her head suddenly pounding with pain, iron spikes driven through her temples and her stomach. Sulfur, bitter almonds, and blood—the smell of the Crusade. Cold, wet, rainy air billowed into the room as Merrick half-turned, knife describing a crimson arc, and one of the things let out a shattering wail. Dappled red light from the knifeblade smashed against the walls.

"Merrick—" It was a stunned whisper. Wet warmth trickled down her upper lip—another nosebleed, dammit. She tried again to make it to her feet, spilled back down to the floor. Carpet rasped against her skirt. It was hard to breathe with that stench painting the air. She coughed weakly and felt icy tingling start in her fingers. One of the creatures let out another shattering howl and thumped onto the floor, lifeless. The other tried to lunge past Merrick. He moved almost too quickly to be seen, the light from his knife glittering off his upraised sword, his feet soundless as he drove it back, feinting, reversing with sweet and natural grace to carve down with the bright length of metal.

Had she ever thought him vulnerable?

Please don't let him be hurt, she prayed, unaware of thinking it. Tried one last time to make it to her feet just as the second Seeker howled, Merrick ripping his blade free and stabbing down with the knife. Crimson light blazed and it howled again, the sound scraping the inside of her head. She slumped against the wall on her knees, her hands clamped uselessly to her ears. *Oh, God. Oh gods—*

Merrick backed up, a quick light shuffle. "Caro?"

Between him and the window, the two sludgy lumps of psychic rot splayed on the floor, soaking into the carpet, scorching as they decayed.

"Merrick," she whispered. "Is it—"

She meant to ask if it was over, stopped as soon as she realized the utter inanity of the question. It would *never* be over, not as long as she lived.

"Just be still, love. Everything's all right." He sounded completely certain, and Caro felt ridiculously comforted. He wouldn't lie to her.

He favored one shoulder, but he didn't put his sword away. Instead, the knife blurred back into its sheath, the crimson light blinking out. She heard the small definite click of a hammer being drawn back. So he'd taken out a gun. Put away his knife and taken out a *gun.* Why?

It meant there was something else out there.

Caro pushed herself to her feet by the simple expedient of mentally repeating every cussword she knew while shoving herself upright. She swiped at the blood trickling from her nose with the back of her hand. "What is it?" Her choked whisper sounded very loud.

"Just stay right where you are and be quiet." He moved back another step, another. Soundless. Then he did a strange thing. He knelt down, crouching. Her pupils dilated and she could see the outline of the gun raised in his left hand, the sword held away from his body and almost parallel to the floor. He looked like he was gathering himself.

But for what? What's out there? I'm on the third story, what can—

Then it happened. A shape filled the hole torn in the wall—no, not *filled*, but simply appeared, the shape of a human creature in a long dark coat. And Merrick leapt, smashing into it as Caro screamed again, pointlessly, and the door to the hall burst open, other Watchers flooding through as Merrick vanished out the window and the sharp clatter of gunfire followed him down.

Fourteen

Falling. Wind in his hair, scars alight with fire, the burrowing shock of agonized pain as his abused body screamed, and the man, whoever he was, hit him again.

Goddamn, he's quick.

Impact. All breath driven from lungs, knocked sprawling, wet earth torn as he rolled, taking care not to hurt himself with his own bloody sword. His opponent was quick, inhumanly fast, with the kind of speed one usually saw only in the Dark. Or in a Watcher.

Gained his feet, but his opponent was on him, gun skittering away, the tearing pain as steel tore through his body. A knifeblade, slid in between the ribs and twisted with inhuman strength, the *tanak* roaring in Merrick's bones.

He hadn't wanted Caro to see how hurt he was, blood dripping from the claw marks on his left leg, ribs broken, head bleeding from a stray strike. Nor had he wanted her to come anywhere *near* the window, not after what he'd seen—the low hulking shapes of two Seekers. The hell-dogs had strained at invisible cords while a figure too tall and graceful to be a Live Knight or zombie and without the white cross blazon of a Bishop followed them with a precise measured step, its aura spreading a black bruise on the face of night.

Cold air. Pain singing along every nerve. Heart clenching in sudden agonized overload, the *tanak* dragging on all available Power and snapping his ribs back out, messily fusing them together, spiking his bloodstream with adrenaline, and sealing the wound as his opponent, with a final vicious twist, tore the knife free. A momentary burning—*you bastard, you have a poisoned blade*—and Merrick heard a welcome sound—boots hitting the ground behind him and the psychic roar of enraged Watchers.

They moved in on the opponent in a loose semicircle, one of them grabbing Merrick's shoulder and dragging him back, sending a tide of Dark-laced Power down his body. It flushed the last burning remnants of poison out and sealed some of the messier wounds. The sound of steel being drawn from oiled sheaths was a low ominous hissing.

Night bloomed and breathed around the Watchers as the ends of the semicircle bowed in and joined, becoming a ring around Merrick's opponent, who stood with his long glittering knives out, his bruised aura surrounded by the crimson-black glows of the Watchers. They pressed forward, and the man who moved like nothing human turned in a slow circle, taking this in. But his knives didn't lower; instead, they lifted a few fractions, defiant. Merrick, his eyes adapted to the soft shimmer of the lamps set on either side of the stone paths winding through the gardens, saw his face. His lips were moving slightly.

Crusade. The word jolted him even as recognition did. *Gods above, they've done it. They've created a Watcher.*

The Watchers struck, a collective force of Dark energy meant to rip their prey apart. Merrick started forward, but Keenan's hand closed around his upper arm. So it was the younger Watcher who had picked him up. "No, Merrick. Let them." His eyes glowed and his face was coated with the blackness of blood, wetly gleaming in the uncertain light. "This is the fifth one we've caught."

Crackling force hummed in the air and the enemy collapsed, twitching, blood exploding from his mouth and nose in a coughing rush. He made a low inarticulate sound of agony, and Merrick's heart chilled with delight inside its cage of ribs. *You would have killed her.* For just a moment the thought of Caro's mouth, her soft sigh, and the feel of her skin drove his anger down. But it returned, circling like a shark, and he started forward again, intent on adding his own force to the circle of Watchers and witnessing the death of this *thing* that would have harmed his witch.

Keenan dragged him back again. "No, Watcher. Let it be."

"*Stop it!*" A familiar voice. Caro's voice, bouncing back from the walls of the safehouse enclosing the garden. "Stop! You're killing him!"

That's the idea, love. Merrick's entire body gave one galvanic soaring leap of pain. The Watchers didn't move, the crackling rush of Power battering the body on the ground. The wind rose, swirling as the enemy convulsed again, screaming. It was the scream of a rabbit caught in a trap.

"*Stop it!*" Footsteps. How had she gotten down from the window? He'd left her safely in her room. Just like her to come running out. "Dammit, I said *stop!*"

Not this time. Savage joy rose in Merrick. He pushed it down and shook free of Keenan's well-meaning grasp.

Caro stumbled over wet grass, more Watchers behind her. One of them must have brought her down. *Better have done it carefully, if she's bruised I'll take it out of someone's hide.* The cold, matter-of-fact bloodlust in the thought didn't frighten him, but he did feel a twinge of . . . what? Concern? A Watcher did not attack other Watchers.

Christ, I'm even dangerous to my own side right now.

Then Caro was beside him, her hair tangling down her shoulders, alive with light in the middle of this cold, rainy night. For the first time, Merrick noticed the rain flirting down, drifting on the cold wind that smelled like the not too distant sea, freighted with salt. He reached out, caught her, and pulled her back against him. The jolt of furious agonizing pleasure from her bare hands reaching up to grab at his was even stronger, if that was possible, scoring into wounds he hadn't even noticed receiving. *Two of them. I held off two Seekers and this— what the bloody hell* is *it? Who is it?*

"Stop!" Caro's voice broke. Merrick clapped his hand over her mouth. He didn't want to. He wanted to stopper her mouth in an entirely different way. He'd been in her bed. She'd allowed him close enough to touch her, close enough to taste, close enough to—

She struggled, he held her back. This enemy was a new quantity. They didn't know what he was capable of. No Lightbringer was getting close until the Watchers were *sure* it was safe. And even then, Merrick wasn't convinced he would be able to let go of her.

The feel of her drawn back against him, her softness twisting as she fought to break free, sent a sharp pang through him. He understood more about the Dark than he wanted to in that one single moment. He wanted to drag her away, find a quiet corner, and prove to himself she was unharmed in the oldest of ways, wanted to touch her and reassure himself. Wanted to catch her breath in his mouth and make her gasp and cry out. Wanted to pull her into him until the light that spilled from her skin was *his*, a lamp to light him back from the darkness of his own fractured soul.

The pressure snapped. The enemy lay broken and useless in the middle of the circle of Watchers, pushed into the damp earth. A thin coil of black smoke rose from him, snarling. Four Watchers snapped the same word in unison, and the flare of knife-edged Power tore through the parasite pulled out of the enemy's body. It took the shape of a wriggling black serpent for just a moment, then stretched, its crimson eyes dimming, the nose-scorching stink of it roiling against the fresh wind. Then the flood of Dark-laced Power from the Watchers shredded it, and clear air poured over the garden.

Merrick's hands relaxed. Caro slumped against him.

"Would you look at that," Oliver said grimly from the other side of the circle. His voice was freighted with harshness, cracking the darkness. "The bastard's still alive."

Caro shook her mouth free. "Let go of me, Merrick." The snap of command in her beautiful voice, so different from a Watcher's, almost caused an instinctive obedience. Merrick glanced over the circle of Watchers, gauging the danger. "It's safe, it's safe enough, let *go* of me!"

"Safe enough," Oliver echoed. "He's only human, and dying."

More Watchers arriving. Where were the Lightbringers? "Slowly, Caro," Merrick found himself saying. "With me."

"Goddammit, let *go* of me before I take your knives!" Her voice broke, command turning to desperation, and every Watcher stilled.

Merrick's fingers loosened even further. But he still didn't let go of her completely. "Take them if you want, they're yours." His throat was suddenly full of stone. "But I will *not* allow this thing to harm you."

A small ripple of motion went through the assembled men, their eyes blazing with the collective fury of the *tanak*. Swords slid back into sheaths, knives too. The *snick* of each blade being pushed home was very loud. Two Watchers moved forward silently and scooped up the ruined, broken body. They brought it to Caro, to show that it was harmless and also to keep her safe, keeping a grip on the enemy just in case.

"We've had it all wrong." Caro's voice broke. "There were two waves of attacks. The seventy-two hour or more incubation period on the normals was for the new *Seekers*. The others, the psychics, they had variable times because they were trial runs for this. For the Crusade trying to make Watchers." She took a deep breath, leaning forward against Merrick's grasp, trying to reach the wounded man. "Get him to the infirmary. Get him to the infirmary *now*."

Oliver cleared his throat. "But—" The word trailed off.

Merrick could have finished the sentence. *He's an enemy, he tried to kill you. If he's a Crusader he will try to kill you again. Better to crush the viper's head than let it bite again. And besides, once we yanked whatever it was out of him, he probably lost his hold on life anyway. He's dying.*

"Take him to the infirmary," Merrick heard himself say.

"Obedience, Watchers."

Because each one of us was once like this. The Lightbringers didn't have to take us in, offer us redemption. The realization stung him far more deeply than claw or knife could.

Another rustle went through the Watchers, and Merrick had the uncomfortable sensation that plenty of the others had read his mind. Silently, the Watchers moved to obey, and Caro finally twisted free of Merrick's nerveless hands.

"I can heal him." Her voice broke again. She was *sobbing*. "I can heal him, I know I can. I know how to reverse the damage. That's what Asher had locked in his head that I had to bring out, it was the *technique!*" She tripped, would have fallen headlong if Merrick hadn't blurred to catch her. The sweater she wore slipped. He slid an arm around her waist and held her up. "The infirmary. Come on, let's go."

"Caro—" He couldn't make his voice work. Irrational fear crowded the clarity of combat inside his head. He'd just disobeyed his witch openly in front of a crowd of Watchers. They would take his knives. They could cast him out or worse, if she told them to. And he would have to fight them, because he couldn't leave her unprotected. He simply *couldn't*, now that he knew, selfishly, how good it felt to be near her. To be with her.

"Come *on*, Merrick! Hurry up!" And, wonder of wonders, she all but dragged him along until he collected himself, steadying her. Blood was drying to a gummy paste on his clothes, and he saw with a Watcher's acute night vision the blood on her own face. Bloody nose, maybe. She'd been too close to the Dark. Or had something hurt her?

At the thought of her hurt, damaged, the rage rose in him. He stopped dead, head down, trembling with fury, fighting for control.

Caro yanked at his arm. The Watchers were streaming away, some to carry the enemy to the infirmary, others spreading out to reinforce the shields and perform other duties in the aftermath of an attack. Twice, now, the Crusade had pierced a safehouse's walls with their new Seekers. The walls and wards that had held for two hundred years were no longer so safe until the Watchers could figure out how to bolster them, outwitting this new peril.

He didn't care. He fought with himself, muscles locked with rage, his bones creaking.

"Come on, Merrick. Please. I need you there to anchor me." She all but hopped from foot to foot with impatience.

"Are you hurt?" The words rose, each one edged with shattered concrete and broken glass. "Are you *hurt?*"

"Of course not." She sounded irritated enough that a thin thread of relief curled under the rage, managed to calm him a little. "Just my stupid nose. What—oh. *Oh.*"

And then, miracle of miracles, she reached up and touched his face, her fingers slipping and sticking in almost-dried blood. The sweet agonized pleasure roared down his skin and calmed him the way nothing else could.

"I'm sorry. I'm all right," she said softly. "I promise I'm all right. What about you?"

As long as you're all right, I am too. "Fine," he managed around the stone in his chest. "Just fine."

"You saved my life. Again." Her fingers shook, a soft flutter of trembling that could have been exhaustion running through her. "Thank you. I've treated you dreadfully."

He almost choked. She'd allowed him into her life, bonded with him in the oldest way known to witch and Watcher, and she called it dreadful? "If this is dreadful, I don't think my heart could stand kindness," He realized he'd said it out loud. "No. That's wrong. I'm sorry, Caro."

She had to stand on tiptoe, but she managed to curve her hand around so her thumb brushed one of his scars and sent another jolt of desire down through his bones. Christ, if this kept up he might snap, and he wouldn't stop until he had her again—and slowly this time, proving to himself with every breath and touch that she was unharmed. His hands curled into fists.

She pulled him down, her mouth met his, and he was lost again. Bloody, battered, and hanging to control by the thinnest of threads, he felt a curious comfort. His hands flattened against her back, pulled her into him. He tasted copper and salt and his witch. When she pulled back he had to restrain himself from trapping her face in his hands and kissing her again.

She sighed. "Better?"

Rain began to come down in earnest. It was too cold for her out here, and she wanted to go to the infirmary. "Better," he rasped. "Are you sure you're all right?"

"Very sure." She eased away from him, but took his arm, her hand sliding through his leather-clad elbow. "Let's go. Please?"

Obedience, Watcher. Obedience. It was a reflexive thought, and one that he shouldn't have had since he'd just disobeyed her in front of everyone. But it spurred him into moving, stiffly at first as the *tanak* settled down to repair some of the deeper and less critical damage. He did make one concession, though. He moved closer to her as they walked and slid his arm over her shoulders, taking her under his wing.

He'd thrown his cards on the table; there was nothing he could do now. If they wanted to throw him out, they were going to have a fight on their hands.

* * * *

"Dear gods." Caro was ashen. She wiped her face hurriedly with the washcloth, handed it back to her brother. Without the dried blood crusting her face, she looked even paler. "You're kidding."

"Nope, they came right through the wall. The Watchers are patching it now. It's chaos." Trev's dark eyes were solemn. He had a glaring-white bandage on his shoulder and his T-shirt was more than artistically torn. He'd been here since just after the attack started, sending his Watcher with the others to take care of the attackers while a contingent of Watchers guarded the infirmary as a last-ditch defense. Now Keenan hovered behind him, face unreadable.

The infirmary buzzed with activity and the occasional cry of pain. "You all right?" This Trevor directed at Merrick, who blinked at a question like that asked so casually. He was a Watcher. If he was still standing he was fine.

Maybe not a Watcher for very much longer. He flinched inwardly. "Yessir." *Fine as a feathered fowl and just ducky, thank you.*

"Where did they take the Crusader?" Caro set off briskly, her sandals shushing over the floor. The healers worked grimly, the air awash with humming Lightbringer magick. Other witches arrived in ones and twos, usually guarded by a Watcher who delivered them to the door and set off to reinforce the walls. Oliver and some of the others had gone to clear the streets outside the safehouse.

"Which one?" He sounded honestly perplexed, trotting to keep up with his sister.

"What do you mean, which one?" Her hair had come free of the messy ponytail and tangled past her shoulders, little drops of water caught in the curls. For some reason that made Merrick's chest ache.

"There are four of the Crusaders alive." Keenan's voice was flat but weighted with terrible fury at the word *crusaders*. "We ripped the parasite out of each one; killed the rest."

"How many?" Caro swung around a healer carrying an armful of linens. The green witch's aura flared and ran with verdant light. She had a spreading bruise over her cheekbone in purple and red. Tears ran down her cheeks, but she worked steadily, determinedly.

They're so bloody brave. Braver than us stupid Watchers.

"Twelve total, last I heard; four of the *Crusaders*," Keenan's lip all but curled at the word, "survived the stripping. North corner, this way."

"Did you recognize the Dark in them?" Caro sped up, Merrick matching his stride to hers.

"No ma'am." Keenan was boiling with silent fury, only barely controlled, his aura a hard, hurtful shine. Merrick understood. There were going to be a lot of very angry Watchers tonight, the rage would translate into Power and go into repairing the walls.

The light glowed in Caro's jeweled hair. "Trev?"

"Yeah?" He snapped to attention, catching the seriousness in her voice.

"Bring me every Mindhealer who's bonded with a Watcher, I think there's two or three of the six here. If they're unhurt, I mean. Set the others to working on the witches here and keeping everyone calm." Caro stopped short as a tall red-haired Watcher, his coat flapping in tatters, strode through right in front of her. He carried a water witch whose long dark hair dripped with blood, her draggled skirt wet and muddy.

"*Medic!*" he yelled, and several healers swarmed toward him. Merrick pulled Caro out of the way and she gave him a grateful glance.

Once they were past that and in a slightly less chaotic section of the infirmary, she caught Trevor's unwounded arm. "Then canvass the Watchers," she said urgently. "See if anyone knows what Dark that was. If they don't, get a good description and call Mari Niege. Tell her to get her ass down into that Library and twist Esmerelda's arm if she has to, but *find out what it is*. Find Fran. Tell her I need her. Got me?"

"Bonded Mindhealers, canvass Watchers, call Mari, twist arm, Fran." Trevor nodded, hectic spots of color standing out in his cheeks. He appeared, other than the bandage on his arm from flying glass, unwounded. "Got it."

Caro pulled him forward for a quick hug. Her skirt was wet, muddy at the hem, her feet were damp too. Merrick longed to drag her upstairs and find an empty room. *Stand down, mate,* he thought ruefully. *Don't even think about that.*

"Good." Caro nodded, and the boy took off, Keenan falling into step behind him.

The enemies were in the furthest corner of the infirmary, Watchers standing guard over their beds and eyeing each with profound contempt. Now there were only two left, Ellis and Drake were busy carrying a wrapped shape that looked like a body away as Caro arrived. She glanced over the two remaining wracked and battered shapes on the two beds set side by side and let out a soft sigh, slipping out of the long sweater coat she wore and dropping it over a forgotten chair. "Which one's more damaged?" she asked, and Hill—a short, muscled, intense Watcher with four instead of two knives and a very short buzzcut—snapped upright, all but saluting.

"Hard to tell, ma'am." His *tanak* gave the words a rough, hungry edge and his dark eyes blazed. "They don't hold on long."

"Better off dead anyway," another Watcher muttered.

Amen to that, Merrick seconded silently.

Caro drew herself up to her full height, her eyes flashing. As she did, one of the battered shapes convulsed, and the psychic dislocation of death smashed inward through its aura, collapsing into the foxfire of spent nerves. A rough stench familiar from any battlefield suddenly roiled through the air. Merrick's hands closed around Caro's shoulders. It was suddenly, utterly wrong. This fragile, indomitable woman should not see this. *Especially* not this.

"No time," Caro snapped, and shook away from him. "Merrick? Anchor me. Please."

"Caro—" *You shouldn't do this, it's dangerous. They're Crusaders, let them die!*

The other thought that rose was just as strong. *Each one of us was once like this. I was like this once. I was bleeding from the* belrakan *and almost dead when they brought me in, too. Though I might not be a Watcher much longer.*

He let out a harsh breath. "Be careful." His voice made the stone walls here at the north edge of the infirmary shudder, just a little.

She looked up at him, her eyes luminous indigo, and the

grateful smile she gave him was enough to make him instantly regret agreeing. His entire body ached, both with combat and with frustrated desire. "I will."

She moved immediately to the bedside of the remaining Crusader. She reached up, touching the silver chain that held the teardrop chunk of amber hidden under her sweater. Merrick almost flushed, remembering the necklace digging into his chest as his body lay atop hers. *Don't die, Caro. Don't risk yourself. God, please, if you're listening, don't take her yet. I need her too much.* He found himself beside her, catching her arm.

"If he dies—"

"You'll pull me back," she said, with such complete confidence she almost convinced him. "You pulled me back before; you'll pull me back this time." She took a deep breath, looking down, and he saw the flash of fear in her, quickly covered as she reached down, exquisitely gently, to take the bleeding hamburger that had once been a man's hand.

All the Watchers tensed. "You can't be serious," one of them said flatly.

Caro smiled. It was, of course, a stunningly beautiful smile, one that almost rocked Merrick back on his heels. "I'm always serious," she replied, her aura meshing with her Watcher's.

He *felt* the touch, against the bruised and sensitive fringes of his mind, the link roaring to life with an intensity that surprised him. Of course, he'd slept with her, completing the bond between Watcher and witch.

Then Caro leaned forward, her entire weight against Merrick's hand on her arm, and leapt without her body, throwing herself into the well of the spreading, weeping wound of an aura that was the shattered Crusader on the bed. She flung herself out into psychic space, trusting her Watcher to hold the other end of the line. Something inside Merrick stretched as darkness closed over his eyes, and he dug his heels into the floor, bracing himself to pull her back as soon as possible.

Fifteen

Falling.

Chaos screaming, chaos dreaming, splotches of color, bleeding wounds and rips in the psyche, a smoking wasteland of jagged rocks and deep bloody clefts still weeping. Down she goes, the rope around her waist sure and strong and tight, the sensation of speed causing a faint flutter in her not-stomach—her psyche is still bound by the fiction of a body and thus, a body's responses. A moment of attention quells the feeling, her descent slows, slowed by will and the rope that rises behind her, a link to the outside world.

The shimmer of consciousness that is Caroline raises her hand. You can hear me, *she says quietly, obeying that oldest of magickal dictums: her word makes it so.* You can hear me.

Noise, then. A cacophony of agony buffeting her, spun and twisted on her rope, reeling as the walls between her mind and the ragged mass that no longer can be called human stretch almost to breaking. The noise is a howl of wind, the depressurization of a cabin, a citywide riot compressed into a bullet of agony.

She spreads her arms, her consciousness thinning, thinning, soaking like honey through a shell. There is no trace of the Dark left here, but the wounds left behind by its ripped-free passage at the hands of the Watchers have smashed this man apart. Who he had been before was gone, and there is no return. He is irretrievably shattered.

Peace floods from her. Calming, soothing, the light in her shining through, a door in the space of this mind filling with sunlight that bursts upon the smoke-scarred wasteland. The deep caverns seem to melt, turning to hands, open begging hands reaching up. A thin longing, a ghost of an echo, reaches her.

Let me die. Let me die. *Moaning. Whispered over and over again, the last prayer of a condemned man.* In nomine Patrie . . . Filii . . . Spiritus Sanctus . . .

Let me die. Beg . . . plead . . . die. *Shattered memories. She reaches for them, ready to knit them together to give her a clue, some story to tell to patch this blasted shattered*

*thing back together. They slip through her fingers like
water. He does not want to remember. And yet, a few of the
memories, the important ones, are caught, enough that
comprehension colors her a deep aching blue that throbs
in the storm-ridden wastes, whistling through the cracked
and parched earth.*

*He wants only to go back into peace. This scorched
and agonized animal wishes only to find a dark hole deep
enough to hide him until he dies.*

Please, *she whispers.* There is so much to live for.

*Her certainty stains the air with gold. A breath of air—
sea air, walking on the beach, sand underfoot and the roar
of waves in the ears, the cry of gulls. Then a wind from a
high mountain, trees bending in their ancient dance and
the plashing of a mountain stream filling the air with wet
earth, pine, and water. She reaches for more images, more
beauty, and it comes—a star-drenched night, the vault of
heaven opened. The glitter of sunlight from skyscraper
windows on a sunny day, the glow of cities at night, the
taste of ice cream, and the touch of sun on the face, the
simple joy of driving with the windows down and the radio
pulsing. There is more, ever so much more, the memories
pouring from her in a tidal wave of color and sense and
impression, laced with every possible shade of peace. And
behind that, her absolute certainty, will translated to
action—life is good. He was still alive, this shattered man.
If he was still alive he had a chance to reclaim everything.*

Beneath her touch, the wilderness bloomed.

Who are you? *she whispers.* What's your name?

*Negation pulsing through the growing vines, the
greening grass, the flowers opening in the cracked canyons
below. Here at Death's door there is no name, merely the
sense of drowning—*

—and her outstretched hand. Take my hand, and I'll pull
you back. *She sends the thought out, a concentrated message
as her healing spreads. Were he to die now, her
consciousness would be rudely jerked back and away, the
garden shriveling as the impulse that gives it life is torn
away. She does not want this. She wants only to heal.* I
promise you, there's hope. No matter who you are, no matter
what you've done, there is hope. I swear it's true.

Indecision, and suddenly there is a new flood of

*strength, other presences behind her, adding their light to
hers. What was once a single floodlight now becomes a
sunrise, light breaking through everywhere, healers adding
their strength to hers, mending the body. And yet, the choice
is his, offered with an open palm. All the light in the world
would not trap him here if he truly wished to leave on
Death's great dark adventure.*

*No time passes in the space between minds, yet it seems
the seconds tick, and tick, and tick while she waits, feeling
the grasp of the rope on her waist and the not-wind moving
through her hair. Her body is numb, a numbness she
accepts patiently. Everything now hinges on this ancient
sorcery, the root of human magick.*

What's your name?

*For the name is the thing that is named, and naming
makes it so. And she feels his decision before it happens
and laughs, joy finally spreading through her as the rope
tightens and she is yanked back, pain blooming through
her like a rose, scattering a shower of fragrant petals down
into the garden that has grown in the wasteland under her
urging. Rising, rising into the blue, pulled and impelled,
breaking into the clear blue sky, through the looking glass,
shattering, and slam—*

—med back into her own body, collapsing against Merrick,
dimly noting the presence of a trio of green witches whose
auras flamed as they repaired the damage done to the body.
The body that still housed a soul and a mind that would need
plenty of work before it was anything near whole, but still . . . he
was alive, and he would mend. There were two other
Mindhealers too, the plump, motherly Lydia and the tall ebony-
skinned woman with long braided hair. They immediately moved
in to continue the work Caro had begun, to make the wilderness
into a garden, to heal his mind as far as they were capable.
Their Watchers moved behind them, keeping physical and
mental contact as well.

Merrick pressed his fingers to her forehead, held her up.
"Caro? *Caro!*"

"I'm all right," she said. "Just a little disoriented. And tired.
Merrick?"

He swore, and folded his arms around her. Breathed
another curse into her hair. Pulled her away from the bedside,
a murmur going through the Watchers as they registered that

the Crusader would survive. Obedience held, though. None of them moved. There was no ripple of bloodlust, though there was plenty of anger that scraped against Caro's sensitized psyche like a wire brush on abraded skin before Merrick's aura closed hard and defensive over hers. She shuddered, fully thrust back into her body.

"His name's Brennan." She sounded strange even to herself. "He didn't do it because he wanted to."

"What?" Merrick's sudden stillness made her very aware that she was exhausted, that her nose was full of dry blood, and her tangled hair was never going to forgive her. She probably presented a very sorry picture of a witch indeed. "Caro?"

"The Crusade," she managed. It was suddenly very important that they *understand*, all of them. "He didn't want this. They forced the parasite into him, once they found out how to make it incubate in a psychic. Whatever that Dark thing is, it *rides* them. It's not like a *tanak*. It's more like a *kalak*, it lives inside." She shook her head, her forehead pressed against his bloody T-shirt. "I don't have it all yet. But I know one thing. They held him down and hurt him, like they hurt the others, and forced the thing into him. He doesn't want to remember that part, he won't remember it." *Not without a few hundred years of therapy,* she thought grimly. Now nausea was returning, as the pattern of his fragmented memories became clearer to her. *There are some things even a Mindhealer can't cure.*

"Bloody hell." Merrick didn't sound half as angry now. Well, maybe he did, but the essential violence had leached out of him. She heard low-toned questions and replies as the Watchers passed her words around.

The nausea spiked and Caro sagged. "I think I have to throw up now," she said primly. "Can you help me?"

"Christ." He half-carried her, her feet dragged uselessly. "You almost stopped my heart. Why do you always find the most bloody dangerous thing to do? Why?"

"Talent, I guess." A jolt of heat speared into her, spread out to push the numb tingling back from her fingers and toes. Merrick, spending Power recklessly, pouring warmth into her. "I'm all right, Merrick. I don't think I'm going to go into shock." *It's a pity. I'd like to have you bring me out. Ugh, no, not really. The end is nice, but I never want to go through that again.*

He found an unoccupied bathroom tucked into the side of the infirmary and pushed the door open. Caro found her feet, gently but firmly shoved him outside, and flipped the light on. A few minutes of dry heaving over the pretty porcelain sink and she was feeling much better, the nausea passing like the weakness, sliding away as the Power he'd forced into her soaked in, repairing, giving her strength.

Caro peered at herself in the mirror. Fever-spots in her cheeks, wide dark eyes ringed with fear, and her hair a tangled mess. She'd put on her sweater-coat inside-out. *What a vision.* The shakes folded away, one wave after another sinking as she clutched the sink. Her knuckles turned white and her fingers creaked, she held on so hard.

I'm alive. I'm alive, he's alive, he's my Watcher and I've slept with him. And the Crusade now has Seekers and parasite-ridden soldiers that can break a safehouse's walls. Oh, God. But I know how to reverse the infection. I know how to get those things out. She could feel Merrick waiting patiently outside the door, so quiet she almost forgot how deadly he was. He fought with the precision and fluidity of a tiger, supple and fatal. No motion wasted, no hint of anger or fear, just calm controlled violence. Just like the other Watchers.

She was an idiot to think she could protect any of them. They were just as determined to risk their lives as she was to risk hers. But still, she shook her head and lifted her chin stubbornly. She would figure out a way to keep them a little safer, if she could.

It was enough, for now, that she'd survived the worst the Crusade could throw at them.

Relief unloosed her fingers. She made it blindly to the door and twisted the knob. He caught her arm as she stumbled, steadied her. "Better?"

"Much." She leaned into him, grateful for his solidity. He loomed over her, his coat creaking slightly, and she saw the shadow of dried blood on his scarred face. He was a little worse for wear too, and her heart lodged in her throat as she saw the rips in his coat and the leg of his jeans, soaked with blood. His T-shirt was in tatters, but he was alive. "God, I'm glad you're here."

He'd shaken his hair down over his scarred face. "Going to take my knives, Caro?"

She winced. *I threatened him right after he saved my life. God, Caro, how idiotic can you get?* "Of course not."

He looked down, his eyes peculiarly dark. "I openly disobeyed you. In front of half the Watchers in the safehouse." His hands were shoved in his pockets, and he looked for all the world like a defiant teenage boy caught breaking a curfew. Behind him, the infirmary bustled with activity, but there were no more screams. The air hummed with the soft music of healers and other Lightbringers, Power throbbing and sinking into pain, dispelling it, soothing. Everything was going to be all right. "I also . . . I've broken my oath."

What? Caro blinked at him. "What on earth are you talking about?"

He shrugged, his tattered coat rustling. "I am not going to let you endanger yourself again, Caroline. If I have to tie you up and sit on you to keep you out of trouble, I'll do it. If you take my knives and the Watchers throw me out, I'll still do what I have to."

Her jaw threatened to drop. "What the *hell* are you on about?"

Another shrug. And then, maddeningly, he shut up. Simply studied her, his scarred face shadowed and unreadable under his shock of dark hair.

Oh, for the love of . . . Screw this. She was tired, hungry, and had the beginnings of a pounding headache from Mindhealing again, with no proper patterning or safeguards. "If I'm too much trouble and you're looking for a reason to leave me, go ahead," she snapped. "I've got to go find Fran."

She brushed past him and stalked away, through the now orderly confusion of the infirmary. There were no more wounded coming in, and the healers were discovering they could treat everyone. Caro hoped there were no casualties, raised her chin, and strode on, her heart threatening to crack.

Sixteen

Well, you handled that as badly as it could be handled. Merrick cursed himself as he trailed her, the throbs and rips of pain soaking in through freshly-healed wounds from the swelling of Lightbringer magick in the air. He should have just shut up, not reminded her of his disobedience. He had only meant to make it absolutely clear to her just what he intended to do.

If I'm too much trouble and you're looking for a reason to leave me, go ahead. Was that what she thought? Well, he'd violated one Watcher oath, maybe she thought he was going to violate all the others too.

Her head was up, her shoulders were taut, and her glorious hair tangled down her back. She walked with long angry strides, barely acknowledging the other witches and Watchers she passed. The halls outside the infirmary were a hive of activity until she took a staircase up to the third floor and started heading for the north wing. The halls abruptly became deserted, her sandals slapping the floor instead of the little clicking sounds she made in heels, and Merrick began to feel nervous for no good reason.

If he was already damned, he might as well try to explain. But what if that explanation irritated her enough to make good on her threat? He knew enough about her stubbornness to suddenly fear that option, and he cursed himself for giving her the idea in the first place.

"Caro?" *Goddammit, I should know better than to open my bloody mouth. Why do I never learn?* But the pressure in his chest *demanded* he speak to her, make his plea, as it were.

Beg for mercy. If she could forgive a Crusader, could she forgive him?

"What?" She didn't sound annoyed, only distracted. She almost turned the wrong way, and he reached out and closed his hand around her shoulder, steering her down the proper hall. "Oh, thanks. Fran should be down in the infirmary, I don't know why she isn't. If she's not in her office . . ."

"Maybe down at Dispatch? There may have been other attacks, Dispatch will know. She might be doing damage control or making a report to the High Council through a safe link-up." He was vaguely unsettled even as he said it. There should have been Watchers sweeping these halls, two of them should have found and attached themselves to the Council liaison— one for protection and one to give a report to Oliver as soon as possible and run other messages.

Caro rounded another corner, sighted the statue of Brigid, and let out something that sounded like a relieved sigh. She didn't sound relieved when she spoke, though. Instead, she sounded nervous and breathless. "That could be it. I'm probably just jumpy. There's her office. We'll check and see."

He shouldn't have asked, but the words crowded his throat, all but strangled him. He had to know. "Are you going to take my knives?"

She stopped and rounded on him, eyes blazing, pulling her sweater-coat together and folding her arms over her chest. "Of *course* not, what gave you such a silly—"

He didn't let her finish the sentence, simply pushed her aside toward the wall and curled his left hand around a knife hilt, instinctively sliding metal free of the sheath. Then he clapped his free hand over her mouth. "Just a moment, love. Look." And he tipped his head slightly, indicating the hall.

Her aura flashed with anger, a sudden sheet of comprehension, and her pupils dilated as a wash of purple fear slid through her. He didn't have time to worry about why he could almost taste each new wave of emotion, because the thing that had alarmed him was a thread of familiar yet out-of-place magick. A throbbing crimson line laid across the door to the Council witch's office. It was a ward, clumsily done like all Crusader ceremonial magicks, and it smoked with evil intent. Merrick wouldn't have seen it except for the fact that it was so sloppily and hastily done. It had started to pulse as Caro approached, readying itself.

Bloody fucking utter hell. Fury rose under his breastbone. If the Crusade had managed to slip another one of those parasite-laden soldiers inside and given him a ward created by a Bishop, the Council witch was probably already dead. And the ward probably hadn't reacted during sweeps because it wasn't meant to kill Watchers. It was meant to disguise itself and spring on the first Lightbringer who approached it.

Thank God Caro's brother hadn't come this way yet.

Caro's eyes met his.

"A ward, probably put together by a Bishop," he said softly. "Meant to kill a Lightbringer. And I'll bet there's something

inside that office, love. Let's hope it's not the Council witch."
His thumb stroked her cheek, a fiery spill of pleasure jolting up
his arm. "Let me deal with it and clear the room. Stay here?"
He made it a question instead of a command, hoping her
stubbornness wouldn't flare. He would put her under a keepsafe
and trap her here if he had to.

She blinked, once. That was horrible, because a tear spilled
out of one eye, tracked down her cheek, and touched his hand.
Then she nodded. Her eyes suddenly swam with more tears.
Her lips trembled, and Merrick took a moment to lean forward
and press a gentle kiss on her forehead. *If I'm going to be
thrown out of the Watchers, I might as well make it worth
my while.* He softly pried his fingers away from her face. His
right hand reached for his sword—not the best weapon in close
quarters, but he had the knife in his left. A little more steel
never hurt anything.

And if it was one of those new Seekers, the knife would
do it more damage than his sword.

He left her standing slumped against the wall, hugging
herself, and eased toward the door. The ward resonated with
her nearness, a few more steps and she might have been in the
critical zone, easy prey for it. The Live Knights of the Crusade
were generally not psychic. It fell to the Bishops to use
centuries-old ceremonial magick texts forbidden by the Church
to create fun little objects—like a little bag of goodies to hang
on a door to ward it; or an amulet to give a Live Knight the
ability to see psychic energy or control the Seekers; or the
geometric tattoos that gave the Live Knights control of the
zombies. Each amulet or physical object took them months to
create, and that was one of the reasons the Crusade hadn't
overwhelmed the Watchers. It was also, according to the
Watchers, one of the reasons why the Crusade hated witches
so much. What came easily and naturally to a Lightbringer
required years of study and sacrifice for a Bishop. Psychic
ability tended to shut down in the presence of the fanaticism
the Crusaders were chosen for—if they had any ability in the
first place, that was.

He walked softly, as if the warding was a wild animal he
didn't want to spook. The analogy was apt. He'd dealt with
plenty of canny beasts in his time, and it wouldn't take much
for this warding to be a pitfall for a Watcher as well as a witch.

His aura hardened, battle-tested combat shielding springing

into place, the *tanak* giving out a slow steady growl of rage.
The sound thrummed in the air, rattled the door, and made the
Crusade warding shiver.

No time like the present, Merrick thought, and gathered
himself. Then he hurled himself forward, shattering the door
and the ward in one movement, ducking under the strike—
slow, human, clumsy—of the Master's broadsword and taking
in the chaos of the office with one swift, merciless look.

The Council witch was a crumpled, bloody shape in the
corner, books flung everywhere, papers scattered, the desk all
but reduced to firewood, and the flowers from the mantel—
lilies—scattered from their broken vase. Sharp sounds bolted
against his ears—gunshots, someone had a gun and Caro was
right out there in the hallway. *Stay put, please God, just let
her stay put until I clear this.* His sword came up in a short
propeller-like movement, carving into flesh with a solid *chuk.*

Then the scream and time slowed down. Because he had
smashed into the Master, greater muscle and bone density
sending the man—average height, close-cropped brown hair,
familiar face, vest with the white cross of the Crusade blazoned
on it under his coat and the broadsword in his capable hands—
flying across the room to crash into the wall. And then, pivoting,
looking for the gunshot, he saw the other Master crouched
over the Council witch's prone, smashed body, knee down,
Glock 9mm in hand, taking careful aim not at Merrick but at
the door.

The door.

The *door*, where Caro stood framed, her hand clapped
over her mouth and her eyes huge and luminous, her aura
glittering with the golden pinwheels of a Mindhealer. The low
bulletlike shape of something Dark, stinking with sulfur and
brimstone, streaked for Merrick's witch, the thin etheric threads
of its connection with the Council witch's battered body
snapping as it lunged to rip, devour, kill. Splinters flew from the
doorjamb—the Master's aim had been thrown off by the sudden
jolting of the Dark parasite he had been planning to put into
Francine now leaping for Caro, slipping the chain of ceremonial
magick that smoked and glittered around its low, unhealthy
neck.

Merrick's knife left his hand, glowing with crimson force
as he flung all available Power behind it. The blade turned into
a red streak painting the air and flushing the walls with rosy

light as he hurled himself forward, what a choice, either the
bullet would get her or the Seeker-thing would. Another
coughing roar as the Master crouched over the Council witch
pulled the trigger again.

Caro screamed, the sound muffled through the hand over
her mouth, her aura flashing. Sudden thumping impact snapping
through his ribs—*he's using hollowpoints, dammit,* as the
bullet meant for her smashed into Merrick's chest and exploded,
blood flying. He met the Seeker with a jarring, rib-shattering
thud. Caro had fallen, was backpedaling furiously, her foot
tangled in the green silk of her skirt. The Dark parasite imploded
under the force of Merrick's second knife, glowing with volcanic
force. *Get up, get up, get up!* chanting in his head, the only
thing that mattered was the Master with the gun.

Another thudding impact, this one tearing into his back, the
sound of breaking glass. Caro's despairing scream turning into
his name as her shoulders hit the wall opposite the office door.
He fell, his head hitting the floor with stunning force. A cool
drench of night air roaring through the room. Merrick rolled,
gun coming free, hands blood-slick, incredible piercing agony
in his chest, smell of copper blood mixing with foul sulfur, the
bitter-almond reek of the Crusade, and the dying, cloying scent
of smashed lilies.

Get up, he told himself. *Get up.* But his body would not
obey him. The *tanak* roared in wounded fury, pumping
adrenaline through his bloodstream, shocking his heart into
beating, squeezing the cardiac muscle with pure Power as it
repaired rips and gouges, sealing bleeding and snapping his
ribs back out into place, small pieces of bone stabbing him as
he tried to breathe with one lung turned to a bloody mess and
punctured with bits of bone. The pain rolled over him, a crested
breaker of red-shot darkness, and he fought for consciousness
even as his wounded body refused to comply for a single
heartstopping moment.

*Get up, where's that fucking Master, get up and kill
him before he can hurt her. Get up, you idiot, get UP!*

Then she was beside him, sobbing, her hands on him,
sending shockwaves of acid pleasure spurring through his
nervous system.

"—gods." Her voice sounded very small after the thunder
of gunfire and the Seeker-thing's snarling. "Oh gods, Merrick,
oh my God, please, don't die—"

Are you joking? I can't die, I've got too much to do.
He wanted to speak, couldn't find the breath, rolled onto his
side and convulsed, blood and clear fluid blown free of his
ruined lung through his mouth and nose as the *tanak* repaired
the organ in one swift vicious lunge of Power. Then, another
convulsion, drowning, he was drowning in his own blood. He
couldn't *breathe*, it was imperative that he *breathe* and get *up*
and kill the bastard who would be coming for the witch—*his*
witch—who caught his shoulders and tried to help, offering a
tide of soft, deep Lightbringer magick that spilled through him
and tore into his wounds, old scars and new dipped in honeyed
fire and scored deeper than his flesh, all the way down to his
bones.

I'll do whatever you want, he thought, clearly and
pointlessly, *just keep her safe. I'll obey, I'll be a good boy,
just keep her safe.*

Silence. Caro's soft sobs. Pain turned to Power, spurring
more rage that twisted into more pain as the wounds healed,
that transmuted into more Power. Cheap fuel, the *tanak* taking
the agony and transforming it into a quick excruciating repair
of major functions. All he needed was time.

Time was the one thing he didn't have if the Crusade
Master was coming for her.

Merrick pushed himself up to his knees, shoving Caro aside,
the gun coming up as he scanned the office. Window broken, a
grapple and line dangling out into the night air. The wreck of
the bookcases and hacked-apart desk. The slumped and
wounded body of the Council witch in a blood-drenched yellow
nightgown. And the Crusade Master he'd thrown against the
wall gasping like a fish as he flopped, ribs and arm apparently
broken, making a small wet sound of a human animal in pain.

Another sheeting of agony providing fuel, and Merrick
found the strength to get up. Running feet in the distance. He'd
made a hell of a lot of noise. Good. He could use a little backup.

"Merrick!" Caro caught him. "My God, he *shot* you!"

*Of course he shot me, love. But that bullet was intended
for you.* He swayed on his knees, eased the hammer back
down. The *tanak* snarled again. Even Caro's touch couldn't
dilute the strength of this suffering.

"Christ, is that what happened?" he managed weakly before
doubling over to retch again, his scars afire and his face contorted
with pain. Immediately he felt the bite of guilt. He shouldn't

have said it. *Got to keep my mouth shut.*

Her hands, against his chest, flooding him with Power. He pushed them away weakly, straightening again. *If she gives me much more she might drain herself, go into backlash or shock.*

"I'm fine, I'll live." *Distract her.* "Check the Council witch, Caro. She's hurt." *God, thank you. Thank you. I will obey, I will never question my duty again, thank you for saving her.* "Go on, love. Go."

She wasn't listening, stubborn Caro. She caught his bloody face in her hands and leaned forward, her kiss landing on his cheek, another on the corner of his mouth because he moved, looking around her. No, the Master was gone. Had he been a Bishop? Likely, maybe, though the Bishops had been awfully quiet since Piers, Jack Gray, and Dante had all bagged Bishops three in a row—the White, the Red, and the Black. Had the Crusade finally started training more than five Bishops? Maybe. He would have to talk to Oliver, see what the—

Caro's next kiss landed squarely on his mouth. Merrick caught her shoulder with one hand, reholstering the gun with the other. Gently, so gently, he pushed her away. "Go check the Council witch, Caroline. I'm all right." *Got to check that window. I can track that bastard, find out where they're hiding. We need to sweep every inch of this city, and the tech witches have to crack the Crusade firewalls again. So much to do, thank you God, she's alive. I will never disobey again.*

She stared at him, and he was taken aback once more by how fragile and stunning she was. Her indigo eyes brimmed with tears that spilled and tracked down her cheeks, her hair tangled madly and glowed with streaks of pure gold, her slender ribs flared and contracted with deep, sobbing breaths. It was hard to fathom how small she was, her force of personality made her seem so much taller. Not now. Now she looked frightened to death, pale, trembling, and saying his name between little hitching sobs. It was unexpectedly sweet, and he felt more guilt for being so nastily glad that she evidently felt *something* for him. Maybe it was just nothing more than a Lightbringer felt for any broken or wounded creature, but if she felt sorry for him he might have half a chance.

"Check her," he repeated harshly, wondering if he could lever himself to his feet. *Of course I can. All things should be so easy. Get up, Merrick. The danger isn't over. The one you knocked into the wall is right over there. Might even be getting a little surprise ready for you and your witch. So get up, get the hell over there, and take the bastard apart.*

The running feet drew closer. Booted feet, other Watchers, the air pressure inside the office dropping as Merrick gained his feet in a convulsive, agonized rush. He brought Caro with him by the simple expedient of grabbing her arm and hauling her upright, hoping his bloody hand wouldn't foul her. Pushed her gently toward the Council witch, which incidentally put him between his witch and the last remaining Crusader, the man from the chapel at St. Crispin's. Merrick had one knife left, and it was in his hand as he limped toward the fallen Crusader, whose breath bubbled wetly in his throat. *Must have broken a rib or two, eh, old sport?*

He noted, clinically, that he'd taken the man's hand off with his sword. *Won't be using those fingers to kill a Lightbringer anymore, will you?* The rush of clean, cold fury *that* thought caused filled his scars with fire and brought him fully upright, every color standing out crisp and clear in his vision now, his boots moving soundlessly through drifts of paper and smashed books.

"Merrick!" Caro's voice, frantic. "Help me, she's fading."

In a second, love. I should have killed this bastard the first time around. He took another step, saw the man's eyes were open and glazed with shock. The white cross on his bloody chest heaved, the left side of his ribs smashed in. It was a wonder he was still alive, between that and the spreading pool of blood from the stump of his right hand. *You stopped me, didn't you. You were whispering "no," and I obeyed. I should have killed him. Maybe the Council witch would be alive if I had.*

"Merrick." Her tone wasn't sharp, but she sounded as if the air had been punched out of her. "Leave him alone. Please. Help me. *Please.*"

She was pleading with him, he realized. Begging her own Watcher, something a witch should never have to do. Merrick's fingers ached around the knife hilt, thin crimson lines running in the black steel, a Watcher's most sacred weapon. Sacred because it was made with his own hands, in a ritual unchanged since the days of Gideon de Hauteville and Jeanne Tourenay,

Gideon the knight and Watcher who had started this whole bloody, impossible thing. A knight's honor, a man's honor. Merrick found himself wondering how a sixteenth-century knight had sworn himself to obedience in an age when women were considered property.

Didn't matter. Not to Merrick, at least. *Duty. Honor. Obedience.*

The Crusader bubbled in another breath, his mouth working like a fish's. He would die soon. And oh, how Merrick ached to speed that process up.

Caro made a single small, pained sound. It sounded remarkably like another sob, a hopeless sound. "Oh, Frannie," she whispered, "hold on. Please hold on."

Merrick's arm ached as he forced himself to sheathe the knife. It went reluctantly back into its dark home, and he consoled himself with the thought of Caro tilting her head back, the taste of the shallow depression above her collarbone, her soft inhale as her body went liquid under his. *Next time I'm going to have to be a little slower, if there is a next time. Make it last.*

The tingle of Lightbringer magick made his scars come alive, throbbing with something too intensely pleasurable to be called pain. But only because it was *her* doing it, and he realized something else—the proximity of the Council witch wasn't filling his nerves with acid. Which meant she was probably damaged beyond repair.

He turned back, every step now fighting against the compulsion to finish the man off. Slowly, making the half-dead body scream for mercy before he was through. Merrick found his hands were shaking. He paced back to his witch, kneeling at her side and examining the damage just as four other Watchers made their presence known by spilling in through the ruined door. And Merrick realized, as he pointed at the window and gave the few clipped words that would suffice to send a team out after the fled Crusade Master, that he had taken the door off its hinges and shattered the wall on either side, leaving a hole like in an old cartoon.

Strangely enough, the thought made him want to laugh, even as he clasped his witch's shoulder and sent Power garnered from the agony of his own wounds roaring through her. He had gone through the worst, might be kicked out of the Watchers, and his witch was probably never going to calm down—but she was alive. The laughter came from a place too deep to be healthy, and had a screaming panicked edge Merrick didn't like. So he swallowed it and watched as Caro worked on the Council witch, more Lightbringers arriving as the Watchers secured the room and the orders were given for every room, every closet, every *inch* of the safehouse to be checked and re-shielded.

Duty. Honor. Obedience. He repeated it to himself, and watched and waited for the axe to fall.

* * * *

"You've got to get some rest," Trev said quietly. "She's going to be fine. I'll stay right here, so will Keenan."

Caro slumped in the chair by Fran's bedside, her cheeks hollow and her eyes shadowed. She bit gently at the nail of her right middle finger, worrying it, her lips tense and bruised-looking. Her hair was still a tangled mess. She made no response. Her gaze was fixed, her hands loose when she wasn't chewing at a fingernail, and her bare feet—she had tossed her sandals somewhere—lay neatly on the floor underneath her chair. One small line between her eyebrows gave her a thoughtful look, and her aura was luminous and thinly sparkling with pain.

Trevor tried again. He leaned close to her, touched her shoulder awkwardly. For a moment, Merrick saw how lost the boy was without the steady compass of his sister's annoyance and crispness, and he began to understood why Caro tried her best never to show any fear. She had probably learned to act fearless very early in life, using certainty and brittle chill to act grown-up and calm her younger sibling.

Merrick's blood was still on her hands. So was Francine's. And a thin thread of dried blood traced her upper lip. The change from her high heels and tamped-down professionalism to this picture of silent, numb grief was almost too much to stand.

"Caro? I'll stay. We'll be right here, and we'll send someone if she wakes up or needs anything. You've *got* to get some rest."

She still didn't respond to the note of almost-panic in the boy's voice. That disturbed Merrick more than anything. Trev gave him a quick, imploring glance.

Fran was in a curtained space in the infirmary, guarded by Watchers and visited hourly by healers. And Caro had maintained a silent vigil here, dry-eyed and silent, her misery radiating out in high-pitched waves. It was, Merrick reflected, almost enough to drive a man mad.

None of the Watchers had made any noises about taking his knives. In fact, Oliver had clapped him on the shoulder and said *good work*, which was as much of a compliment as a Watcher could hope for. Drake, his scorpion tattoo writhing visibly through a hole torn in the shoulder of his blood-soaked coat, had nodded, dark eyes alight. Merrick's scars still burned with shame, fiery stripes down his face and chest.

The Samhain celebration would be tinged with sadness this year. Four witches had died in the attack, and two Watchers. The shock of an attack that could pierce a safehouse's walls was still reverberating. The High Council was sending reinforcements and investigators. Merrick had missed and would continue to miss most of the investigating. His responsibility was the witch who sat staring and chewing her fingernails, refusing to leave the Council witch's bedside. In the busy slew of activity, nobody had approached him to strip him of his knives yet.

He was grateful for that. It gave him time to think. Of course, he wished it was over. The silence gave him . . . too *much* time to think.

The Crusade Master was alive, tended by Lightbringers and under heavy guard. So was Brennan, the one Caro said was innocent, or at least hadn't willingly become a parasite-driven killing machine. He couldn't speak yet to defend himself, but a Lightbringer's word was almost as good. Then again, Caro wouldn't lie, but she might interpret the evidence in the best possible light for the wounded man. Time would tell.

I've had about enough of this. She needed sleep and food, and perhaps a crying fit. This numb, silent grieving was not healthy.

Merrick moved forward. He closed his hand over her delicate shoulder. "Time to get some rest, love." He had to work for the right tone, soft but inflexible, one equal to another. If this didn't work he was going to pick her up and drag her.

Caro shook her head slowly, as if trying to dislodge a particularly ugly thought. His heart ached for her. No witch should have to see what she'd seen.

"Did you get hold of Mari?" She gathered herself up out of the chair slowly. Like an old woman.

"Not yet," Trev said. "Her home phone just rings and her cell puts me over to voicemail. I left a message on her cell and another one at the Rowangrove. Emmie at the safehouse is supposed to give me a call when she hears something."

Trev sighed. "There's been a lot of activity there, too. The last Emmie heard, the Guardians swear the borders haven't been breached, but there have been attempts that look like the Crusade. They're probably holed up somewhere safe, working. You know how Dante and Hanson are, they like everything played close to the vest." He scrubbed at his eyes with his palms, skinny dark-haired boy in a red sweater and a leather cuff closed around his right wrist. His aura was just as thin and drawn as his sister's. "The tech witches are still working. They just sent out a request for a new kind of hardware and more coffee. Looks like the Crusade's gotten better firewalls since last time."

Caro's shoulders slumped as she looked down at Fran. "Dominion." Her tone was dull. "What do we know about them?"

"Nothing yet." Trev looked relieved. At least Caro was *talking*, that was a step up. And it was apparent she'd been listening to the snippets of information being thrown from mouth to mouth. "Tech witches working on it."

"The Watchers?"

Trev glanced at Merrick, whose hand had fallen back down to his side. Caro barely reached his shoulder. It was amazing, once again, to see how small she was. "Nothing yet, they're squeezing all their contacts for information. But it's slow."

She nodded, her tangled hair moving, pleading for his fingers to straighten it. Or at least, touch. Offer some comfort, anything. The suffering printed on her face was enough to make him want to find where they were keeping the two Crusaders and kill them both. Slowly. Then start tracking the one that had gone out the window, the one that had almost shot her. "All right. Come wake me up if anything happens, okay?"

Trev nodded, didn't dare give Merrick a grateful look until Caro had turned away, her head down, starting for the end of the bed where the Council witch was drawing her smooth breaths, no longer tortured. The damage wasn't as bad as Merrick had feared, and with healers visiting every hour and pouring Power, antibiotics, and pain meds into her, the witch would probably pull through and be little the worse for wear. If you had to be attacked and beaten, inside a safehouse was hardly the worst place.

Still, this is *a safehouse. They should have never gotten inside. We should have done something, seen something, stopped it somehow.* The voice of responsibility spoke up insistently. It hadn't gone away for hours. *Caro should never have seen this, should have never been in danger. I should have done something more, known something.*

The waiting was killing him, too. Each moment he expected to turn around and see a pair of Watchers, solemn-faced, and hear the words, *We're here to take your knives, Merrick. Don't make a scene. Don't embarrass yourself.*

Caro stopped. She sighed, her shoulders slumping even further. "Trevor? Thank you. I . . . thank you."

Her brother nodded, his hair sticking wildly up in every direction, his small gold earring winking in the clear light. His aura scraped against Merrick's freshly healed wounds, Caro's glow providing comfort he didn't deserve. When would she remember his disobedience? Would her stubbornness flare up again?

She threaded through the infirmary, head down, wanting to be ignored. He followed, steps silent after hers. Out into the hall, up the stairs, and in the stairwell's dimness, she stopped, rubbing at her temples. Merrick eased closer to her, as close as he could, hoping his silent bulk wouldn't be a reminder of all the hideousness she had been forced to endure.

When she turned back, standing on the step above him, and looked up, all he could think was, *Here it comes. Brace yourself.*

Caroline studied him, thoughts he could almost decipher moving behind her dark blue eyes. The high arches of her cheekbones, the soft, lush print of her mouth, the bruise-dark circles under her beautiful, beautiful eyes, the pulse in her fragile throat—it was a continual surprise to see, again, just how lovely she was. It wasn't just the flawlessness of her skin or the architecture of her bones; it was the light shining out from her core. The light, and the indomitable will you could see in the lift of her chin, the flash of her eyes.

Finally, she spoke. "Merrick."

As if reminding herself of something. Who he was? What he was? What she intended to do with him?

He simply watched her. His scars were alive with pain,

almost seeming to writhe on his skin. Burrowing deeper. *Just let me look at you. Please, just let me stay near you.*

She took a deep breath, gathering her courage. *Merrick, I'll take your knives now. Don't let me see you again.*

"Thank you." Her voice broke. "For—for everything. I should have stayed where you told me to. I was stupid, I was careless and thoughtless, and I could have gotten you killed. Or both of us killed. I'm so sorry."

Huh? If she had informed him that the moon was made of green cheese and she intended to go up in a cracker-filled rocket and have a slice, he might have been less surprised. As it was, he stared at her, truly speechless for once instead of simply refraining from opening his big mouth.

She didn't seem to care, because she went on, the words spilling helplessly out. "Trev was right, damn him. Vince would have been very disappointed in the way I've behaved. I just . . . I don't want anyone else to get hurt. But I could have killed us both, I wasn't even watching where I was going and I could have run right into that ward and Fran would be dead now, too, because you would have been busy trying to take care of me." Her sweet, husky, tired voice bounced off the wooden stairs with their strips of sandpapery anti-slip and the smooth white-painted walls. Claustrophobia was probably affecting her right now, but she spoke even faster. "I've been an idiot, and a royal pain, and I'm sorry. I just hope—I mean, I don't want you to feel . . . obligated."

Obligated? What the bloody blue hell? "Obligated?" *I sound like I'm choking. Again. What is it about this woman that reduces me to slack-jawed dimwittedness?*

She shrugged, color rising in her pale cheeks. "You really don't have any control," she said quietly, her voice a sweet purr in the echoing well of the stairs. He should get her moving, up to the third floor and then through the halls to the room they'd moved her to—down the hall from the blue room with the Cezanne that had been broken into twice. Caro hadn't protested, just nodded wearily when Trev told her they were moving her luggage. That had filled Merrick with an uneasy wariness. "What you feel when I touch you, I mean," she continued. "You can't be sure if it's me, or if it's just the fact that I don't make you . . . hurt."

He had to work it around silently inside his head for a few moments before comprehension struck. *Women and their*

*convoluted brains, I will never understand females. I will
never understand this female in particular. She thinks I
just fell into bed with her because it doesn't hurt me to
touch her, is that it? Christ. Well, I've been a big dumb
idiot in interacting with her anyway; I can see why she'd
think I was a brainless pudding when it came to that too.*
"Ah. Well, Caro—"

"You don't have to say anything," she interrupted, chin
high and shoulders drawn back. But her eyes were soft, and
just possibly wounded. Hurt. Hiding her fear again. What did
she think he was going to do? "I won't ask you for anything. If
you want to, you can go back on patrol. Or we can find some
way for you to live a normal—"

That did it. His long-abused patience snapped. He lunged
forward and caught her midsentence, helped by the fact that
he was on the stair below her. She went over his shoulder in a
trice, and he was up the stairs and into the deserted third-story
hall before she collected her wits and began to struggle.

"Merrick!" She sounded, thank God, furious. Not wounded
and broken, but absolutely incensed. He felt a hard delighted
smile tilt his lips as she began pounding on his lower back.

He found the room Trevor and Keenan had moved all her
luggage to, opened the door with a quick twist of his wrist and
a palm flat against the heavy wood. Everyone was in the
infirmary or doing something else. The suites up here were
quiet as a mouse. He carried her into the twilit darkness of
another room that smelled of disturbed dust and the faint rich
smell of fabric softener, beeswax, and vanilla. The light was
dying in the gray, rainy sky, another winter storm sweeping in.

This room was done in spring greens and soft yellow
touches, a reproduction of a pre-Raphaelite *Sleeping Beauty*
hung over the fireplace where sunlight would catch it in the
early afternoon. Merrick kicked the door shut, locked it, and
proceeded across the thick green carpet to dump her on the
bed, a queen-size four-poster with a quilt worked in sunflowers.
Rain slapped the windows, the storm gathering strength.
Thunder rattled in the far-off distance. *This city isn't a good
place to live if you like sunlight,* he thought, and looked down
at his witch, who pushed herself up to sit on the bed and glare
at him, all but sparkling with indignation.

"You drive me to absolute distraction," he informed her
before she could catch her breath. "I have *never* in my life

met a more stubborn, infuriating, absolutely charming female. Are you going to take my knives or not, Caro? I'd counsel you not to, since I plan on protecting you one way or another. But you're my witch, you do what you like. Just understand this— *you are stuck with me.* I am not leaving you under any circumstances, and you can rant and rave about it all you like. I'll listen. I'll even help you along when you run out of words."

He had to take a breath, dried blood crackling on his clothes. He hadn't had a quiet moment to clean up and repair anything yet. "And don't worry yourself over whether or not I feel *obligated.*" His hands had curled into fists to keep from reaching out and cupping her face, holding her still so he could kiss the smooth arch of her forehead or the soft lushness of her mouth. "Obligated isn't the word."

"What's the word, then?" She tossed it at him like a challenge, and relief bloomed inside his chest.

"Infuriated," he supplied immediately. "Awestruck. Bloody out of my mind with fear. And completely, utterly mad for a witch who doesn't have the sense to let a brick wall win in a contest with her head."

There. I can't get any plainer, can I? Can I, Caro?

"Oh." A small, hurt little word. She sagged back against her arms as if too exhausted to hold herself up. She probably was. Thunder bloomed, slid through the sky, and taunted Merrick's ears. "Well."

"You're *my witch,*" he said, as softly as he could. Still, the glass in the window rattled, and the floorboards groaned as if something heavy had come to rest on them.

"He shot you twice." The same small, hurt little voice, the voice of a child. Her aura sparked, ran with pinwheels of golden light. Merrick slid his coat off his shoulders, watching her face. "Because I didn't stay where you told me to."

He let his coat drop, heard the clinking metal of gear shifting inside it. His hands moved easily, naturally, unbuckling the weapons harness just like he'd done hundreds of times since he'd become a Watcher. But his hands were trembling. "It's all right. I'm hard to kill, love. You don't know *how* hard."

"What were you? Before?" She bit her lower lip as he carefully, gently, let the harness settle atop his coat. The slim length of the sword, the knives, the guns, the leather straps. It was the question every witch asked her Watcher sooner or later, and it was never easy to answer.

"I killed people for a living." It didn't get any simpler. "I started out in the army. Rifles, knives, bare hands. Anything to get the job done. Track the target and take them out. Then I went into the private sector after my own government cut me loose. They tried to kill me, thought I knew too much. I kept one step ahead of everyone until the day I accepted a job—kill a woman with a rifle. Fee was enough that I could retire." He let his hands dangle at his sides. "They didn't tell me the woman was a witch, and she had a Watcher. He was good, really good. Inhumanly good. Damn near killed me, but she told him to stop. I was just a dogsbody anyway."

"Oh." Comprehension colored her tone. "The Crusade."

Might as well tell her, Merrick. Not like you have anything left to lose. "The bloody Crusade. It was one of their attempts to see if a mercenary with a long-range assault rifle could do what Seekers couldn't. She told the Watcher to let me go. She was so goddamn naïve she didn't know I was liable if I didn't finish the job. Nothing left to do but beg to be a Watcher. They wouldn't take me."

"Until?" And, wonder of wonders, she patted the bed next to her. He lowered himself down cautiously, the mattress making slight sounds as it accepted his weight. And then, completing the cycle of impossible events, she leaned against him, resting her head on his shoulder.

"Until they were sure I was serious." The words stuck in his throat. "I ran foul of a *belrakan* while I was trailing a witch. That's how I got the scars." They were throbbing and twisting with shameful warmth even now, reacting to her nearness. He wanted to put his arm around her, stroke her hair, pull her back down on the bed and get her out of that skirt. Wanted to comfort her, too.

"You weren't a Watcher?" She rubbed her temple against his ripped shirt, against his shoulder. He had to fight down the flare of sugared heat that went through him. Her breathing slowed, evened out. She was sleepy. No wonder.

"Not then, no. They brought me in, fixed me up, and let me take the training." He swallowed against the dustiness in his throat. He couldn't tell her the rest of it. *Please, God, don't make her ask. What do you say? Let me be lucky for once.*

"Are you sorry you did?" At least she didn't sound numb or frightened. She leaned heavily against him, and he found his arm settling around her naturally, easily, as if it had just fallen into place.

"Not now." *Isn't that strange. That's the truth.*

"Oh." She yawned. "I'm tired," she announced, as if he couldn't tell. "I have to sleep. Don't go anywhere."

"Of course not."

"I mean, really. Stay here. With me. Right here. We still have things to talk about." Her words slowed, almost slurred. He wasn't surprised; she must be worn out.

Like what? "Like?" Cautious, the word hung in the air. *I thought I was clear enough for even you to understand, you obstinate little witch.*

"Like the exact meaning of the word *foreplay*," she said, in a heavy, I'm-almost-asleep voice.

By the time Merrick had finished wrestling down the desire to laugh like a lunatic, Caro was asleep against his shoulder. He didn't want to move, but he laid her down and got the covers over her. Then he worked his boots off and settled himself, bloody clothes and all, on top of the quilt. So he wouldn't be tempted. And he willed himself into the dark mind-resting trance a Watcher could use to repair his mental acuity, listening to her breathe while the *tanak* continued its patient careful repair of his scarred flesh and broken bones.

Seventeen

She woke slowly, in stages, warm and feeling somehow cleansed. More peaceful. She lay on her side, snuggled against something warm and wrapped in blankets, her cheek against something hard and her arm thrown over another something hard. Her nose wrinkled. She smelled smoke and the copper of dried blood, as well as her own unwashed hair. Thunder rumbled, she heard the muted pounding of rain.

Where am I now?

Memory returned, and she jolted into full wakefulness, jerking herself upright, her breath coming hard and fast and her heart suddenly pounding.

Merrick curled up gracefully to sit as well. He was lying on top of the quilt.

What the hell?

"Easy, Caro." His voice was a soothing rumble, deep in his chest. "You've only been out a few hours. Nothing's happened."

What do you mean, nothing's happened? Fran's beaten almost to death, there's a Crusade Master you nearly killed and another one I had to talk you out of killing in the infirmary, and the safehouse might not be so safe. What am I doing sleeping? Dear gods.

"I'd better get back to Fran," she heard herself say mechanically. The room was dark, only the faintest reflected gleam of citylight coming in through the window, no night-light in the bathroom. They'd moved her luggage, and Caro hadn't protested that hard. There was bravery and then there was stupidity, and she had probably been practicing more of the latter lately.

Merrick had apparently taken the sweater-coat off her, He pressed his hand against her shoulderblade and sent a heat-tingle through her aura. It hit her softly in the solar plexus and spread out to fill her fingers and toes with warmth. She also caught a glimpse of what he was feeling. *That* brought a hot flush up from her neck to drench her cheeks.

"Be calm, love. Breathe." He sounded a lot less ironic than he usually did.

Stubborn resistance rose inside her, but she forced it down

and took a deep breath. Another. It did help, a sense of calm returned. With it came renewed acuity, as if a fog of cotton wool had lifted away from her brain. She literally hadn't been thinking straight before, too tired and punch-drunk with one crisis after another.

She leaned back into Merrick's hand. It felt good, she decided. He paused, then slid his hand up under her hair until he cupped her nape. The feel of his skin against hers sent a wave of tingles down her back, and she was fairly sure that if she simply *reached* she could find out what it felt like to him. She was, after all, a Mindhealer.

And he was her Watcher.

He kept his hand there for a good ten minutes as Caro breathed, then reluctantly took it away. It was odd how such a lingering release of the pressure of his skin against hers could feel more intimate than a caress.

"Better?" He moved restlessly, as if he was planning on getting up off the bed.

Caro gathered her courage. "Much." She pulled her knees up, got her balance, then reached down for the hem of her sweater and pulled it off over her head. *My hair's a mess, and I'm all bloody and I probably smell. Gods, I hope I'm not disgusting.*

Merrick froze. Caro almost wanted to laugh, decided she'd better not. "It's the middle of the night," she said, in a very low, very clear voice she hoped wasn't shaking. "If anything happens, Trev will come find me." *What do I say now?* "You want to take your shirt off?"

Great, Caro. Wonderful. That's really, really slick.

She was saved a great deal of embarrassment when he almost tore the rags of his shirt off. *Certainly didn't need to ask him twice, did I?* She wondered how she was going to get out of her skirt, but didn't have much time to figure it out, since his fingers brushed her back and a jolt of lightning went all the way through her. He trailed his fingers up her spine, just lightly skimming, and her breath caught in her throat. Her pulse rocketed into orbit, tingling that had nothing to do with magick racing through her.

She actually giggled when he cursed, struggling out of his jeans. Her own fight to get her skirt off was less protracted but more tangled. She was still all bloody and would have worried about dried blood on her face if there had been any light to see it by. She would have worried again about her hair or about a hundred little things if his mouth hadn't found the sensitive hollow between her neck and her collarbone, just exactly the most vulnerable spot.

Caro's entire body turned to warm oil. She was only barely aware of curling her fingers in his hair and moving to get as close to him as she could, despite the fact that there were still tangled sheets and a quilt in the way. The bed was probably going to be covered in dried blood and she would have to strip it, carry the sheets to the laundry room and—

He bit her lightly, in just the right place, and Caro heard herself moan. *Good God, whoever knew he had it in him?* The covers were beginning to be a major irritant, especially since his callused hands were roaming her torso, finding the most sensitive spots and teasing at them. His thumb brushed her nipple lightly, and she surprised herself by arching her back and hissing in a sharp breath. *Did I really think he'd need a little coaching in the foreplay department?*

Guilt returned, sharp and deadly. Here she was in a Watcher's arms, enjoying herself, while Fran was unconscious on pain meds down in the infirmary, under heavy guard. It was only small consolation that they hadn't had time to beat her as badly as they had Colleen or Nicolette.

She stiffened, and Merrick seemed to catch her mood, because he stopped. Simply held her, even though she could feel his readiness through the layers of rucked sheet and blanket and quilt between them. He rested his chin atop her head and stroked her back, evenly, smoothly, his calluses rasping. Said nothing.

Oddly enough, that managed to make her feel even guiltier. "I'm sorry," she whispered against his throat, his pulse throbbing under her lips. The shiver that went through him echoed in her own body. It would be so easy to drown in what he was feeling, the feedback squeal of pleasure that was a Watcher's reward.

"Why?" He sounded baffled.

She shrugged, shifting awkwardly. She was half in his lap, and the covers were all tangled. "Want to lie down?"

"I thought you'd never ask." He tried to make it sound like a joke, and her hitching little laugh sounded more like a cry of pain. She let go of him reluctantly, tossing her skirt to the floor. *I'm never going to get the wrinkles out of this. It probably has blood on it. Maybe I should burn it.*

In less than thirty seconds he had magically restored order to the bed and tucked her in, sliding in next to her and pausing for only the briefest moment before she cuddled up close to him, throwing her leg over his hip and hugging him as hard as she could. Her fingers found his scarred shoulder, and he tensed. "Caro—"

"I'm such an idiot," she whispered. "I feel like a teenager again."

"Really?" His fingers polished her hip, drifted up the curve of her belly, found her ribs, tickled slightly.

She tried not to squirm. "Like I'm going to get caught. Like I shouldn't do this while so much has gone wrong." Her breath caught, and she realized she was crying. The tears rolled silently down her cheeks. She tried not to sniffle and warn him. She hadn't ever wept willingly, not even during her childhood.

Marvelously, blessedly, he didn't speak. Instead he turned on his side and kissed her, gently. It was like the first time, awkward and tender. He didn't tell her not to cry; he didn't tell her it was going to be all right. At least not in words. And when the tears stopped and she shook with the slanted white fire of climax, the only thing he said was her name, whispered raggedly as the bright flame of the link between them became a star in the dark. It was all the promise she needed. There, for that moment, the darkness was kind instead of dangerous, and she fell asleep with her head on his shoulder, trusting that promise for a few hours until she had to wake up and be responsible again.

* * * *

The next morning, a knock at the door brought Caro to a complete standstill from the rut she'd been wearing in the carpet, pacing from the window to the empty cold fireplace. A shower, a pot of coffee, and some peanut butter toast had restored her to some kind of normalcy. She stepped into her heels and met Merrick's eyes squarely. He had already unfolded himself from the neatly made bed, where he'd been sitting cross-legged, repairing his T-shirt with flickers of Power and infinite patience. She reminded herself, once again, to get him fully outfitted. He shouldn't have to repair a blood-sodden rag like that, but Caro didn't have a shirt that would fit him.

"Keenan," he said, his green eyes glowing. His scars flushed for a moment, and muscle moved under the bare skin of his chest. "Probably with news."

Caro nodded, biting her lower lip. She'd managed to fight her hair back into behaving, mostly with Merrick's help. He had actually laughed at her discomfiture while he patiently combed out every tangle. Properly dressed and in her heels, she felt a little more ready to face the next crisis.

The door opened, and Keenan's dark-blue eyes flicked over the room. "Duty," he said, quietly.

"Honor," Merrick responded. "Come on in, mate."

Caro was sure she saw a look pass between them, Keenan's eyebrow raising a millimeter and Merrick's infinitesimal shrug. "Good morning, Keenan. Would you like some coffee?" *How's Fran? What's going on? Why do you look so worried under that straight face of yours? Is Trev okay?*

"No, ma'am, just had breakfast with your brother, he's fine. The Council witch is better. The healers say she'll definitely pull through. She's out of the woods and resting comfortably."

Relief weakened Caro's knees. "Any other news?" *Gods, please. Let it be something good, not another crisis.*

"Lots. The tech witches have been busy, and the Crusader—Brennan—has been talking. There's also . . . other news."

Caro folded her arms. A weak rectangle of sunlight lay against the green carpet, and the air stiffened with heat from two Watchers. Merrick pulled his repaired shirt over his head and bent to pick up his weapons harness. It came alive in his hands, a supple thing that curled around his body. She leaned back on her heels, one hip stuck slightly out, and wished the shoes didn't make her lower back hurt. It was a tradeoff, feeling a little bit of professional confidence hand in hand with an aching lumbar spine. "All right. Give it to me straight."

Keenan clasped his hands behind his back, stood at parade rest with his shoulders pushed back. "There's been another wave of attacks," he said, with no discernable emotion. "Up north, in Saint City. The Guardians are all right—Theo and the baby are fine, Elise has a broken arm and a severe case of frustrated rage but she's otherwise in fine fettle, and Mari's down in the Library, digging. Jack Gray took a lot of damage getting Anya to safety. Apparently this organization—Dominion—is the Crusade's new best friend, and they're paramilitary. Bunch of evangelical Protestant fanatics. The Crusade funds them, and they've been training for a few years to strike. The tech witches cracked a major Crusade node last night and got us a list of targets. The Crusade's targeted a whole roll of Lightbringers we didn't even know about. The High Council is mobilizing every Watcher they can to stand guard and bring them in." He took a deep breath. "The tech witches also got us translations of the texts used to create the new Seekers. The bad news is, the Crusade's going ahead with creating them, and their version of Watchers too. They've perfected the process. They call them Slayers."

Caro almost swayed. *Oh, God.* "I know how to stop the infection," she heard herself say, in a cool businesslike tone. "I should report, and I need to see those translations to figure out if there's a better way to combat it."

Keenan nodded. "You're now a High Council special deputy. To teach every Mindhealer and anyone else you can how to—"

"*What?*" She was vaguely surprised the window didn't shatter under the force of her screech. "I mean, *why?* For God's sake, I nearly got Merrick killed and didn't figure anything out until it was too late, and—"

"Begging your pardon, ma'am." Was Keenan trying to hide a *smile?* "You almost single-handedly solved the mystery, and if you hadn't kept your head and gone to find the Council liaison, we would have had two Masters and another one of those new Seekers loose in the safehouse. You also saved Asher. All in all, the Council's very impressed. So's everyone else."

Caro's jaw threatened to drop. "You can't be serious."

"Rarely anything else, ma'am. I've got to get back to the infirmary. Trev wants me to spell him at the Council liaison's bedside. With your permission?"

She waved him away. "Special deputy? What am I supposed to do? They *can't.*"

"They just did. Honor, brother." Merrick held up his ripped and tattered coat, returned Keenan's nod.

"Duty, brother. You're in for commendation. Oliver sent word for you to stop worrying." And with that, the younger Watcher ducked out the door, shutting it softly but decisively.

Caro hugged herself, cupping her elbows in her hands. "Gods above." *I sound shocked. I feel shocked.*

"Going to be interesting," Merrick remarked mildly. "Watchers bringing in witches instead of just standing guard and waiting for a Lightfall witch to make contact. A whole list

of Lightbringers we didn't know about and the Crusade did."
He shook his head and laid the coat down on the bed, a blot of
darkness against the sunflowers. "Caro? You all right, love?"

"No. I'm not all right. There aren't enough bonded
Mindhealers to treat all the cases in time if the Crusade's really
serious about this." She crossed to the window, unsteady on
her high heels, finally kicked the damn shoes off. Maybe she
should start wearing flats.

"Bonded Mindhealers?" He sounded curious.

"Of course. That's the trick. It has to be a bonded
Mindhealer linked to her Watcher before she goes in, or the
parasite can drag her down and her heart stops. Not to mention
the risk of being knocked out of her body and other fun and
games." *Fran's going to live. Thank you, gods.* "That's why
Danica died. She wasn't linked to her Watcher while trying to
heal Colleen. The parasite simply dragged her down when she
disturbed it. It went dormant until I disturbed it again—as luck
would have it, on the final day of its incubation. If I hadn't
been linked to you, I'd be dead." *And I feel like such an
idiot, I should have pieced it all together sooner. All the
clues were there. I'm getting dense in my old age.*

He was silent for a long moment. Then, dangerously quiet,
"You're just telling me this *now?*"

"Well, you didn't ask." Caro swung away from the window,
stepped back into her heels, and headed for the door, pausing
to glance at him over her shoulder. "I want to go see Fran,
make sure she'll be all right. And Trev's been down there all
night. I'll need to bully him into bed. Then we'll get those
translations, and—what?"

Merrick glared at her, his eyes bright and piercing under
his messy hair. "Tie you up," he muttered. "And *sit* on you."

"Ha." She shook her head, and glared right back. "Just try
it. I know where you're ticklish. Look at it this way, I'll be so
busy inside the safehouses I'll barely be able to step outside."

"No consolation. You could get into trouble in a nunnery."
He shrugged back into his tattered coat. At least he'd been
able to clean the blood off it, the smoky smell of Watcher magick
hung in the air.

"First things first, though. We'd better stop by Requisitions
and get you some new clothes. And a haircut wouldn't be amiss,
either."

Merrick drew himself up. Nodded, his eyes fixed on her

face.

Caro held her hand out. "Are you coming?"

His eyes dropped to her hand, flicked back up to her face. He took four long steps and his fingers slid through hers. His skin was fever-warm and dry. The carefully reined strength was reassuring, and she let out a sigh as their linked hands dropped between them.

"If you'll have me. Lead on, witch."

But she paused, looking up at his scarred face. "You're sure? I mean, I'm not the easiest person in the world to—"

"Caro," he said, gently, "you're my bloody witch and you couldn't pry me away with a chainfall. Let's get to work."

Well, that answers that. So she gave him a worried smile and led him out the door. Let's hope I'm smart enough to keep us both out of danger and find a way to stop the Crusade this time.

Printed in the United Kingdom
by Lightning Source UK Ltd.
129926UK00001B/76/P